The Daughters of Avalon

Book 1 of the "Seven Sisters
of Avalon" Series

By Katrina Rasbold

The Daughters of Avalon

ISBN-13: 978-1493785728

ISBN-10: 1493785729

ACKNOWLEDGEMENTS

My deepest gratitude to George Taylor for his meticulous editing and discerning eye. He finds and fixes the multitude of typos and proofing errors I leave in my wake as I write in a white-hot frenzy of storytelling. Truly, he makes me look so much better than I am and for that, I am eternally grateful.

This book's beautiful cover artwork is a combination of two photographs by Marcus J. Ranum (mjranum) of Deviant Art. Thank you, Mr. Ranum, for sharing your talent on this website and allowing your beautiful work available for other deviants to use without restriction.

Table of Contents

The Daughters of Avalon

The Daughters of Avalon

Introduction

The stories that we, as a culture, elevate to the status of fable have always fascinated me from childhood to current time and so it is within those time-honored tales that I decided to work my craft. My favorite movies are often these stories we call "Fairy Tales" as envisioned and retold by modern day filmmakers. I love how a story can become so woven into the fabric of our history in such a way that nearly everyone knows it and some might not even be completely sure what is fiction and what is history. Seeing such a legacy tale told through new eyes with a different perspective is fascinating to me.

As this story began to come to me, I found myself besieged by several different insecurities. A period piece opens the author to the scrutiny of the perfectionists, the purists who frown self-righteously and criticize every flaw and weakness in a work rather than enjoy the work for its own story. These are who came for me in the night as I wrote this tale.

An example of this is one of my favorite movies, *Robin Hood: Prince of Thieves* starring Alan Rickman and Kevin Costner. At the time the movie released, I spent a good bit of my life around Renaissance Faire people. One of my favorite scenes in the film was when a very frustrated Sheriff of Nottingham (Rickman) told a comely servant to be in his room at a 10:45 and "bring a friend." The people I knew *lost their minds* and sputtered, "But…but…there WERE no 'o'clocks' in that time period!!!" their eyes wide with righteous indignation and the thrill of *being right*. The actual fun of the scene was completely lost on them because *oh my God, they got it wrong!*

It is specifically a challenge to write about the fifth, sixth, and seventh centuries because largely, there is no history. Most of what people think is history comes from works of fiction such as Geoffrey of Monmouth's *Historia Regum Britanniae* (History of the Kings of Britain) and *Le Morte d'Arthur* (The Death of Arthur) by Sir Thomas Malory. While it is tempting to fall into the luxury of poetic license and simply "make stuff up" about how things were in that time, period writing itself brings with it certain landmines in the most innocent disguises. Our heroine looks sorrowfully out the window. *Did they have windows? When did paned glass come into use? How transparent would the glass be? Would there be only shutters? Where would the window have been placed (possibly at the top of the room, prohibiting her from looking out of it without standing on a few chairs).*

As you can see, a whole can of worms is opened with almost any thought. She is given a mirror? *What would a mirror have been made of in that time and how much could she see in the reflection? How were kingdoms divided amid the Saxon, Jute, and Anglian sprawl? What would they use to light a torch? What were the politics of the time? How did people of that time prepare for a wedding? What medical practices were in use?*

Love scenes were a challenge because I am not given to the "purple prose" of "throbbing manhood" and "tangled secret garden of delight." This led who a whole mind-thrashing number of days researching when words such as "clitoris" and "penis" came into use and since that was not until many, many centuries later, *what the heck did they call that stuff?* As it turns out, they didn't talk about it *at all*, but I needed to! Again, quite a trap.

Before long, you start to over think every line you write, looking for the trigger that will set off one of those purists and in doing so, it becomes a real feat just to keep the story afloat. For a person such as myself who is accustomed to writing non-fiction, I felt as though I had to untangle a Gordian knot of facts just to get the story told. In the end, I did what one does with a Gordian knot: I pulled out my sword and started hacking away at it. My husband laid it out perfectly when he said, "It is easier to write non-fiction because all you have to do is give the facts. When you write fiction, you have to remember every lie."

This introduction is my apology to you, the reader, because it is very possible that this book does have historical errors and that I did not take every single aspect of living in the Dark Ages into account. I accept the disdain of those who know more about this than do I, but I ask that if the glaring misrepresentation tears you violently out of the scene, that you please just pat me on the head and consider me to be just an ignorant little thing and move along with the story. If you are able find where the story picks up again after your mortal literary and historical wounding, the characters and I will thank you kindly. It is a good story, I feel, and the characters wanted come to life, so here we are.

What I did in the end was research as best as I could and let me tell you, I could not have managed this book at all if I had needed to trudge through a library card catalog to find out if clitorises existed in the sixth century and whether anyone cared if they did. *Goddess bless the internet.* Aspects of the story I did invent where I thought it was fair and safe to do so... Some I pulled from what seemed like endless numbers of Arthurian legends, both modern and ancient. I value your patience and understanding.

My approach to this period work is less like "There were no o'clocks!!" and more like the serving wench in *The Cable Guy* who tells Matthew Broderick's character that there were no forks and knives in Medieval times and therefore, there ARE no forks and knives AT Medieval Times and then offers him a Pepsi. Yep. That's me. Just go with it and you will enjoy the story more. If you start to feel yourself getting into a twinge about some tidbit of history I did not get exactly right, just relax and drink your Pepsi and find out what happens next in the story.

This book is the launch for the series called *Seven Sisters of Avalon,* following our girls into many adventures, some of which will ring to you of an old tale retold in a new way and from a different perspective. I hope that you will go on this journey with me and will come to love the characters as I now do.

As my mother used to say, "I told you that story so I could tell you this one..."

Katrina Rasbold
November 2013

Prologue

"Curse it all," the old midwife muttered as the left side of the laboring woman's face went slack and she lost the ability to speak. There would be no more pushing then. Moments later, the mother let out a long breath that sounded for all the world like a moan of pleasure and went limp as the life left her. Just like that. Damned cold it was in this godawful stable and here she had been about to take her supper and settle down for a nice quiet evening. Oh well. What's done is done. Thinking quickly, the midwife pulled the sickle shaped knife from her belt and with the speed of experience cut into the skin of the mother's belly, through layers of body material, until she revealed the tiny baby inside. So small for such a big belly, but isn't that how it goes? She sighed as the warmth from inside the mother's body wafted over her in a comforting wave.

Blood ran down the midwife's hands and steam rose up out of the woman's still contracting body to meet the frigid air.

So...not quite completely dead, she guessed.

Never mind. She would not have survived anyway and certainly would not now. The midwife worked the baby from the woman's body and pushed away the birth sac that covered its face with a gentleness she did not feel. A baby born with the caul comes forth from a dead woman on the Winter Solstice with a Full Moon ripe in the sky. The portent caused a shiver to go up her spine.

The baby's father was unknown because his mother had been unknown, having only arrived in town days before seeking work as a servant in the home of a local merchant. The merchant had been reluctant to take her in as she was obviously far gone with pregnancy and would be of little use to him in the coming days. Still, something about her had moved him to bring her into his employ and it had been he who summoned the midwife when the groom found the woman enduring the throes of labor without so much as a sound in a mound of hay in the horse stable.

As the midwife gently blew puffs of her own breath into the baby's lungs, she was relieved to hear a soft gasp and musky sigh from the baby's mouth. She glanced down and saw it was a boy baby, then pulled back and looked back at the dark, solemn eyes that silently surveyed her. The wee one was so quiet that she feared his lungs would take the sick and he would yet succumb to death. But no. He simply stared at her as if memorizing her face. Again, she shuddered because it seemed that this baby looked into her very soul and knew her every secret.

The merchant returned just then and she told him what had transpired, letting him know that she would arrange to have the area cleaned and the body removed. He nodded his thanks and passed a gold coin off to her, which she accepted, knowing it would sustain her and her husband for at least another week during these hard times. As he turned to leave, she stopped him.

"Beggin' yer Lordship's pardon, sir, but the babe bein' born in your stable and having no earthly parents no more... It's to you to tell me what to do with the wee one." She offered up a silent prayer to the Goddess that he would not tell her what many men in her position would say to do. She could do it, but she cared not for it and felt it beyond doubt cursed her of any small hope of redemption she might have left.

The merchant paused and closed his eyes. It was very late. He was tired, having haggled his way through a brutal marketplace day and now, not only did he have a dead servant cast onto the horses' hay and bloodying it, but he also had to make a choice that could prove life or death for a newborn baby. The old woman eyed him, waiting for an answer. Finally, he asked, "Does Gretchen, the kitchen help, still have her baby abreast?"

"Aye," the midwife confirmed. "She come t'see me just t'other day as her wee one was not taking well to suckle anymore and he not even a year old yet. She is still with milk, I can say."

"Take the babe to her for the night," he decided. "Ask her if she would be willing to give him suck until I figure out what to do. Tell her I will increase her wage and she's not to work tomorrow, but instead, to care for the child. Can you do that?"

The old woman grinned, relief showing in her toothless gape. "Aye, yes I can do that. She'll be pleased to have a bitty one to cuddle again and also for the day without kitchen work. I'll get right to it." He passed her another gold coin and her eyes lit up.

"That," he said quietly, "is for your silence until I figure out what to do next."

She nodded and turned her back to him, dismissing him outright.

"Here," he said, handing her the long, warm, woolen scarf from around his neck. "For the babe." As the merchant left, she tore off a length of her own inner shift and swaddled the newborn snugly, then wrapped the scarf around her own neck. No one would ever be the wiser. She had turned herself to the odious task of clean up when movement caught her eye from the bloody pile of straw and human remains.

"How so?" she wondered with curious awe.

"How so?"

Lillian

Chapter 1

Arthur, the once and future king, the greatest of them all, was dead. He had been dead for more than forty years and although the simple people needed to believe that he would return with the desperation of people who had no other hope, Lillian doubted it would ever be so. Certainly, his bones still lay in the burial area of Avalon where his sister, the Lady Morgan, had interred him with honor all those years ago. Ample time had passed for one to come forward as the king reborn, yet none had done so.

The Merlin had returned as confirmed by the Druids of Avalon, and as was foretold in prophesy, in fact, by Taliesin himself.

"I will come forth born of no living woman," he had predicted and so it had been. After a scandal before Arthur's death left Britain without a Merlin, there had been none for many years, much like the Lady of the Lake. It was remarkable to all to think of this handsome, young man, swarthy and dark, as The Merlin Reborn where The Merlin of Arthur's time had been old for as long as anyone could remember.

Upon meeting the young man, the Druid leaders of The Temple of the Sun had accepted his claim, although still they put him through test after test to confirm that what he said was so. Such a miracle, of course, could not be fully endorsed without intense scrutiny and given the unrest in Britain, the Druid leaders could take no chance of endorsing a fraudulent claim in their desperation and enthusiasm.

Time and again, the young man proved himself to be genuine and after a year and a day of ongoing trial, he was proclaimed to be The Merlin Reborn. Lillian had never met him herself, but despite the discipline and training of both Druid and Priestess, or more likely *because* of that very discipline and training, there were few secrets on Avalon. Word of the arrival and testing of the strange young man was of tremendous interest to those on the island, which had for years now fallen into quiet routine with little to no variation.

The Druids and Priestesses of Avalon had remained faithful and strong, even as the fervent Christian zealots had stormed the sacred groves, destroying the oak wood circles and tearing apart the sacred arbors on the mainland until little but ruins remained. Each time, they rebuilt so the common folk would have a place to worship. Although mourning the giant oaks and ceremonial groves, they knew that magic was present in the tiny seedling just as well as in the ancient trees.

After Arthur's death, the ensuing political chaos left Avalon at tremendous risk as the fanatical, crusading followers of the One True God sought to destroy all that was magical and of the Old Faith. In her last act as ruling Lady of the Lake, the Lady Morgan herself coupled with the Arch Druid in a powerful magical congress to regress Avalon even further into the mists, leaving it completely inaccessible to all but the most highly initiated. The island was now essentially isolated from the rest of the world.

It was this very isolation that provided the first indication that life as they knew it on Avalon was changing. The story, as Lillian heard it, was that one of the elder Druids had come upon the strange, woaded people who ferried the barge preparing the large craft for a trip to across the lake. No one on Avalon had asked for the barge, so he questioned why it would be prepared to go to the mainland. They told him only, "The barge has been summoned."

Word spread like wildfire through the island that *someone* from the mainland summoned the barge, yet there was no known person *on* the mainland with that degree of power. With nothing short of breathless anticipation, the Druid and Priestess leaders of Avalon waited to see who would step off when it returned. They would never forbid the ferrymen from taking the barge to a summoning, which was an act possible only by those who were of the Great Goddess Herself.

They waited for the better part of the day and dusk was beginning to settle when they saw the dark form of the barge moving through the veil of the mists. Silently, it brought its mysterious passenger to the shores and the leaders could not have been more shocked when a young man, scarcely out of his teens, came forward and greeted them by kissing the ground in front of them. He shared his story and the Council of Druids immediately took him into seclusion for vetting.

Quickly, news had spread throughout the island. Not only was he claiming to be The Merlin Returned, but he was also born and bred *off island*. For many of the young priestesses, there was only second-hand knowledge of what existed on the mainland. Most had been born on-island or had lived there for so long that they remembered little of their life before coming there.

Now that the island had moved so far into the mists, it was rare for mainland dwellers to send their children for training among the Druids and Priestesses on Avalon. Children, however, were born to the Avalon priestesses, oft times from the coupling that took place each year at the Beltane fires, but sometimes from quiet rendezvous between the Priestesses and Druids throughout the year. There was no law forbidding either Druid or Priestess from marrying, but few did and instead preferred to keep their options open to the will of the Goddess and the flow of the life tides within.

All children born of the Avalon priestesses were Children of the Goddess and as such, were subject to the rule and claim of no man. The retreat of Avalon further into the mists protected them from not only the Saxon marauders, but also those who sought to destroy all magical people. It also served to further the distance between the common world and the world of magic. Once, the people of Avalon had been well versed in matters of state in Britain. The common knowledge of British politics and news of that known as "the world beyond" trickled in from time to time but was usually outdated by the time it reached Avalon.

Many lamented a time when the two lands were one, but as they say, "What is done, is done." It was rare now to hear the Glastonbury bells ringing out to invite the devout to services. Silence enveloped the island except for the birds and the sounds of voices and daily work. Although travel was still possible for the elders between Avalon and the mainland, the amount of time the trip took constantly shifted. At one time, a week would pass as the barge drifted from one shore to the other, even the ripples making not a sound. At others, a month would go by and still others, only a day or so. There seemed to be no rhyme or reason to what drove the time shifts as they occurred. Lillian had heard her own Elder Priestesses talk about traveling to the mainland and that while their visit there would last a week or a month, when they

and buried her head under her pillow to escape their clucking. Had they never seen a man before?

Now, Danu led her toward the Temple of the Sun in silence. Lillian wore her finest gown and Maia had woven golden ribbons in her dark hair and braided it in an intricate fashion, creating a crown effect on her head. One of the attending girls from the House of Maidens darkened the mark of the crescent moon on her brow that identified her as a daughter of the Goddess and it stood in stark contrast to her creamy white skin.

She always envied the flaxen-haired maidens who would tan as brown as hazelnuts in the summer while she remained whitest white. She was short, round, and soft where they were long, lean, and lithe. It took a tremendous act of self-discipline for her to resist caving to painful insecurity regarding her physical differences from the other girls. The challenges of having memories from multiple lives constantly spinning and colliding in her mind caused her to appear eccentric and strange. Although they were kind to her, most of the maidens distanced themselves from her and she often felt lonely, even while living in a dormitory filled with girls.

After the Elder Priestesses started the process of grooming her for this very moment, the distance between her and the others had grown greater still. The women and especially the children in the House of Mothers loved her well. The grandmothers in the House of Crones found her fascinating, especially since many remembered her from her previous physical incarnation and when they happened to float to the surface of her consciousness, she could carry on full conversations with them about experiences they had shared with her in that life before. It was only with people her own age that she felt an estrangement, although there were times when even about the older women she felt valued more as a novelty than for who she was as a person.

As they approached the Temple of the Sun, she saw a crowd of robed men waiting by the door, talking amongst one another. Her mind flashed to the enormity of what was about to transpire and she pulled in a sharp, involuntary breath. Danu, who was walking ahead of her, stopped and turned to face her.

"Are you alright, dear?" she asked, motherly concern softening her usually stern face.

Lillian smiled reassuringly. "I am," she said, but noticed quickly that her voice was barely above a whisper. "Danu…" she said, touching the older woman's arm. "What if..?" she struggled to find words to explain herself without appearing weak and fearful. "What if I am not who I believe myself to be and who you believe me to be? What if I am but an addled girl who heard bits and pieces of lore and filled in the right blanks? What if you are wrong? What if all of you are wrong?"

Danu gently took her hands. "I knew you before," she said. "You were my dear friend, my mentor, and my Goddess on earth and when they brought your body to Glastonbury after you were murdered in such a brutal fashion, it was I who traveled there to pay you the honor of Avalon. You have told me things that only she and I knew and that you could not possibly have heard elsewhere. I was the one who caught you when you pushed screaming and red-faced out of your beautiful mother's body in this life. I believe in you and you must believe in yourself."

Lillian bowed her head so Danu would not see the doubt on her face and said, "Even so, I have not the political prowess that is needed for such a job as this! I know little and nothing about the world beyond and Avalon's place within it. I have no knowing of kings and wars and diplomacy and negotiations. I know of weaving and herb lore and healing."

"You have her memories," Danu assured her. "That is all that matters. The rest will come to you in time as it is needed."

"That's just it," Lillian whispered, and her voice took on a fierceness that caused her to wince. "Her memories are a jumble in my head! I can rarely make any sense of them. Things float to the surface at their own bidding, not mine."

"That too will come in time," Danu said softly. She reached to straighten the veil around Lillian's face. "You would not have come to us as you did knowing the things you know had this not been meant to be. We will be here with you. You are not alone." She smiled and patted the girl's cheek. "Now come along. Those old Druids do not like to be kept waiting...and neither does your destiny."

Lillian drew herself up to full height and found herself wishing she had more height into which to draw herself. She was far from slight, but she was small in stature and as she stood at the temple doors, she felt miniscule and insignificant. Every eye turned to her as she crossed the threshold.

The woad he used to paint his face made him look primitive and fierce, but magical at the same time. His cloak lay loosely across his strong, wide shoulders and revealed his smooth brown chest. Feathers and beads were woven into his hair, which was blackest black and braided in an odd fashion. Her breath caught in her throat at the site of him and despite her training and determination to remain stalwart, her lips parted and she found herself, for once, at a loss for words. She stared at him and he at her as ripples of recognition raised the hairs on her arms and the nape of her neck. She felt the strong, insistent pulse of magic at work and closed her eyes to compose herself in the privacy of darkness. When she opened them again, she saw that his eyes had not left her. His gaze was warm and reassuring as wave after wave of familiarity washed over her.

She licked her lips nervously and said the first words she could form in her mind, "Is it you?"

He drew in a long breath that seemed to fracture slightly in the middle and then let it out slowly. She sensed that he as well was attempting to maintain his composure in this potent moment.

"Yes, dear one," he said, his voice barely above a whisper. "It is I."

Behind and around her, Lillian became aware that the Druids and Priestesses were whispering softly, but urgently, to one another. Danu came forward and said, "Lillian, this is The Merlin of Britain, who is called Bran." Still locked in the hold of his eyes, Lillian extended her hand to him and he took it between his own. She felt the firm warmth of his skin wrap around her fingers as he bent to kiss it.

"I greet you in honor, Lillian. It is my deepest pleasure to meet you." As soon as he lowered his eyes to her hand, Lillian felt as though a cloud had passed over the sun and she longed to return to the engaging light of that intense gaze. He lingered over her hand and the moments felt like hours to her. She was very aware of the warmth of his breath against her skin and of the odd, tingling sensations the pressure of his fingers on hers created throughout her body.

When at last he looked up and found her eyes again, she felt the flood of the tides rush through her as never before. Every fiber of her being cried out that the Goddess had made her for him and him for her. All thoughts of her previous life on Avalon fled her mind. Any sense of the gravity of her presentation to the Druids was lost. Any apprehension dissolved and for the very first time in her life, all that existed for her was this one moment. So ingrained was her priestess training that she managed the self-discipline to refrain from flinging herself into his arms and immersing in the comfort and excitement of his embrace…but just barely.

Although only a few minutes had actually passed, to Lillian, it felt as though she lived a lifetime as they stood there looking at one another. At last, Danu smoothly walked between them, blocking her view of Bran. Seeing her Elder Priestess's expression allowed Lillian to recover her composure and stand taller in her soft, doeskin shoes. It was a priestess trick not of glamoury, which was a whole other process, but of claiming one's own power to the fullest. Shoulders back, head tall, spine straight, chin high, she pulled herself up and connected with the life's energy that flowed through her and provided her true substance.

On one hand, the power she felt in the gaze of The Merlin, which she still felt glancing her skin through her clothing, told her exactly why she had been brought to this exact place at this exact time. Formally, however, it was for the presentation. She had not known until earlier that same evening the purpose of the meeting. When she asked Danu and Fi, another of her teachers, why she was making the trek to the Temple of the Sun to see the Druids, both had replied using precisely the same words with precisely the same intonations, "All will be revealed in time."

She knew better than to push the issue at that point, so she tempered her natural curiosity and opened herself to whatever was to come. They refused her right to go to the Beltane fires that year, despite the fact that the tides ran fiercely through her. She asked permission both that year and the year before and was frustrated that they denied it to her. "The Goddess will call you when it is time," Fi had told her gently.

Urgency ran through Lillian's voice as she argued, her eyes locking onto Fi's to convey her intense meaning, "If the Goddess calls me any louder, dear Fi, I fear my loins will catch afire...if you know what I mean." Fi had only smiled, patted her hand, and assured her that she would understand the need for this sacrifice later.

Would she be the Virgin Huntress for a new king to come as she had done at other times in her previous life? As Lady of the Lake before, she had worked the Great Marriage with both High King and lesser kings on five different occasions, both before and after her coronation. Would she – *please Goddess, no* – be called to go on a mission in Britain on the mainland, away from Avalon? She used every discipline she possessed to still her mind from courting too many possibilities and instead, to be present in the now, as she had been trained to do for so many years. As the sun was about to set and the party was ready to leave the House of Maidens that evening, Danu and Fi had at last told her what was to be.

Lillian was speechless.

She? Lady of the Lake?

She still resided in the House of Maidens! She had only taken her vows as a Priestess of the Goddess two years before! Certainly, the words of magic came to her easily and the power coursed through her as truly as did her own life's blood. Yes, she had the sight when she chose to use it and no, it never came upon her unbidden as it did many of the girls her age. Indeed, she had thousands of memories of governing this beautiful and sacred land in lives past scattered around in her mind. That in no way changed the fact that she was but a girl of eighteen! Many women her own age already had borne children, two or three even, but to sit as Lady of the Lake?

Early on, when the Elder Priestesses discovered that Lillian inhabited two worlds in her mind, they worked long to train her to isolate the two; to know what was of this world and what was of her past life. Her ability to process memories from both lives often caused her brain to work faster than she could keep up. If she did not make a conscious effort to tame and sort her thoughts, her mind would be in a constant state of chaos with many thought tangents streaming at once. She often heard voices from her previous life, which Danu told her were like echoes and while useful in the cause of understanding the past and providing prior wisdom on which to build her current training, they were of little other practical value. Many nights, Lillian had lain wakeful as she listened to conversations that had taken place many years before her birth, wishing the voices would find their peace so she could sleep.

After the initial full stop of her racing thoughts, she now found that impressions, voices from both the past and the present, and thought were colliding into one another more so than ever before. Here, in the presence of her mentors, of the High Druids and of The Merlin Reborn, she called upon all her strength to still the thoughts that trafficked through her mind.

She came to this place knowing that what happened there would change her life forever more. Although that very thing occurred the moment the breath left her body under Bran's strong gaze, she now forced herself to recall that she was here for another purpose entirely. Vaguely aware that Danu was speaking, she trained her thoughts on the words her Elder Priestess said.

"...since a young child has spoken intelligently about events of the past, both personal and matters of history and state that are not of public record or common knowledge. She has demonstrated an aptitude for magical arts beyond that which any of us have seen and her sense of diplomacy and honor have been well established, even at this early age. It is clear, not only from our own study and determination, but from what we have just witnessed between Bran and Lillian, that she is of the old royal line and is, in fact, The Great Lady herself returned to us just as Bran is the greatest Merlin Britain ever knew returned to us." Danu paused as a wave of murmurs went through the roomful of men. "After considerable conference and Divine congress," she continued, "It is the decision of the Elder Priestesses of the Temple of the Moon that Lillian should be immediately placed into the long-vacated role of Lady of the Lake with, of course, a counsel of Elder Priestesses to act as her consultants."

Lillian's head reeled and again she used breath control to still her mind and remain focused in the moment. She allowed herself the luxury of seeking out

Bran's gaze from the corner of her line of vision. It was there and warmed her spirit, as she knew it would. His face was still and calm, but his eyes were dancing. He looked at her with what appeared to be tremendous pride.

Pride? He barely knew her in this life!

"…of Avalon owes her conscience to no man and we, the brotherhood, are honored that you share with us this monumental decision you have reached." The man who was speaking was familiar to Lillian, but she could not bring his name to mind. In fact, she could bring very little to mind, even though her thoughts were racing…racing too quickly for her to catch. The older Druid looked at her critically. "We understand the gravity of your decision as we were recently faced with our own similar circumstance when Bran came to us. Magic and wisdom know no boundaries in terms of age and the Goddess works in mysterious ways. The experiences these two young people recall from their previous lives, partnered with the support of their teachers from whom they may seek counsel will do much to rebuild the strength of Avalon and to return the voice of the Goddess to the world. Truly, we stand breathless at a critical and magical precipice in time."

His hand gripped the top of an intricately carved cane made of ash and polished to a high sheen. Although the cane was clearly aged, the carefully wrought magical symbols carved into it still showed deep and strong. Again, the hair prickled on the back of Lillian's neck as she felt the power he conveyed. She felt the Goddess again come up in her, responding to the powerful force of his male energy and the gravity of his words. He took his time in continuing, seeming to arrange his thoughts while working his gnarled hands over the handle of the cane that supported him. His mouth moved without words and he worked to bring his thoughts into words. "As you know, Lady Danu, it is written in sacred text that two will rise up from the mists to restore hope to the land and propagate magic throughout the world during its darkest days. Deferring to the wisdom of the Elder Priestesses of the Temple of the Moon, there can be no question that these two youngsters are, in fact, the fulfillment of that prophecy. These are majestic and potent times when so many of our prophecies are coming to fulfillment."

Priestesses and Druids alike whispered intently all around them as Danu dipped her head in respect. "We are in agreement and I am certain you understand the need for urgency in this matter, given the unrest that has once again come to our doors."

The old man shook his head grimly. "Agreed. Avalon must be restored to power soon or I fear that it will, at last, be no more."

"Father, what do you hear?" Danu asked her voice temporarily plaintive. "You are in closer contact with those on the outside than are we. Tell me, will the tribesmen support a return of Avalon to power or have they buckled under the weight of persecution?"

The old man startled everyone in the room with a burst of laughter. "Dear Lady, the tribesmen would joyfully welcome a return of Avalon to power. They only appear to be subjugated and apart from their Goddess and the Old Ways. Their hearts lie with us even as the priests burn and ravage their sacred places. They will support us. Concern yourself not at all about that."

"Then we must make haste," she said resolutely. "It will take time to re-establish our position and move the message through the tribesmen. The work must begin at once. Will you join us for the crowning?"

"Aye," he nodded. "Will we follow the old rite, then?"

"We shall," she affirmed. "The Moon of the Strong Sun is upon us. We will then begin."

Lillian's mind could barely process what she had heard. The enormity of what had been said pounded through her mind. She could still feel the heat of Bran's eyes upon her, but also because even more than usual, her head was filled with voices from the past, all clamoring to be heard. They raged against the assault on the Goddess in the world beyond. They demanded that the magic find its release and move throughout the world unimpeded and that all be free to worship as they chose to do so. She needed to be alone. She needed very, very much to be alone.

She barely remembered leaving the temple. No one among their group, not Fi nor Danu nor Lillian, spoke as they made their way along the path that led back to the Priestess quarters on the other side of the island. At last, as they came upon the spiral path leading up to the Tor, she excused herself, much to the surprise of the two older women, and started up toward the circle of standing stones. She had climbed the steep path many times over the past eighteen years, but today, her energy was waning from the tension of the presentation and she felt as though her legs would relinquish their support at any moment.

She was grateful to at last reach the top and approached the heel stone with reverence. She closed her eyes, touched the back of her right thumb to her brow, and said, "I bid enter this sacred space." After a moment, a soft breeze fell across her face in welcome and she entered the ring of stones. Three times, she walked the perimeter of the circle, then approached the central altar and spoke the sacred names. As always, she felt the rush of the tides within her as the power rose up all around her. She had no idea what she would do here, but she knew that *here* was where she must be.

The altar before her was a large, flat stone, a little lower than her waist in height. It was smooth polished and as she ran her hand over the surface, she knew it looked the same now as it did when she stood in front of it in her previous life. She climbed up onto the altar and stretched out on it, her face kissed by the setting sun as pink and purple hues transformed the sky. As more of her body met the stone altar, memories flooded over her. She saw blood, as though in projectile from her own body, spill over a throne. She heard a woman scream, her voice ragged and rough from years of silence. She saw an ancient man, older than time itself, sitting up in bed chattering incoherently, his eyes fixed on something she could not herself see. A gleaming sword flung end over end into the lake spun wildly and then caught a blinding flash of sunlight before falling smoothly into the watery depths. The Avalon barge, draped all in black, slid through the water where the sword had fallen. A young girl, small and pictish, her solemn eyes filled with sorrow, stood in the marshes where the waterfowl gathered and watched men battling on the far shore.

She knew these were visions from the other life, not this one, and experience taught her over the years that now and then, she had to allow them the freedom to play out. She heard voices in her head, whispering that the King was a cuckold and worse still, forsworn, followed by wicked laughter. She saw a fair woman with a sad face slip into the large doors of a church without looking back. Saxon armies rushed over the land, bringing death and destruction to all they touched. She saw the sacred groves alight, the holy trees screaming like women as the flames took them down. She heard a harp playing, more sweetly than any she had heard before.

So lost was she in this unfiltered and unmetered flow of memories from her previous life and visions of what had been, that she did not notice when a tall shadow, maroon in the quickly fading light, fell over her.

Chapter 2

Bran drank in the sight of Lillian, stretched out on the altar stone like a beautiful sacrifice. Her body was full and soft, round at the hips and breast, with skin as smooth and white as a summer cloud. The sun was moments away from setting into full darkness and the play of residual light and shadow on her face shrouded her in mystery, yet a mystery that he knew well.

Her brow furrowed and she made a small noise of distress in her throat. He knew that look well. More than anything, Bran wanted to soothe away any thoughts that might cause her fear or pain. He knew better than anyone did what she was experiencing, for memories of his previous life had besieged him for as long as he could recall.

How many times he wished over the years that someone, anyone could provide him with wise counsel through the visual and auditory sendings that he had considered a plague for most of his life. Many thought him to be mad, possessed by demons and visions that others could not perceive.

The sense of immediate recognition he felt when he first saw Lillian was easily the most profound emotion that he had ever experienced. Until he came to the Druids a year before, his life had been one of servility and duty. He had served Lord Seaton well and later, the priests of Seaton Abbey. It had been Father Francis, his mentor, who had come to him late one evening. The concern on his friend's face had disarmed the usually composed Bran and he listened intently as the older man described the turmoil that was coming over the land.

"Bran, my son, you know that Seaton Abbey is, well, it is different than other churches. There is a certain level of, um..." he hesitated, choosing his words more carefully than usual. "...there is a certain tolerance here that is not common in the faith of our Lord and Savior." He rested his hand affectionately on Bran's shoulder. "You have studied well with us, son. In fact," he shook his head in wonder, "you have taught many of us a good deal and we are all better men for having known you. There is, however, a growing unrest in our country and the brothers and I fear that you may no longer be safe here."

Bran startled at his words. "Not safe? I do not understand."

"The church is becoming more aggressive, Bran. They are determined to wipe out all of the Old Ways that have survived beyond the purge that took place under and since King Arthur's rule. King Constantine is away and the zealot priests are free to conduct this assault on Britain's people with impunity. The outlying tribes, the people of the fields, still meet secretly to honor their Goddess and practice the magical arts that were part of their existence for time untold. The Church is determined to exterminate these people who will not convert to Christianity and it is our fear that they are going to target you as well."

"Me?" Bran laughed. "Why would they come after me?"

Father Francis drew in a breath. "There was a time, Bran, several months ago, when you and I were engaged in a conversation about the potential fallibility of God. Do you remember what you said to me then?"

Bran searched his mind. "I honestly cannot recall," he said.

"You said, 'All Gods are one God, Frank, and they most assuredly cannot all be wrong at once.' Do you remember this?"

Bran laughed in spite of himself. "I do now, yes. Quite clever that one, was it not?"

Father Francis looked at him with an expression Bran could not read. "It was, but it was also not the first time I heard it."

Bran blinked. "I do not understand. I certainly never imagined that the idea was original by any means. It was simply a jest."

"It was a jest I heard before…*in those very words* and even in this very room."

"Now I am more confused than before," Bran said, nervously running his fingers through his long dark hair. "The same words?"

"Why do you call me Frank? No one living calls me Frank."

"I don't know," Bran said thoughtfully. "I mean no disrespect. It is a term of endearment, truly."

"I understand," he said. "Bran, what do you know of the last true Merlin of Britain?"

Bran let out a heavy sigh and searched his mind. "I've read many of his works. He was a talented philosopher and diplomat who served under three different kings, who were Ambrosius Aurelianus, Uther Pendragon, and Arthur Pendragon. He died during Arthur's reign at an advanced age. He was a gifted bard. He was an advocate for spiritual unity and a good bit of his writing focused on the encouragement of both Christians and people of the Old Religion to embrace the commonalities in their faiths rather than denouncing the differences. I found him to be a little long-winded, but he had an eloquent turn of a phrase and his teachings are unparalleled for his time or, as nearly as I can tell, for this time as well. What am I missing?"

"Nothing at all," Father Francis chuckled. "As usual, Bran, your information is quite comprehensive. There are, however, things you might not know, like that he was, in fact, my own mentor and confided certain, well, personal details to me. For instance, many did not know that The Merlin was reborn with full memory of his past lives."

This information was stunning to Bran. Raised in a devoutly Christian manor under Lord Seaton, such heretical talk as past lives was forbidden. After leaving Lord Seaton's employ, he went directly into Seaton Abbey to study with the priests there, who also did not entertain such notions. He listened as the older man continued.

"For as long as time itself, The Merlin of Britain was born and reborn into consecutive bodies, each time finding his way to the Druids on Avalon to complete the education he started in the outside world. Taliesin, for instance, spent his younger years in the forests and many considered him a lunatic before he made his way to the Druids and learned the disciplines to arrange his memories of his prior lives and access the wisdom they brought. The Merlin has, throughout the ages, come to the world as both nobleman and pauper and he himself explained to me when I was no older than you are now the turmoil he felt when he was a young man, struggling with the memories of lives he had not experienced and knowledge he had not himself gleaned."

Bran closed his eyes and considered this thought that someone else had walked this earth awash in the madness he had felt his whole life. Someone else had heard voices in his head that were not in the same room with him…or even in the same time with him. Someone else had seen visions of things he could not possibly know. More importantly, someone else had effectively managed two lines of progressive thought at once, his own and The Other, and gone on to achieve greatness. He chided himself for the turn his ego took and reminded himself that greatness is not an ambition, but a calling.

He swallowed hard. "He was like me?" he finally asked.

"Bran," Father Francis continued and leaned in closely for impact, "I believe he *was* you…or *is* you… or you are he. I believe you are the same and that his mind has somehow come back in your body." He poked Bran in the chest with his forefinger.

Bran was confused. "Father, the church does not condone the idea that a person is reborn into another body. How can that be possible?"

Father Francis sighed, feeling older than his years. "Son, the truth of the matter is that Christ is perfect, but the Church is flawed and is very likely no closer to the truth of God's mysteries than are those little tribal people dancing around their balefires. The Church knows no more of what God can or cannot do than they know why the sun rises and sets or why the cows know to come back to the barn at night.

"I sat at that very table…" he gestured toward one of the few items in the sparsely furnished room, "and had The Merlin say to me, '*All Gods are one God, Frank, and they most assuredly cannot all be wrong at once,*' the very same words you said to me *verbatim*. That is not the only time that your words have been his words and to be honest, several of the older priests who knew The Merlin have remarked about it both to me and among themselves.

"Bran, you play the harp with greater skill than anyone here and not because you labored away in your practice, but because you knew how to play it that well within minutes of picking it up. The way a man plays his instrument is unique and you play exactly as he did. You have confided to me in confession that you feel as if someone else is inside your head and that you have knowledge that you could not possibly possess by ordinary means. Does that not then, son, suggest something *extraordinary?*"

Bran took all of this in, his thoughts racing and colliding into one another even more than usual. "What do you want me to do?" was all he could manage to say.

"I want you to allow me to put you into a trance," Father Francis said simply. "If The Merlin is in there, I want to talk to him."

"Then it shall be done," Bran said without hesitation.

Moments later, his eyes were fixed on the gold cross from Father Francis's waist that was now between his fingers, swinging back and forth. Bran followed the movement of the cross carefully, relaxing and tuning into his mentor's voice. As the older man's lulling words coaxed him deeper into trance, the voices inside his head became still and attentive. It was as though the whole world become quiet for what was to come next.

"Now," Father Francis said softly. "Are you in there you old Druid?" He leaned forward and whispered a name into Bran's ear: *"Gwion."* Almost immediately, Bran's face visibly changed. His bright, dark eyes took on a pale blue color and receded deeper into his skull. His nut-brown skin loosened over his strong, defined cheekbones and the hollows below them deepened. The skin on his face became white and paper-thin. This was not painful to Bran but felt extremely odd as his field of vision shifted and clouded.

"Frank," Bran heard himself speak in a melodic, although slightly broken, voice, "For the love of the Gods, man, what took you so long?"

They talked through the night and through the next morning. The church bells tolled, but they did not move to go to morning mass. By the time the sun was setting that second day, neither had eaten nor had drink for many hours. One thing was clear, however. The Merlin was absolute that if Bran did not go to the Druids to complete his training, not only would he be in danger from the rise of the Church, but all of Britain would suffer.

In addition to the sage warning he received, he left Bran with another gift: all The Merlin's memories of life after life after life were not only in his head, but nicely organized and accessible when needed them instead of forever and constantly racing and colliding with one another.

A year later, Bran looked back on that moment as the most important of his life...until today. Lillian lay so still on the stone altar that at first, Bran was not certain that she lived. As the sun surrendered into the darkness, he fumbled for the flint stone in his pocket and used it to light a torch kept among the standing stones. Lillian wrinkled her face at the sudden light and gasped when she saw him, sitting bolt upright.

"How long have I been here?"

Bran smiled. "At least as long as I have been here and you were already sleeping when I arrived."

"I was not sleeping," Lillian said. "I was trancing, trying to sort things out in my mind."

She slipped off the altar and brushed the dirt from her tunic. Bran was suddenly acutely aware that they were alone together on the Tor and he drew in a ragged breath. "I thought you might be ill."

"No. I come up here to think, sometimes," she said softly. "Why are you here, anyway?"

"I came up here to be alone, he said…and to think." His gaze met hers and she dropped her eyes away, turning to hide the flush that crept into her cheeks.

"You have been on Avalon for a year, they said?"

"I have," Bran answered. "Just over, in fact."

"Why is it," she asked, "that I have not seen you before today?"

"I can only wonder myself," he said softly. She was so close to him that he could reach out and touch her if he dared. His hands trembled at the thought. He could smell her scent on the air. It was as though the very apples of Avalon had mated with the fragrant flowers. He drank in her appearance hungrily, feeling that if he did not commit it to memory now, in complete detail, he would not remember her when he left. The thought of having her absent from both his presence and his mind was exquisitely painful, surpassed only by the pain of knowing they would part again.

"Lillian, I…" he closed his eyes as the words he wanted to say jumbled in his brain, lost in translation between thought and speech. "Lillian…"

She looked up at him, her eyes wet and her breath ragged and shallow. Gently, he reached to touch her cheek, his hand still shaking. He sighed audibly as he touched her smooth, cool skin. She raised her own hand to cradle his against her face. "I...don't know what this is," she said, her voice so quiet he could barely hear her. "I have never experienced anything like this before."

"Nor have I," he replied. "I am quite accustomed to my thoughts not always being my own, but from the moment I saw you, my heart has been filled *with just so much*."

Never in his life had he had an unrestrained moment. Never in his life had he lacked the discipline to command his emotions and his actions, even as a young child. His foster mother, Gretchen, had always remarked on what a controlled and solemn child he had always been. Now, in this moment, he could no more restrain himself than could he command the tides to cease their movement.

He swept her into his arms and kissed her deeply, passionately. His mouth sought hers in fierce abandonment before he even realized he had moved. She opened her lips to him, not in surrender, but with tremendous aggression, which caused the hunger inside of him to rage even stronger as his tongue slipped around hers in a dance of desire. Her hands never stopped moving, now with nails digging so deeply into his back that he could feel their sting through his robe and cloak; now twining in his hair and pulling his face even closer to her own. At first, her reaction was so intense that he thought for a moment she was resisting. When he realized that her need was as fervent and enthusiastic as was his, he cupped his hands around her full, round bottom and lifted her effortlessly until her legs wrapped eagerly around him. Carefully, he sat her down on the stone altar, never breaking the heated contact of his mouth on hers.

Urgency swelled within him such as he had never known. In a moment, he finally understood how men could kill in the name of love. "You are mine," he gasped against her lips. "From this day forward, you belong to me and me to you."

Holding her buttocks firmly in his hands, he pushed himself against the warmth of her dampening tunic and moaned with pleasure at the pressure against his wanting, urgent erection. He lost all conscious thought as her hands began to frantically unlace his belt and reach into his clothing. His hands found her round, full breasts and he moaned aloud as his thumbs touched the nipples, hard and erect. He wanted them in his mouth, but he did not want to leave her eager kisses to satisfy that craving.

Finally, her warm, firm hand found his smooth, engorged shaft and the shock of her touch was almost more than he could bear. "I want you inside me…now," she breathed against his mouth.

He was perfectly happy to accommodate that wish. He quickly slipped his hand up her tunic and was in the process of removing her small clothes when he heard her gasp and felt her pull away from him.

"Lillian," a voice said from the edge of the stone circle.

Chapter 3

Danu stepped into the torch's light. "Bran?"

Bran took a breath and hurriedly adjusted his clothing. "Lady Danu," he said in greeting, surprised that his voice sounded so steady.

"Lillian, we were concerned when you did not rejoin us by nightfall," she said, her voice on the edge of reprimand.

Lillian was grateful that her position in relation to the torchlight concealed her disheveled appearance. She adjusted the veil she wore over her hair and smoothed her tunic. "I needed some time on the Tor," she said. "Much has happened today and I wanted to be alone to think."

"But," Danu observed, "You are not alone."

"No," Lillian agreed. "I am not." She looked at Bran helplessly, the tides still flaring madly inside of her.

"Come home, girl," Danu said simply, and turned and left the circle.

Bran did not take his gaze off Lillian and when her eyes met his, he mouthed, "Soon." She nodded and went silently with Danu to the House of Maidens.

Soon. The word should have comforted her, but instead it served only to fan the flames that raged inside her.

She and Danu walked silently down the path that led away from the Tor. She hazarded a glance back and although the torchlight was faint at this distance and angle, she could make out the dim outline of him standing by the heel stone, watching her go. When he saw her turn, he raised his hand in the gesture of honor and then placed his palm over his heart. Her body continued to ache for release the rest of the walk home; even as her head swam and her skin tingled in every place where he had touched her.

When she entered the sleeping area of the House of Maidens, her Sister Priestesses were already sleeping. She made her way to her own bed without a sound, but then decided to forego sleeping alone, despite her desire to contemplate and process all that had happened that day. Another desire took precedence that she could deny no more.

She took off her clothing and folded it neatly onto a chair by the bed, but not before cupping her tunic against her face and inhaling deeply. As she hoped, the front of it still conveyed Bran's scent and the musky, earthly aroma sent her urges coursing even stronger through her loins. Her thighs, her belly, and her heart all cried out for the consummation of her pleasure. Completely naked, she slipped into bed behind Maia and pulled the young woman's warm sleeping body against her. She let out an involuntary sigh as their skin touched and as she knew she would, Maia immediately took her hand and wrapped her arm around her, pushing backward against the front of Lillian's body.

Within moments, Maia's mouth and fingers were busy, skillfully sucking and biting at her swollen, stiff nipples, kissing her, massaging her sweet spot with her quick and deft fingers and then slipping her fingers inside as her tongue and lips brought Lillian to a blinding release that rocked her to her very core. Maia kissed her lips gently and brought her drenched fingers up for

Lillian to taste. "You were so wet, my girl. You must have had an interesting visit with the Druids."

"Indeed," Lillian agreed.

The sole of discretion, Maia did not press her friend for more information and gently declined Lillian's offer for reciprocal pleasure. "I was with Cara earlier. The height of pleasure you reached tonight is tempting, to be sure, but you have had quite a day and I am sated. Sleep, my sweet."

…and sleep, she did, without dreams and in complete peace.

Chapter 4

"I still can't believe it," Maia said, her quick, deft fingers braiding flowers into Lillian's hair. She was far more fine-handed than any others in the House of Maidens and Lillian was pleased to have her help in the initial preparations for the ritual. She had received no instruction for what she should do in preparation for the ceremony other than fast for three days prior. In her training as a priestess, she had learned to control her body's needs and so fasting was not an effort for her. Her stomach would rumble in protest for the first day and she would fatigue more easily, but it was no true challenge. She drank plenty of pure sacred water from the holy well and herbal teas to keep up her strength and enrich her blood.

"Lady of the Lake," Maia continued. "I am excited to live in a time where there is one at all, much less have it be someone who is so dear to me." She continued to chatter, but Lillian's attention waned with the anticipation of the ritual bearing down on her. What would it be like? What vows must she take? She reflected on her dedication to the Goddess, which had taken place among her Sister Priestesses and the Elder Priestesses. She had been marked to the Goddess at that time, had sworn to be obedient and to pursue her magical education throughout the rest of this life and into the next. She had taken the sacred drink and visioned for hours while a scribe recorded her words to enter the holy writ of the island.

She tried to follow the trail of memories from her other life back to a similar experience, but the other many rituals of great importance kept blending in her mind to the point that she could not separate out one from the other. She saw a blood covered man in a headdress bearing the horns of a great stag, saw him over her, mounting her, and crying his pleasure in primitive grunts and moans. She saw an elderly woman muttering chants and blessings as she rubbed dyes and scented oils over her body. She saw luminous faces, painted with some sort of paint to cause them to reflect the light and the glowing, disembodied around her. Again, she heard the harsh screams of a woman that she had heard a week before while in the sacred circle on the Tor. She saw herself reaching upward to the clear, blue sky, speaking words of incantation and watching as a lightning bolt stabbed into the cauldron in front of her, igniting the wood and twigs within. She saw herself under the sword, her arms raised in the Goddess position speaking words she could not hear.

"Lillian," she heard Maia say firmly. "Lillian, you're done." She shook herself awake and realized she had dozed while visioning. It took her a moment to separate out realities and come fully to her senses. "You're exhausted, Little One," her friend said kindly. "Danu will not call you to her quarters until almost sunset. Go. Sleep for a while and I will wake you when it is time."

Lillian nodded and slipped into her bed. She was asleep the moment her head touched the pillow.

She started awake an undeterminable time later when she felt a hand cover her mouth and a voice whisper, "Ssssh. It's me."

She was shocked to find that the room was dark and she was otherwise completely alone. Where were the sisters and why had she not been roused before sunset? "Bran?" she whispered. "What are you doing here? How did you get in?"

He took his hand from her mouth, reluctantly it seemed, and caressed her cheek, then her hair. "I had to see you," he said softly. "My heart aches from being without you."

She took his hand in hers. "Mine as well," she whispered. "I want to know you, to know everything about you. We have spent so little time together and yet...," she faltered as words failed her.

"...and yet, we are bonded in such a way as no others have ever known." He finished and she nodded. "I do not know how much I will be able to see you after the ceremony tonight," he said, his voice filled with regret.

"Why?" she asked. "You will be The Merlin of Britain. I will be the Lady of the Lake. Whether it is meet and right that we do so or not, we will rule over this land. Bran," she said excitedly, "We can do whatever we want to do. After tonight, we can be together...always." She brought his hand to her lips and kissed his strong, slender fingers, searching his eyes for affirmation.

In the darkness, she could barely make out his features. "My dearest," he said with pain evident in his voice. "Would that we could, but I am not completely certain that it works that way. There are plans afoot, I fear, that may separate us for a time."

"Plans?" she asked, feeling indignation rise within her. "What plans are there for my life of which I have not been informed?"

"Sssh," he whispered. "I don't know, sweetling. If I did, I would tell you without a moment's hesitation. It is outside of my influence. Something, however, is in play and I feel changes in the air. Whatever it is, I want you to rest assured that my heart is yours, dear Lillian, and I will never, ever love another so long as you live."

His lips met hers in the briefest sweetness and then he said, "They are coming. I have to go now."

"Bran…wait…" but then he was gone into the darkness. She fell back onto her pillow, her arms draped over her face, and wondered how it was possible that in the course of but a fortnight she could become so much more confused than she had ever been before.

The next thing she knew, Maia was waking her from a tremendously sound sleep. She woke to find the twilight sun easing lazily through the windows and casting odd, dancing shadows into the floor.

"Oh look," Maia said. "You've mussed your hair." Tenderly, she began pushing the flowers back into the carefully structured braids and smoothing loose tendrils into the folds of her hair.

Lillian looked around, confused and disoriented from the abrupt departure of deep sleep. Twilight? It had been completely dark a few minutes before. Did she dream?

"There now,' she smiled. "You look as good as new. Danu is ready for you. Let's go change your life profoundly, now, shall we?"

Chapter 5

Lillian was carried to the top of the Tor in an enclosed litter. She insisted that she preferred to walk herself, but Danu and Fi were absolute that she would be carried and wait within until called into the ceremony. Attending Priestesses had scrubbed her clean from scalp to toes, rubbed her skin with grit, and then nourished it with balm until it very nearly glowed under the Summer Full Moon. As soon as she came to the Temple of the Moon for preparation, someone pushed a cup into her hands that contained an herbal drink. She drank it all down at once and almost immediately, her head begin to swim. Several of the Elder Priestesses anointed her body at each of the magical points with scented oils and then painted her face, shoulders, hands, and arms with the holy, magical sigils. As they worked on her body in silence, Lillian found herself slipping in and out of trance, the voices in her head so distinct and insistent that at times, she could not tell what was real and happening in front of her and what was an echo of memory that only she could remember. It was as though all those familiar voices in her head were chanting in harmonizing cadences. The combination of strong herbs in the drink, the scent of the oils, the rhythmic lull of the voices in her head, and her long fast blurred the lines between the worlds for her.

Before the priestesses lifted her into the litter, they blindfolded her and gently turned her nine times in a circle, furthering the disorientation even more. The litter lurched and shifted through the long walk across the island and up the hill to the Tor and several times, Lillian feared she would wretch. She lay back and forced her breathing shallow, mentally counting the breaths as they came and went. It was hot, so hot, within the enclosed litter. The Midsummer heat played upon the rain from the week to make the air damp and cloying as the scent of the sacred oils hung around her. She wore very little and felt nearly naked compared to her usual dress and tunic covering. Dissatisfied with the braids Maia had created, Fi loosened Lillith's hair and secured small flowers within the waves the hair arrangement had created. Her dark hair fell to her waist in rivulets, but in the heat of the litter, it felt heavy and sweaty.

She must have dozed because she jerked awake when the priestesses sat the litter upon the ground. After several minutes, she heard voices speaking in the litanous tone of ritual. She could smell sage, lavender, and other herbs burning and the scent carried thickly through the air, overpowering the fragrance of the oils that anointed her body. Carefully, she used one finger to feel along the dark back window of the litter and push aside the curtain a tiny bit. She gratefully breathed in the cooler air as it rushed to her through the tiny gap she created. Now, she could better hear words, but still, could not decipher what the speakers were saying. She could tell a call and response was being used and she clearly heard a man's voice speak and others answer in cadence, then a woman's voice speak and the same group respond.

After a period of time - it could have been minutes or hours - the curtains on the front of the litter opened and a rush of cooler air flooded over her as a hand reached inside to assist her in leaving the enclosure. She took it firmly and was pulled into a standing position and led away from the litter. Without the benefit of eyesight, her other senses were much stronger. She felt the power current as she passed between the large ring stones and knew was nearing the stone altar.

Voices were chanting around her and she could now make out that they were saying, *"Lady wise and lady strong. Lady lead us far and long. Lady wise and lady strong. Take the place where you belong."* The guiding hands backed her against the stone altar and there she stood, pushing aside the moments of fear and apprehension that arose and stilling her mind to the profound experience going on around her. Such a thing had not happened in the lifetime of most of the people here and would not likely happen again at all if Avalon fell to ruin.

The chanting stopped and for several minutes, there was silence ringing in the night. She could hear movement, first far away and then close by, and could sense a presence near her.

The chanting began again, this time saying, *"Lord of wisdom, Lord of fate. Lord of honor at the gate. Lord of justice, Lord of song. Lead us far and lead us long."*

The pungent smell of resin incense became stronger and Lillian knew that a censor moved around her to bless her. To confirm this, she heard a man's voice say, "Blessed are thee with the Air and with the Fire."

Warm, wet fingers traced the shape of the solar cross on her forehead, followed by the grainy rub of dust into the wet path and Danu's voice said, "Blessed are thee with the Water and with the Earth." Lillian felt the ancient, primal power rush through her.

Someone, Fi, she thought, knelt before her and lifted up Lillian's feet one by one, placing each one in a ceremonial bath and washing them gently. When she finished, she said, "I humble myself before thee and call thee The Lady of the Lake."

Some distance away from her, she heard words being spoken by a man's voice but again, could not make out exactly what was being said. She swooned slightly from the energy of the ritual and was grateful that no hands reached to steady her. She did not want to appear weak or infirm in this moment.

She felt the touch of steel between her breasts and automatically raised her arms in the sign of the Goddess, out, spread wide and reaching upward toward the sky. She felt as if she could reach her hands all the way up to the heavens and touch the starry breasts of the Mother Goddess. A man's voice said, "Lillian of Avalon. In as much as the Goddess has chosen you to wear the mantle of leadership for this island and represent Her on this earth, to speak Her words, to know Her mind, and to follow Her will in all things, I ask of you, do you accept the providence of Lady of the Lake and all that the title conveys?"

Lillian's voice was strong and absolute as she said, "I do. So mote it be."

"And do you swear by your very life and your soul through this life and all other lives past and future to defend Avalon in all things, to place the will of the Goddess above all other considerations, and to give of all you have, including your life, your love, and your very spirit in service to the Goddess?"

"I do. So mote it be."

"Do you enter into this binding congress and contract of your own free will and without coercion, doubt, or hesitation?"

"I do. So mote it be." The pressure of steel on her breastplate increased and she felt a trickle of blood run down the wispy thin shift she wore.

"For verily I say to you, Lillian of Avalon, that it is better to rush upon my blade and perish than to enter into this congress and contract with fear in your heart. Do you wish to proceed?"

"I do. So mote it be."

"And what is the password to your sovereignty?" He asked.

Password?

Lillian knew she should have stumbled as no one had given her a password to use, but the words came to her as if she had spoken them every day for her entire life. "I have sworn by vows of four to rein as The Lady forever more."

She felt the man kiss her right hip, her forehead, her left hip, her right shoulder, her left shoulder, and then her right hip again, forming the sacred star upon her body. Her arms should ache from holding them upright for so long, but she felt strong and solid. He kissed her lips to complete the blessing and she tasted the pungent combination of cloves and ale on his breath.

"The Druid Fellowship of Avalon names you to be Lady of the Lake from this day forward," he said loudly. A group of men's voices repeated what he said. "The Druid Fellowship of Avalon names you to be Lady of the Lake from this day forward."

Away from her, she heard women's voices say, "The Priestesses of Avalon name you The Merlin of Britain from this day forward." Her blindfold was removed and she saw a large circle of Druids around her. Of course, she thought, chiding herself at her lapse in memory and training. This induction was a duality ritual. Males coronate the female leader and females coronate the male leader, thus honoring the duality of leadership and service. Normally, the Druids dressed in robes of color according to their avocation: blue for bards, yellow for scribes, green for arborists, and red for healers. Tonight, however, they all wore black hooded robes. She knew this was to strip away all hierarchy from each man and humble him in the presence of the new leaders of the island and, in fact, of magic. The Elder Priestess who had washed her feet had symbolized the humbling of the priestesses of the island before delivering her to the males for induction.

She lowered her arms and watched as the circle of priestesses on the other side of the circle of standing stones filed into the circle around her, moving interstitially among the men in a male-female configuration. *Again*, she thought, *perfect duality.* When the circle was complete and now doubled in size, the last male and female to link together dropped their hands and created an opening. In the light of the Full Moon, she saw Bran enter. He, like she, was sparsely dressed, wearing little more than a loincloth. He too had sigils painted on his skin, which gleamed as darkly in the moonlight as hers was pale white. The oils rubbed into his body caught the light and accented the curves and angles of his body. He joined her at the stone altar and the circle of men and women closed around them.

The chanting began quietly and gradually, the volume and intensity increased. "The Lady is with us and magic is born. The Merlin is with us and magic is born." Three, maybe even four, or five drummers began to beat out a loud and steady heartbeat to punctuate the chant.

"The Lady is with us and magic is born. The Merlin is with us and magic is born." The power within the circle rose higher and higher. Bran came to her and lifted her effortlessly, placing her on the end of the stone altar. He raised his arms into the air and called loudly, "I now erect the ancient altar where man and woman have long worshiped. Woman is the altar to man that he might pay honor to the Goddess, for I say unto you, all acts of selfless passion and devotion are Hers and all moments of pleasure belong to She whose silver face lights the sky this night."

Although she had no idea of what was to come, the words came easily to her as if she had spoken them many times. She suspected it was the same for him. "I now give life to the sacred altar where man and woman have long worshiped. Man is the altar to woman that she might honor the God, for I say unto you, all acts of selfless passion and devotion are His and all moments of pleasure belong to He who runs with the stag and gives life to my seed." She lay back on the stone altar and as she parted her legs, he moved between them. Her eyes met his and held him fiercely in their gaze. He found he had no hope of looking away from her.

The chant within the circle changed, but the heartbeat of the drums stayed the same. *"Lance to grail. Lance to grail. Lance to grail."*

She was naked beneath the airy shift and she felt Bran's body, warm and smooth, as he lay upon her. His hard shaft, covered in softest leather, pushed eagerly against her soft, dampening folds. He kissed her deeply and as he started to pull his mouth away from hers, she whispered to him, "I am virgin."

He pulled back and looked at her, then whispered softly, "As am I." He slipped off the stone altar and grasped her hips, pulling her to the end. Her hands cupped his firm buttocks and brought him in closer to her. He lifted the loincloth and she felt the smooth, heat of his hard cock press against her. His hand slipped between her legs and stroked her gently and she moaned aloud, pushing eagerly towards him as his fingers touched silky wetness. "Lance to grail," she whispered. "My Lord Merlin, Lord of my heart, so mote it be."

She gasped loudly as he pushed into her and felt a moment of pain and then nothing save exquisite pleasure throughout her body, from her loins to her nipples and throughout her very skin. She wished she could be closer to him. His position standing at the end of the altar as he thrust into her repeatedly had him at a right angle to her. She could not kiss him, touch him, or hold him as she wished, but the fierce sensations coursing through her did not allow for rational thought of any kind.

"Lance to grail, lance to grail, lance to grail."

She felt her release approaching and looking into his eyes, she knew that he was on the verge of completion as well. His face contorted and his body shuddered violently as a primitive, ear-shattering roar burst from his throat. Her orgasm came at the same time and she felt wave after wave of pleasure and power course over her as never before. The body jerked and contracted around him and she felt her womb throbbing inside her. His arms reached around her and he swept her up off the altar, still pulsing inside her, still hard and thrusting into her, and roared again, a guttural, animal sound that seemed to come from deep within his very soul. The change of sensation sent her into yet another wave of pleasure and she cried out again in passion. This was as it should have been two weeks ago here, in this sacred place, but this was also why it could not happen before now. This culminating moment of magic and power is what would propel Avalon back into power and begin the process of returning magic to the land. She realized the chanting around them had stopped and they were now in silence, the last echo of her cry the only sound moving through the air.

Shaking and weak, she fell against him and somewhere in her mind, she wondered at his incredible strength to hold her there after such an experience, the two of them still connected lance to grail. She was no slim flower, but he cupped her in his arms with ease and held her close, kissing her hair and whispering words of love and adoration to her. With soundless steps, the men and women in the circle came to the altar and pressed their middle finger into the small stream of blood that creased down it. Her chest, she thought dimly, must be bleeding more than she thought from the final challenge and vow at the point of the blade.

No, she thought. That is the blood of my maidenhead spilt upon the altar.

Bran gently lifted her off his deflating penis and stood her beside him, her shaking legs hardly finding strength to hold her upright. She leaned against him, sensing that her knees might buckle at any moment. She was sore inside already, but pleasantly so. She watched as the men and woman used her blood to mark the sign of the solar cross on their own foreheads using the middle finger, which runs closer to the spirit than the utilitarian forefinger. Gooseflesh rose on her arms as she realized the potent magic of what they were doing. She was now a part of them all and a stream of consciousnesses opened in her mind as she connected with each one.

As the last woman anointed herself, Bran turned her to him and caught her eyes with his own. "Lady Lillian," he whispered to her. "I need for you to focus for a moment. I am going to give you a gift."

She smiled coyly and whispered, "My Lord Merlin, what you have already given to me this night is a treasure beyond value."

He broke into a smile and for a moment, he was not the Merlin of Britain, but a young man who had pleased his lover.

"Lillian," he said, serious once more. "Close your eyes."

She did and then felt his breath warm on her ear. He whispered a name to her: *"Evienne."* Immediately, her eyes flew open as she drew in a surprised breath. If the world had not stopped for her in the flames of their ritual consummation, it certainly did now. The name echoed through her mind repeatedly and abruptly, all of the random, detached thoughts that had plagued her since her birth began to organize throughout her mind. She opened her mouth to speak, but nothing would come out. There was no thought behind the action. There was no thought at all, in fact. Her head spun and she felt faint as memories of the other life and lives even before it fell neatly into place. She could feel her own heartbeat pounding in her temples. Then, there was silence, not just in the circle, but also in her mind as well. She felt tears of relief and gratitude slip down her cheeks. It was done.

The priestess she was before, the Lady of the Lake she was before, was still inside of her. She held every memory, every echo, every bit of wisdom stored safely within her. Like a book, she could open it at any time, but at last, meticulously indexed so that she could access the exact memory she needed with ease. If she wanted to, she could read through her past life from beginning to end and know every thought, every sensation, every fear, every moment of longing, every regret, and every joy she had experienced in that life. It was at her command and within her control.

Finally, the cacophony of voices and emotions in her head quieted and only *she* remained. She, who was Lillian, The Lady of the Lake, and this man who created such blessed refuge in her mind and such grand pleasure in her body, he with whom she had spent her entire previous life, was now hers forever more.

Chapter 6

Lillian resisted the urge to massage her temples, knowing it was essential that she maintain a priestess level of poise and confidence. The summit had engaged at sun up and now it was well past evening mealtime. Maia brought her a bit of cheese and some bread to soaked in wine at the midday and she had nibbled at it through the afternoon. The opinions of the Druid High Council and the Priestess Elders divided not only between one another, but also, among themselves and there seemed to be no hope of reaching a unilateral decision on how to proceed anytime soon.

Her back ached from sitting so long and the oppressive heat, combined with the wine she seldom took, left her stomach pitching and rolling. A steady throb had taken up residence deep in her head and she found it hard to concentrate around it.

She found herself wishing fervently that Bran could be here to lend his wisdom to the proceedings. She had not seen him since the night after their inductions. He had come to her formally and asked for an audience in the antechamber of the Great Hall of the Temple of the Moon where the summit was now taking place. She and Maia had that day moved into the long-abandoned quarters of the Lady of the Lake. Her first act as the island's female royalty had been to name Maia as her personal lady-in-waiting and install her into the home. Maia had her own quarters inside the house. The Attending Priestesses would come and go to bring food, clear away dishes, tend to the fire when needed, and make certain the home always had clear, sweet water from the Sacred Well available, but she and Maia would be the only ones permanently in residence.

She was grateful for the company because she had never lived alone. Lillian was born to Leya, a kind and gentle priestess who considered well past the age of childbearing. No one was more surprised than she was when she unexpectedly conceived from a night at the Beltane fires. Because of the nature of the evening, she had no knowing of who might have fathered the child. All men were as Gods on that holiest of evenings and all wore masks to heighten the mystery, intrigue, and excitement of the tides that coursed ravenously in the coupling that occurred.

The delivery had been complicated and strenuous and had ultimately taken Leya's life. The boisterous baby girl burst forth from her and went eagerly to her breast. She tucked the baby into the crook of her arm to give suck and as the afterbirth slipped from her, so did a blood flow that would not cease, despite the admission of the most aggressive herbal anti-hemorrhagic agents and highest magic of the priestesses. She was gone before the child finished her suckle.

There were several priestesses with babes at the breast ten moons after that particularly boisterous Beltane night, including Danu, and all took turns giving suck to little Lillian. Her name was a gift from the First Elder Priestess because the night she was born, a shock of calla lilies suddenly burst forth with countless blooms where none had ever been before outside the hut where Leya had labored. The Elder Priestess had gathered the other priestesses around the lilies and decreed that surely this was a very special child sent to them at the cost of their dear sister.

After she weaned, Lillian spent time in both the House of Mothers and the House of Maidens and at the age of nine, she moved permanently into the House of Maidens, as did all young girls.

She had a quick mind and was a fast study at any lesson or task she was assigned. She was fine-handed and could weave, spin, and embroider with the most intricate stitching the priestesses had ever seen. She played the harp beautifully and her knowledge of herbs was immediate and comprehensive. It seemed that only her thirst for knowledge surpassed her capacity to learn.

Though she was energetic and had a busy mind, she was an obedient child and well-tempered. She always had a twinkle in her eye and a ready smile. Even before she moved into the House of Maidens, the comments she made caught the ear of the Elder Priestesses, who then began their study of her extraordinary mind and the memories it contained.

After living her entire life with a bevy of females around her, it was strange to her the first night she slept in the quiet quarters of the Lady of the Lake. It had been many year, decades even, since anyone had used the little house, so Attendant Priestesses spent the day prior to the ritual scrubbing the little house from roof to cellar. They stocked it with every kind of fruit, dried meat, bread, and vegetable that she could ever imagine to want. The bed had new straw and fresh bed clothing and the sweet smell of the hay permeated the room. The house was sparsely furnished, but she needed little and even the small hut seemed huge to her with only the two of them in it. She bade Maia to sleep with her that night so she would not feel so alone and Maia readily agreed, likely feeling as isolated and she did herself.

Before sleep, a young Druid arrived at her door and told Maia that The Merlin wished to see Lillian in the antechamber of the Great Hall of the Temple of the Moon. It was late and Lillian was tired, but her heart leapt at the knowledge that he was here, so close to her. She thought of little else the entire day but the feel of his arms around her as he had swept her up and thrust into her during the ritual. She replayed that moment often in her mind.

The Druid bowed to her and extended his arm for her to take. They walked across the courtyard to the Great Hall and she entered, as always, with a sense of reverence that could still her very breath. In a show of discretion, her escort excused himself at the entrance and she made her way with the soundless steps of a trained priestess to the antechamber.

A solitary candle burned in the room and in its glow, she saw Bran rise as she crossed the threshold. He opened his arms to her and she rushed into them with her heart pounding. She savored the feeling of his embrace and nestled to his chest, breathing in his musky, male scent. He kissed the top of her head and then seated himself on one of the many small benches that constituted seating in the room, pulling her onto his lap.

"I just want to hold you forever," he murmured into her ear and she closed her eyes and allowed the pure sweetness of the moment to envelop her. Her skin tingled with electricity at the nearness of him and the intimacy of their closeness. For the first time in her life, she was in love; deeply, passionately, unquestionably in love. She allowed it to wash over her like a gentle, Summer rain. How was it possible that she had ever lived, nay had even drawn a breath, without this feeling in her life?

After a few minutes, he said, "As much as I love being this close to you, my dearest, I want to be able to look at you while I talk to you." He eased her off his lap and onto the bench beside him. He took her hands in his and smiled at her. "I do not believe there was ever a time when I did not love you, Lillian," he began. "Even before I knew there was you, I could feel you there, like a promise in the darkness that I could not yet see. My heart is so very full and although I consider myself an aptly gifted wordsmith, I cannot find the right words in any known language to convey the depth of what I feel for you. My heart is yours. I am yours. I think of nothing but you, day and night, night and day and every single moment of both. Holding you, touching you, wanting you is the most powerful and delightful thing I have ever done or ever known. I have never experienced anything close to the thrill and pleasure I felt last night as we coupled."

He stopped and closed his eyes for a moment, seeming to be lost in the memory. "I will not lie to you. The sheer power of our conjoined forces was delicious and addictive. I felt we could rule the world and none would dare challenge our claim."

He brought her hand to his lips and kissed each finger. "My beloved, I know that pride brings the quickest fall and that the Gods love to toy with a man given to such ignoble egotism as such. Still, I could not refrain from stepping into the force, the sheer *command*, that joining with you in such a way provoked within me. Darling Lillian, please say that you think no less of me for my indulgence of such base and selfish thoughts." His eyes sought hers in pleading.

She reached up her hand to cup his cheek against her palm. "I too," she said. "I was completely overcome not only with the physical magnificence of the pleasure you awoke and released in me but yes, also the magical power we together invoked. I truly felt as the Goddess before you and you the God within me. I have thought of nothing, not one thing more, than of you and of us since that very moment. If you are damned for celebrating your own ego and pride, then I am also so damned and we shall meet our fates for such thoughts together."

"I love you, Lillian," he said. "I love you so."

"And I you," she replied and looked into his eyes, in some ways trying to convince herself he was real and not a dream she had conjured from her own desires. How her life had changed within only one moon's cycle through her faces!

When they spoke, they both spoke at once and said different things.

He said, "There is something I must tell you."

She said, "Marry me."

Again, they spoke at once, but this time, said the same word.

"What?" Followed by…

"You go first," at the same time again.

"Marry me," Lillian repeated. "We will have the grandest hand-fasting ever. We can do it on Mabon and celebrate the blessings given to us. We can have it up on the Tor and welcome all the Druids and all of the Priestesses and the stag and the wildings and the bird of the sky or, if you want, we can have a grand ceremony in the Temple with candlelight and the holy regalia and the moonlight shining down on us through the stained glass. Oh, Bran, I don't care where or how we do it, but marry me."

Bran dropped his head and her heart sank. "Oh no. Oh no. Bran, I am so foolish and headstrong and giddy, I did not even imagine that you might not want to marry. Please, my love. Please forgive my impulsiveness." She pulled his hands to her lips and covered them with kisses.

He looked at her with tears misting his dark eyes. "Lillian, oh my precious love. There is nothing, *nothing*, I would love more than to be your husband."

She almost collapsed with relief, "Then you will? Or…can The Merlin of Britain not take a wife?" She closed her eyes and went into the past life files in her mind. "No, The Merlin can marry. By history, it is the Lady of the Lake who remains without a partner for she is to be claimed by no man and is Goddess unto herself. Oh well," she said with a flip of her hand, "I will change that."

"No," he said. "You are correct. There is nothing that forbids marriage between us that cannot be changed and if you wish to change tradition, I will change it right there with you and yes, believe me, when that moment comes, we will have a wedding like no other; like none that has ever been and none that will be again. Kissed by the Gods, it shall be."

"But…" she said nervously.

"But I have to leave at daybreak and," he tilted her chin upward so she looked at him. "Lillian, I do not know when or if I shall return."

She felt as if someone had pulled the firmament of the world out from under her feet. "What? Leave? Where? To where do you depart so abruptly?"

"As The Merlin, I must leave Avalon immediately and attempt to broker peace with the Glastonbury priests and then with the priests further into the country, to all seven kingdoms of Britain... It is to me to play the diplomat in this conflict before war again comes to our very doorstep. We not only have the war on magic and the Old Ways at hand, but the defense of Britain against the Saxons and other enemies. Our country is frighteningly vulnerable and it is essential that the lesser kings join not only to protect *our* people, but to protect *all* people of Britain. The lesser kings answer to the Christian priests."

"Then I will come with you," Lillian said resolutely. "What stronger front could we present to the priests than The Merlin of Britain and The Lady of the Lake? It is Arthur who broke his vow to protect Avalon and he died for his error. Surely, all will see that to deny the Goddess brings only chaos and despair! I will tell Maia to make arrangements to ride out with us at first light."

"No, love," he said sadly. "Your place is here. The Druids and the Priestesses need your wisdom, your leadership, and *yes, your memories* to solidify their position. We cannot both leave and I am the one called to go and you are the one, my beloved, called to stay. Dearest, this venture may, and no doubt *will,* be treacherous in so many ways. I cannot and will not subject you to that."

"That is absurd!" she protested angrily. "I am trained in warfare and can handle a sword as well as any man and as for Avalon, the elders managed for tens of years without a Lady of the Lake and without The Merlin of Britain. We can do the God and Goddess's work in the world together."

"They need you here," he insisted. "I – *I* – need you here. I must know that you are safe and cared for every day. If I take you with me the danger we will surely face would be a distraction I cannot afford. The task I must attempt is simply too great to bear it. I need to know that you are here, safe, and taking care of business on Avalon."

As painful as it was, the priestess and diplomat in her saw the wisdom in what he said. It was the woman and lover within her who cried protest. She felt the heavy weight of their circumstances on her shoulders and she the calmness with which she accepted it was in no way reflective of the inner battle that waged between her heart and her good sense.

"So explain to me what will happen, then," she said.

He feigned a look of shock. "Are you serious? Is that all of the fight you have in you?"

She managed a half smile. "I'm saving my energy for when you return."

He shook his head in amazement. "I love you."

"I love you too."

He explained that he and two of the Senior Druids would take the Avalon barge to the shore at daybreak. She and an advisory group consisting of the remaining Senior Druids and the Elder Priestesses would develop an effective defense strategy for Avalon should his diplomatic mission fail or should he be unable to complete his tasks. They were to assemble the information he relayed back to Avalon and determine a wise course of action. When he had met with each of the primary churches and their leaders, the Kings if possible, and assessed their position, he would return to Avalon. It could take months or it could take years.

Her heart broke at the prospect of not seeing him for so very long and she could tell from his expression that he felt the same. Her limited experience in relationships provided no course of behavior, so she instead sought the guidance of her heart and simply said, "I will watch and wait for you every single day until you return, but I do have one condition and I will not compromise on this."

"Anything," he said.

"I know of something from the memories that you organized from me and I want you to use it. Come." She led him out of the antechamber and together they walked towards the Lake itself. Stepping into the water's edge, she felt the cool sand under her feet and the tiny, wet movements coursing against her ankles. Unsure of exactly how to proceed, but picturing the result in her mind, she raised her arms spread into the Goddess position and said in a firm and commanding voice, "I bid you come forth. Sister, give of your bounty!"

At first, there was nothing, but then, a series of concentric ripples began at the center of the lake. Gradually, they became stronger and within moments, they could see movements on the surface. *Something* was moving along the lapping water with the ripples pushing it toward the shore. Lillian bent down and retrieved a large item from the waters at her feet.

"This," she said, "is the sword *Excalibur*. A priestess here on Avalon created the scabbard around it and according to legend, the sword itself was forged by dragon's breath. So long as the bearer holds the sword and wears the scabbard, no blood will be lost. I want you to wear this always."

She pulled the sword from the beautifully made scabbard and held it into the air. Forty years in the embrace of the lake showed no ill effect. It had been reborn in the watery womb of magic and was again a sacred and empowered tool. It was large and her strength to hold it surprised him until he took it in his own hand and saw that it was perfectly balanced and very easy to manage. He had himself watched it drawn from the Lake; however, it was as smooth and shining as if newly forged. The scabbard was of the finest cloth and thread, which was still bright and neatly sewn. If this was truly Arthur's scabbard, it must be at least sixty years past since it had first come to Arthur's hand and the sword itself was of the ancient holy regalia and had not been seen since his death. Most presumed it interred with him on Avalon. Yet here it was in his hands.

"I will do so and honor your request," he said.

"It was less of a request and more of a..."

"I understand," he interjected. "Historically, it is not for The Merlin to bear weapons as logic, wisdom, and diplomacy are his skills. In these treacherous times, however, I have to bow not only to your... *non-request*.... but to common sense as well. *This* Merlin of Britain is willing to defend Avalon with his very life should it come to it. He does, however," he smiled, "have so very much to live for that this sword will never leave his side."

They spent that night on the shore of the Lake. He put out his cloak on the ground, which was already damp with dew, and they laid together, each entwined in the arms of the other, until the sky began to lighten.

Since that time, the moon had twice gone from Full to Dark and already Bran sent word that the priests of Glastonbury had grown increasingly contemptuous of Avalon and refused him an audience. He learned from groundskeepers and other staff on the holy compound, that on a regular basis, the people of the Heaths and outlying lands who still practiced the Old Ways were brought to the temple for torture and ultimately, for execution.

The Druids and Priestesses were stunned that torture would occur on the sacred grounds – any sacred grounds - themselves and were of a divided mind for how to proceed. Some felt that they should take military action by organizing the practitioners of the Old Ways and training them for battle. Others felt that an aggressive military maneuver would spell disaster and result in the annihilation of the few remaining who were faithful to The Goddess and kept Her name and Her secrets alive on the mainland. When further word came that there were rumors Glastonbury was actually of those most kindly deposed to those who still followed the Old Ways, it became difficult to quell the thread of panic that ran through Avalon.

Lillian called the meeting of her advisors to attempt to form a unilateral mindset on the problem and instead found that if anything, hours and hours into the process, they remained more divided than ever. Each attempt to find threads of common ground on which to build a strong foundation of unity seemed to crumble like sand between her fingers. How must it be for Bran attempting to negotiate with their adversaries and find their common interests to support when she could not even do so amongst their own? She had drawn extensively from her own past life memories to find equating circumstances and wisdom developed over oceans of time and still came up dry at the well of cooperative thought and effort.

As Priestess argued with Druid, Druid argued with Druid, and Priestess argued with Priestess, Lillian's stomach continued to argue with the bread and wine. At last, she reached her limit.

"Enough!" she said firmly and was pleasantly surprised when immediate silence fell on the group. She wondered if she would ever become accustomed to commanding such power over people who two months before had been her authority figures. "For all that is unclear and unresolved in this lengthy discussion, there are three premises that are quite galvanized.

"One is that it is fruitless to expect that we are going to come to an amicable conclusion on how to proceed today or possibly any day in the near feature. It is obvious that the wise ones around me are committed to their perspectives with tremendous passion and I honor that in you. There is, however, no sign of compromise or adjustment in sight and I know that we are all weary from the day's discussion.

"The second is that while the Dark Moon is an appropriate time to bring forth our innermost thoughts and agendas, the Full Moon will shine light on the subject and potentially bring new information to consider."

"The third is that we are engaged in a fearful situation that puts us at a obvious tactical disadvantage. In addition to the mundane practicalities of what *could* happen, we also must remember that we are magical folk and that magic is where our strength lies, not in warfare. Although many of us are trained in weaponry, we are not soldiers, we are healers, bards, and teachers. We must consider ways to use our own strengths rather than attempt to work outside of our scope of power.

"I hereby call this meeting to a close to reconvene at the Full Moon. In the interim, I will consult with the oracles at hand to see what else can be determined. We will also hope to hear news from our Lord Merlin and consider his own input and advice." She picked up her dagger and tapped the table with the hilt three times. "This circle is open, yet unbroken. Leave one another with peace between you and no malice in your hearts for your divergent opinions."

As the senior Druids and elder priestesses began to drift away from the table, Lillian stood and immediately felt a swoon come upon her. Clearly, she was more exhausted and undernourished than she thought. Her stomach gave forth a violent lurch and she barely made it outside the Great Hall before all she had eaten in the day left her body in an urgent heave. Her face broke out in immediate sweat with large droplets falling into the ground around her sick. She felt a wave of chill come over her and she leaned against the cool, marble wall of the building. She felt she had no strength in her body at all.

She felt firm hands slip around her waist as Maia steered her away from the hall and toward their little house. "Come," her friend said. "You are exhausted and you must rest." Lillian had no protest in her and allowed Maia to lead her straight to her bed, gently undressed her, and tuck the covers around her as if she were a child. Minutes later, she returned with a large, steaming cup of broth brewed from the waterfowl brought in by the younger priestesses earlier in the day. Lightly seasoned with herbs, it tasted delicious. Lillian sipped it, whispering her thanks. Afterward, Maia took the cup away and slipped naked into bed next to Lillian. She wrapped her arms around her friend and pulled her into the warmth of her body, stroking her hair until they both fell asleep.

Chapter 7

The next day, Lillian was supposed to lead the young priestesses in training from the House of Maidens on an herb identification walk on the shores of the Lake near the Faerie country. Odd plants with strong medicine grew in that area, but it was unsafe for the girls to venture forth without an experienced priestess to guide them lest they be enticed into the Faerie country and be lost for years within their oddly timed world. Not long after she woke, Lillian asked Maia to offer her apologies and then fell back into the bed. All she wanted to do was sleep and sleep for ages.

She was tired through to her very bones.

Lillian found that having a lifetime's worth of memories of leading the people of Avalon was a tremendous asset to her in her new capacity as Lady of the Lake. What she struggled with, however, was that those memories were through a filter of the emotions she experienced when she lived that life. She had to separate out what she felt then from what she knew to be true now, from the historical vantage point, and realize that while there had been wisdom and justification, most of what had occurred by her hand in that lifetime served as a cautionary tale rather than an instructional manual. Because she did not live as the Lady Morgan, the most recent Lady of the Lake, she did not have her memories, but in her past life, she had shared many of the same experiences and could easily understand that there too, ego, pride, and a quest for vengeance created disaster and tragedy. She knew that those dangers would take her away from the voice of the Goddess in short time.

One of the most valuable lessons that her memories provided her was that one should *not* work beyond one's physical limits. She knew that in this leadership capacity, she had to focus on the long run, not the short sprint. Endurance would be far more valuable than anything she could accomplish by over-extending herself.

Later that afternoon, she called Maia to her and said, "Please inform those who need to know and any who ask that I am in seclusion and will not receive guests until further notice."

"Are you all right, dearest?" her friend asked, concern evident on her face.

Lillian smiled. "Exhaustion is taking its toll on me, my friend. I feel my physical reserves are depleted. I believe rest and some of that amazing broth you make will put me right in short order."

Maia gave her a warm hug. "I will take care of everything. You…into bed and rest."

Lillian climbed into the covers and did not come out for five days. During that time, she sipped bits of broth and nibbled at the hard bread soaked in wine or milk that Maia brought to her. She drank plenty of the holy water from the Sacred Well, known for its healing and restorative properties. Although she kept down the broth and water, the bread and wine or milk would come back up within minutes of eating. On the second day, Maia began bringing her sprigs of dried peppermint to chew, as well as other antiemetic herbs. As Lillian's strength lessened instead of improving, she also included valerian root to help her sleep, giving her body time to rebuild and restore.

On the sixth day, Maia found Lillian out of bed and dressing herself in the late morning. She was about to ask if she felt better, but a quick look at her friend told her that such was not the case. Her face was much more gaunt than usual and her eyes were sunken with dark smudges beneath them. Her hands shook slightly as she tried to braid her own hair, so Maia took over and quickly plaited and pinned her hair into place. She knew better than to question Lillian's decision to leave the bed and suspected that her physical illness would have her out of sorts, so she did not press the issue.

"What is our status?" Lillian asked.

"Lady Danu has been here three times, asking for an audience. I told her I would send an attending priestess to get her when you were out of seclusion. Brother Gaedyn has been here twice and was turned away. There is no news for Lord Merlin since the summit. I sent the Maidens into the orchards to tend the trees and check the ripeness of the apples. Lyndle is already planning the Mabon feast and is driving everyone mad with her preparations and here we are not yet even to the First Harvest celebration."

Lillian placed her hand atop Maia's, which was resting on her shoulder. "Please tell Lady Danu that I will see her right away and have one of the priestesses bring tea and fruit to the table."

"Right away," Maia said.

"Maia," Lillian said, calling her back. She turned and looked back over her shoulder as she opened the door. "Thank you."

Maia returned to Lillian and gave her a warm hug, noticing how thin her friend's shoulders and chest felt when she held her. She must have lost a stone's weight in the past week. "You are so very welcome," she answered, and kissed her on the lips.

An hour or so later, Lillian sipped her herb tea and tried to focus on what Danu was telling her. It was something about the Harvest ceremony, scheduled in three days' time. At last, she realized the older woman was no longer speaking to her but was instead, looking at her intently.

"Child, are you ill? I thought your seclusion was for rest and restoration, not recovery."

"I do not feel well at all, Mother," Lillian said, using the term of affection she reserved for the elder women who had raised her. "My strength seems to decline more each day. My belly rejects almost everything I put into it and I can barely hold my eyes open, much less focus on the matters I need to attend."

She began to weep softly and Danu rose from her chair and pulled the young girl into her arms. "You know, Lillian, because of your unique situation in the world and all that it lends to your position as The Lady, I forget that you are still a young girl. This must be such a weight for you to carry and what a tremendous responsibility we have placed on you."

At the woman's loving words and embrace, Lillian turned and sobbed into her soft, fragrant breasts. "I don't know what to do. I cannot think clearly and my head swims. The will is strong, but my body weakens more with each day."

She heard Danu pull in a sharp breath.

"What?" Lillian asked. "Am I dying? What have you seen, Mother?"

To her surprise, her mentor was smiling. Danu wiped the tears from the young woman's face with her two thumbs and cupped her face in her palms. "Lillian, are your breasts tender?"

Lillian pushed against them with her palms and winced. "They are," she said.

"Did your Dark Moon courses come this month? That would have been at the time of the summit."

Lillian looked stricken and a memory flashed into her mind of Bran's roar of pleasure as he spilled his seed into her when they joined during the coronation ritual. "No," she confirmed. "I had not even for a moment considered…they did not come, Danu." Her thoughts reeled, banging into one another in chaos she had not once felt since Bran had whispered *that name* in her ear. She found her breath getting away from her as it came on in ragged, uneven gasps. "My Goddess… Great Mother…Beloved Ceredwyn…It cannot be! It cannot!"

"Dearest child," Danu said, her grin nearly pushing off her face in its reach. "You are not dying. My love, *you are breeding*. You, our Lady of the Lake, are carrying the child of The Merlin of Britain! Goddess be praised!"

Chapter 8

Lillian woke abruptly from a bizarre and very lucid dream that had something to do with counting the rings on the back of an exceptionally large tortoise. While there could perhaps be some significance to the dream, it faded so fast after she opened her eyes and oriented herself that she could not quite catch it. She realized that she had been sleeping in a chair by the fireplace.

Someone had banked the fire for the night and there was a warm quilt tucked around her. The attending priestesses had long left and she was alone in the room without so much as a candle for light; only the smoldering coals of the fire. It was cold outside, but the small house she shared with Maia was comfortably warm with only a slight chill in the air. She thought of the girls in the House of Maidens and those women in the House of Mothers and House of Crones who would have removed the straw bedding from the frames and used it to create a large group bed in the middle of the room. The bigger buildings were more difficult to heat and the women and in the case of the House of Mothers, the small children, enjoyed the closeness of others in the Winter months not only for warmth, but also for companionship.

She found that once she got used to it, she liked living alone with only Maia for company in the little house. In the larger houses, there was always noise of some kind and the erratic energy of many different people in one place. The house was never truly still.

Here, however, it was so quiet you could actually *hear* the silence. Occasionally, an ember popped or hissed in the fire and sometimes, she could hear Maia's rhythmic breathing in the next room. It was peaceful, meditative, and motionless...

...unlike her belly, which never stopped moving. She had the advantage of knowing exactly when she conceived since she had only been with a man the one time. By her calculations, the baby should come by Spring Equinox. Belen, one of the midwives who cared for the breeding women on Avalon, would press hands against her swollen belly and cluck, shake her head, and then insist that the baby would come early.

She was big, although big seemed like too small of a word to convey how huge she looked and felt. Her skin stretched further than she thought it could possibly go and here she was with three or maybe even four more moons to go, during which, the baby would grow ever so much bigger! Several times a day, she rubbed her itchy and overstretched skin with balms made by the midwives. She felt if the skin stretched any tighter that she would be able to see the baby inside.

The pain in her back never ceased and as of late, her hips had joined in on the complaining. A few weeks before, she had to stop going to the Sacred Well to vision and call upon the sight. The walk was too much for her and the last time, she almost did not make it back down the hill again. She found that the distance she was able to walk at all, much less up hill and down, was ever decreasing. Now, she lost her breath just waddling over to the Great Hall.

Considering that everyone on the island had seen the conception, there was no denying the paternity of the baby. Many of the elders had encouraged her, some to the point of uncomfortable pressuring, to send word to

Bran that he was going to be a father. She refused and forbade any of them from disclosing her condition.

As the months wore on, she knew her instincts had been correct and her decision a wise one. As she told the Council of Elders, "The Merlin has very delicate and dangerous matters of state to attend and will need all his focus to make wise choices not only for the good of Avalon, but also to keep himself safe. It took more than forty years for a new Merlin to be revealed to us and we do not have the luxury of waiting that long for another one should he perish because his attention is diverted. As Lady of the Lake, I directly command each and every one of you into my confidence and bind you to the silence I require." It was strong magic and a lot to ask, but necessary for the good of the island. More importantly, she could not bear the thought of anything happening to Bran because he was distracted on her behalf.

They heard no world from him since the end of Summer and now it was nearly the mid-Winter. She felt as though surely she would know if something happened; if he had been harmed, imprisoned, or worse. His last report had detailed horrific tortures of the follower of the Old Ways and anyone deemed a follower of the Goddess or sorcerer. Every day that he was away from Avalon left him vulnerable to tremendous danger. Although he noted that some priests were still hospitable and kindly deposed to him as The Merlin of Britain, many had never met the one that came before and therefore, had no frame of reference for his position in the land. Too much time had passed with the position empty and now many did not remember a time when The Merlin of Britain was valued as an esteemed scholar, strategist, and advisor.

Moreover, he reported that so immersed was Constantine, the current High King, in pursuing vengeance against the followers of the Sons of Mordred that it was rumored his throne was all but abandoned. After Mordred and King Arthur inflicted fatal wounds on one another at the Battle of Camlann, Mordred's sons continued their father's legacy of insurrection against those who supported King Arthur or his legacy.

Saxon born, the Sons were fierce and unrelenting in their campaign to wipe out all of Arthur's legions and any who swore fealty to him, even in his death. Many followed the Sons of Mordred on their murderous campaign and as a result, the Lesser Kings of Britain turned over in rapid succession since most had given sword fealty to Arthur. Kings and their sons died violently and with alarming frequency. Arthur's companions were no more, vanquished by this murderous duo and the growing army of avenging Saxons they assembled. The companions of Arthur and many of their sons fell victim to the Sons of Mordred who were determined to wipe out any and all who supported Arthur and his reign. In complement, Constantine IV determined do the same to the Sons of Mordred.

While most considered this an honorable quest, the result was that the land fell into ruin as war raged in very nearly all parts. When at last, Constantine and his armies pursued Mordred's actual Sons into what had been Londinium, the great city was already in ruins following the withdrawal of Roman occupation. Some said he cut the traitors' throats, letting the blood spill forth onto the church altar and proclaiming them damned for all time. Although he ended their own personal rampage by spilling their blood on the altars of the churches where they sought sanctuary, their followers continued with their gruesome mission and he stayed on their heels. It did not escape Lillian's attention that as the grandchildren of the Lady Morgan, Mordred's own sons, who Constantine IV had gleefully murdered, were actually closer kin to Arthur, and therefore, Duke of Cornwall and High King by right. The result of the quest of Constantine was not only the blood of two Saxons staining the floors of churches in Londinium, but the near abandonment of the seven kingdoms of Britain.

Lillian was surprised to hear that the increasing Saxon invasion that infiltrated in the East now extended well into the north so that the country was now half the size it had previously been. Relatively new lesser kings, all ruled the seven kingdoms of Britain autonomously, according to their own consciences and without an overseeing government. Essentially, Britain was now a collective of sovereign kingdoms, all ruled individually by men who could not possibly be less like-minded from one another. Because of the rapid turnover of kings, little or no training was afforded to those now in charge of governing vast amounts of territories. Gone were the days of princes being prepped from birth to ascend to the throne or winning the crown through military prowess. Now one could become a king by being of the proper family and simply surviving longer than those before, which did not typically take an extended time investment.

This made Bran's job all the more difficult because the new kings were eager to prove themselves to one another, which brought about a posturing game of one-upmanship among them. To Lillian, who had never once stepped foot off Avalon, it was no more than a pissing contest among male egos. The problem was that their currency in this ego game was often the persecution of non-Christians and this did not bode well in Bran's quest for allies. Internal conflict was rife through the land and there was little doubt that a civil war was brewing with the followers of the Old Ways caught in the middle.

With Constantine's focus on his crusade against the Sons of Mordred, which the avenging marauders still called themselves even though there were no more actual Sons of Mordred, the defense of Britain fell to the individual kings. In addition to this fringe element focused on kings and their heirs, the threat of the ever-growing Saxon expansion loomed with raiders still ravaging the countryside at will, pillaging and plundering. A few of the kings allied with one another to protect their conjoined lands. Focused unity and defense, however, did not exist in Britain and left the country unsafe for all concerned.

Lillian's back ached from holding her position in the chair for a good bit of the night and she longed to walk for a while and stretch her legs. In the past few months, she had learned more about the politics and history of Britain than she ever wanted to know or ever imagined she would need to know.

She hoisted herself from the chair and on a whim, walked out to into the night. She brought with her the small quilt that someone, likely Maia, put around her for warmth and pulled it tightly around her shoulders. The Moon was in its fullness and the courtyard was illuminated as if it were dusk outside rather than the wee morning hours. The bracing cold felt wonderful on her face, which seemed to flush with heat on a regular basis since her pregnancy. The back of her neck rejoiced to feel the cool breeze upon it. She thought with a smile that it would not surprise her to see steam rising up off her skin in the cold night air.

Having lived out her entire life on the island, she realized that she often took for granted the beauty and the relative safety of the place. Magic was definitely alive here, present in every Winter flower, the trickle of the streams yet unfrozen, and the near constant movement of the air in gentle breezes that playfully caressed the skin. It seemed that nothing was ever harsh on Avalon. Not a sound stirred within the courtyard and she moved on whispered feet along the cobblestone path.

Her steps led her toward the Sacred Well and she paused, remembering the last time she had ventured forth to look into its reflection for what visions the sight might offer her. Now that she had access to her past life memories in some organized fashion, the sight came more readily for her than ever before. Still, she used it sparingly because she knew it was not good to have much foreknowledge of your own life and those around you. So strong could be the compulsion to course correct that those who sought out the sight on a regular basis often managed to get in their own way much of the time and delay experiences that were essential to one's own life mission. The sight never came to her unbidden as it did so many. She knew of several sister priestesses who wake in the night with their sleep disturbed by sendings or visions, or else would fall into trance accidentally while spinning or fire gazing. She never did. The sight was waiting for her when she sought it and otherwise, did not impose itself upon her.

She had specifically not looked for Bran in the reflective waters of the Sacred Well. The degree of self-discipline she had to employ to keep from doing so was monumental. Her need to know about his location, his progress, and more importantly, his safety was tremendous; however, she knew that regardless of what she saw, her ability to change what he was experiencing was extremely limited. She also knew that using the sight to connect with him and learn of his circumstances would create a link between them that neither she nor he could afford. The sight merely showed her what was happening, what had happened, or what would happen; it did not explain to her how the situation developed or one could alter what was shown. Sometimes, what the sight showed her was part of the Divine plan of the Goddess and as such, was destined to occur in some fashion or another. Other times, what she saw was mutable and could change by even a moment's breath of free will. Although her sight was always true, the immutable fact of The Universe was that while some things could change and others could not, too often, we do not know the difference until the moment has passed.

The Sacred Well was not nearly so far away as the Tor, only at the far edge of the courtyard and a bit up the hill. Still, as she reached the bottom of the climb, she already felt a pulling sensation deep within her and a nagging ache in her back. She was grateful that she thought to pick up her walking staff as she left the house. She paused often, keeping her breath slow and rhythmic even after it wanted to come in ragged gasps. The weight of the baby was more than she ever expected it could be. She thought back to all the times that she had observed her Sister Priestesses who were with child and felt tremendous compassion for them. She knew these discomforts were common to all childbearing womankind and she thought of the childless who would give anything for the privilege of feeling that discomfort. Because of the walking distance, her trips to the Sacred Well were becoming more infrequent. Of late, most of her scrying was done in silver bowls of water or mirrors.

At last, she reached the Sacred Well and sat down gratefully on the carved bench beside it. Her thoughts slipped, as they so often did when she was here in this place, to her *other* life here on Avalon...her life as Evienne. She thought of how Evienne had mourned the lack of daughters in her life and most deeply, the one she had lost to death while still a tiny babe at the breast. She thought of her child's translucent eyelids, her rosebud lips, and the golden cap of silky blond hair. Her daughter had not been dark as she had been in that life, but the picture of golden, pale beauty. She had given birth to sons for certain; some who were big men with rough features like the men of the North and one who was more slight and delicate, as had she been in that life. Her daughter, however, had been like a little ray of sunshine. Even after she had surrendered her short life back to the Goddess, she had only looked to be sleeping with pink cheeks and skin that looked as creamy as milk.

No daughter had come to her in that life to inherit the throne of Avalon. Would this child be a daughter to whom she could pass the honor when she herself advanced into her crone time to the point that it was no longer prudent for her to lead? Or a son, who would become the Merlin of Britain himself? There was little denying the power of a child conceived between the two leaders of Avalon during such a sacred ritual and the impact of such a fortuitous omen was not lost on the Council of Elders. They hovered over her like hens, monitoring what she ate or did not eat, whether she had slept well, how much fresh air she took in daily, and how soon she felt movement from the baby. She suspected they secretly kept score of how many times she made her way to the privy and the amount of each of her leavings. They performed countless blessings on the baby, holding hands to her belly as if it were the only fireplace in the dead of Winter.

Early on, when the nausea and weakness had been so intense that she could not leave her bed, they had rarely given her a minute's rest. Potions, herbs, and different types of palatable foods arrived nearly on an hourly basis. Maia could hardly keep track of it all and finally, Lillian had to insist that they give her time to rest and focus on balancing her energy between herself and her baby.

Thankfully, midway through her pregnancy, only a moon or so before, the nausea abated and she could tolerate food once more. She had grown thin and wan during that time and no sooner did her strength return from her early pregnancy illness than it drained away from the weight of the huge child she carried. Often, it felt as though a giant, ever-shifting boulder had taken up residence in her womb.

The moonlight reflected into the water in the well and as she peered into its mirror-like surface, she cleared her mind completely of thought and opened to whatever the sight chose to show to her. Often, she would see the face she wore before speaking to her, instructing her in ways of leadership and magic. She valued these times because her position, although important, came with very little in the way of guidance. Although she could access memories from her previous life, it was much more helpful to have one-on-one discussions with someone who had actually lived the role.

She had never known the sight could work in such an interactive capacity and finding this facet of magic available to her was a tremendous benefit. She valued the ability to consult with her predecessor but was aware she must filter the responses and guidance she received with regard to the different times and personal agendas. Her predecessor could be ruthless and single minded and ultimately paid the price, but she sat on the throne of the Lady of the Lake longer than anyone since and many before, so her influence was most definitely valuable, even if Lillian must translate the knowledge to current times. Even her predecessor urged her only to consider what she said and to include it in the sum of knowledge and experience afforded to her.

This time, however, the sight did not take her into instruction. She first saw the barge of Avalon, draped in funeral black, moving smoothly across the lake. Her heart nearly stopped as her immediate thought was that this was Bran, coming home for the last time already departed back to the Goddess. But no, there was a woman at the bow that she recognized from other visions; a woman with gray hair and blue robes. She knew this was King Arthur, coming to Avalon after the Battle of Camlann. She wondered why the sight would show her something from the past instead of the present or the future.

She passed her hand over the water and the vision rippled. This time, she saw a tall, large-boned woman close to her own age working at a spinning wheel. She passed her hand over the water again and she saw two women speaking to one another. The older one said, "You, sister, will bear this great king. You will be mother to the one who will save Britain." Oddly, instead of addressing the women who spoke to her, the other woman looked directly through the waters at Lillian and said, "Not this time, Lillian. My son has come and gone. This time, it will be *you* who gives birth to the salvation of our country and of the very Goddess Herself."

Lillian pulled back from the vision, stunned. She had only ever interacted with her own past selves through The Sight. This woman, although not one of her former selves, had looked directly at her, called her by her own name, and spoken to her. She knew her child would be sacred to the Goddess, but *save Britain? Save the very Goddess?* How in the world does one do *that?* Lillian sat on the earth and leaned with her back against the well, pulling the little quilt around her.

She felt overwhelmed with longing for Bran and closed her eyes, allowing herself the luxury of conjuring his features in her mind. It seemed unthinkable that she had only seen him a handful of times in her entire life and here she was heavy with his child and so full of love for him that at times she felt her heart would burst apart from it. Although she could easily summon the memory of his touch and the warm glow of his physical nearness, she found that it was more difficult to remember what he looked like.

Long hair of blackest ebony, dark eyes that danced with joy and were an unexpected contrast to his swarthy skin that almost looked Egyptian, a wide, generous smile, high cheekbones, broad, muscular shoulders...she wanted to take the image and wrap herself in it until his arms could be around her once more.

For the first time ever, she wondered what her father had looked like and for that matter, her mother. She had been told her mother had stunning red hair that fell down her back in a shimmering cascade. Her mother supposedly had delicate features, yet she herself did not. She was anything but slight with her round, curvy shape and strong, sturdy frame. She was normally quite physically strong, although her pregnancy had compromised that strength somewhat from the very beginning. Would the baby have her green eyes or Bran's dark ones? Were there physical features of her parents or her grandparents that would come through to the child? Would the Goddess ask her to give her life as her mother had done when she was born? She cradled her belly and thought what a strange mystery this baby was to her in so many ways.

The sunrise was a dim glow on the horizon as she made her way back down the path to the little house. Her bed waited for her and she longed to rest after her walk. Although she could feel the fatigue settling back into her body, her mind was full and she doubted sleep would come easily to her.

Chapter 9

Lillian tried not to squirm as Belen the midwife pushed her fingers so deeply within her that she thought she must be up to her elbow by now. It was uncomfortable to rest on her back and the position caused her to feel light-headed, but the exam was necessary. Finally, the old woman withdrew the encroaching hand and began to massage Lillian's very large belly with a thoughtful look on her face.

"How often do you need to relieve yourself?" she asked.

"You don't know? I thought all of you kept track of that," Lillian thought to herself, but aloud said, "Too often. It seems as though I barely have left the chamber pot when I have to go back to it again. I might just as well just stay there."

"The baby's movements are often?"

"The baby never, ever stops moving. My insides are in constant motion."

"Hmmm." Belen pressed at her belly firmly from all sides. "And how much blood was there?"

Lillian winced as the probing fingers dug deeply into the skin and muscle over her pubic bone. "Some on the sheets when I woke. Some on my nightdress. They are all still on the chair. I kept them for you to see."

"Good," the midwife smiled, then rose to look at the blood-streaked items. "The blood was dark red, not bright."

"It was and almost brown in color."

"Like mud?"

"Mostly, yes, but a little red."

"You'd been walking before it happened?"

"Yes. I walked to the Sacred Well and back."

"Any back pain?"

"Always."

"Dizziness? Fainting?"

"No, only now when I rest on my back."

"Are your stools loose?"

"Not particularly."

"How is your appetite?"

"It's good. Impressive, even. I want to eat everything I see."

"Any belly pain at all?"

"No. None other than some feelings of pressure. Is my baby well? Tell me, Belen."

The older woman patted her on the leg and indicated that she could get dressed again. "Your babe is well as nearly as I can tell. The womb is not yet opening, so that is good. There is some thinning of the opening and it is a bit early, but I do not believe there is yet cause for alarm. The bleeding was likely just a rupture of the tiny blood vessels. It happens sometimes.

"I do, however," she continued, "want to call Danu in to feel your belly. I'd like a second opinion given the importance of this little one." She patted Lillian's bulging midsection again.

Within minutes, Danu was pressing on either side of her large tummy, pushing this way, probing that way, pressing into the area above her pubic bone with great interest, and massaging where her swelling belly pushed into her ribs. Without speaking, she nodded briskly to Belen, who nodded back. This exchange did not escape Lillian's attention.

"What? What was that nod about?"

Danu pulled Lillian's tunic down and brought the bedclothes up over her lower body. "My Lady," she said with great aplomb, "There is no easy way to tell you this." The two older women exchanged an amused smile.

Lillian's eyes grew large with fear.

"There is more than one baby in there." Danu grinned broadly as she delivered this news.

Lillian felt her jaw drop and then closed it abruptly. "Two babies?" she said quietly.

Belen cleared her throat. "Well," she said hesitantly, stealing a glance at Danu, who again nodded. "Perhaps...more than two."

"More than two," Lillian repeated dully. "More than...*two.*"

"Perhaps," the two older women said in harmony that in other circumstances, Lillian might have found amusing. "Perhaps only two," Danu finished.

"Or more," Belen said. "Possibly more."

"But at least two," Danu added.

Maia covered her own mouth to stifle a laugh and Lillian shot her an unforgiving look. Lillian drew in a breath, closed her eyes and let it out. "I have had sexual relations with a man once in my entire life," she began. "You all were there and the *one time* in my life I knew a man's body intimately, I was surrounded not only by a circle of my nearest and dearest, but also by complete strangers, many of whom I had never seen before that night and have not seen since. For three years prior to that night, I asked for leave to attend the Beltane fires and you denied that privilege you give to every young girl of breeding age. Now, after having only *one time* enjoyed the intimacy with *the love of my LIFE,* that experience that other women so take for granted, you are going to tell me that not only am I vastly, immensely pregnant from *that one time*, but that I am pregnant *with two babies?"*

"Possibly more," Belen said.

"Possibly more," Lillian repeated. "Danu, how many priestesses in the House of Mothers have delivered more than one baby with a pregnancy since you have lived here on Avalon?"

"Well, um, My Lady. One…who lived."

"One who lived," Lillian said, her voice remarkably level. "And when was this?"

"Oh… I was a young girl, so probably thirty-five or forty years ago, I would guess."

"So," Lillian continued, "What you are saying is that one woman among us delivered more than one child at a time *and lived* and that was as long ago as *when the Lady Morgan ruled here?"*

Danu hesitated and then said, "Yes, that is correct as best as I recall. In fact, 'twas the Lady Morgan who delivered the two."

Again, Lillian closed her eyes before continuing and pinched the bridge of her nose in consternation. "So there is not one person upon the island of Avalon who has the skill and experience required to midwife two babies," Belen opened her mouth to speak and Lillian held up her hand, "or possibly more."

The two older women looked at one another and Danu admitted, "I would say that is accurate. Yes, My Lady, but truly, catching one baby or catching two…"

"…or possibly more," Belen interrupted.

"…or possibly more is not much different one from the other. You push…we catch. The mechanics do not change…only the results."

Lillian fell back onto her pillow, her arm resting across her eyes. "Leave me," she said clearly. The women looked at one another in confusion. Lillian peeked an eye out from under her arm. "Go. Off with you then."

Belen gathered her medicine bag and she and Danu quickly left the small house.

Lillian lay as she was for a few minutes, but then felt Maia nudging at her belly. "Hellooo in there," she said whimsically. "Hellooo babies."

Lillian could not help but laugh. "Stop it!" she said, pushing Maia's face away from her tummy. "I want to be completely miserable for a little while." Maia gently brushed back the hair from Lillian's face and smiled. "Little Mama," she said. "You never do anything halfway, do you?"

"Two babies," Lillian said in wonder.

"Possibly more," Maia said softly.

"Oh, great Goddess. Maia, what am I going to do?"

Maia wrapped her arms around her friend and held her close. "You're going to have babies," she said simply, then started to giggle. "Lots and lots of babies."

Her laugher did not cease even when Lillian pushed her off the bed.

Chapter 10

At long last, there was news from Bran. King Linus in Rheged swore fealty to Avalon and agreed to station troops on the mainland shores around the lake to protect the island. His alliance with King Letholdus of Elmet would ensure ample defense of the borders to the North, as well as sending soldiers South to protect Avalon and its border people. Rheged was historically the kingdom most closely aligned with the magical people and securing even two of the seven kings' support was monumental. There would no doubt be conflict between the defending army and the Glastonbury priests, but the priests would in no way be able to stand against the number of soldiers that would soon be in place.

King Constantine continued his relentless pursuit of the supporters of the Sons of Mordred and seldom now returned to Carmeliard. Although King Arthur once ruled from Camelot and before that, Caerleon, Constantine moved his court deep into Wales, nestled between Gwent and South Wales, which he considered to have the military advantage.

While one would think that once he vanquished the true Sons of Mordred he would eventually return home to rule his lands, he instead he moved deeper into this quest to find their allies and eliminate them. He was a man obsessed. Although his court remained unattended, it was a staunchly Christian court and the people who remained at Carmeliard and Gwent were devout to the point of fanaticism. The court priests refused to give Bran audience and he advised the council that he was a prisoner there for a short time.

King Gwynedd in North Wales was reluctant at first to hear Bran's entreaty, but after days of discussion, he ultimately rode out with Bran to meet with his ally, King Aurelius in South Wales to guarantee his allegiance with Avalon, which Bran secured. This was a particularly valuable victory because it ensured not only safety for the entirety of the North shores of the mainland near Avalon, but also because it gave the incoming soldiers a clear and safe path for most of their journey. With the entire North in alliance, there would be no need to station soldiers on the mainland near the North shores and those troops could instead be sent to protect the mainland on the more vulnerable shores to the South of Avalon.

The fact that the Northern kings all welcomed Bran's attempts at unity told him that the time was right for harnessing the strength of Britain and putting it back into power, even within its shrinking land holdings. The Saxon expansion was pervasive, but if treaty troops were willing to accept Arthur as their king, perhaps they would make peace with the existing kingdoms of Britain as well. As difficult as it was for land-hungry nations to stop and listen to reason, they still might be just as weary of battle as were the Britons. The difference, of course, being that the Britons were losing and the Germanic tribes were winning. It seemed as if on a regular basis, reports came in that another village, another kingdom, fell to the hands of the vicious invaders.

Only two kings remained with whom Bran must attempt liaison: King Lucius in The Summer Country and King Marcus in Cornwall. King Lucius was the newest of all the lesser kings to take the crown and as such, sought to garner favor with the High King and to do so, initiated aggressive persecution of the magical people. He was in fact, the third king of The Summer Country in two years' time. Rumor had it that he was ambitious and duplicitous and it was known that while he had never fought in battle, he had no compunction about using his sword. Beyond this, there was little known about him and it was hard to tell where his favor would lie.

King Marcus was the Regent of Constantine and as such, faithful only to the line of Arthur and his Christian banner. Bran held out little hope for alliance with Cornwall, but intended to try, nonetheless.

Already, he had been away for more than half a year's time and Lillian felt his absence more greatly than ever before.

The Council of Elders met in the Great Hall to discuss the news. Several of the younger Druids carried Lillian to the hall in a large chair because she could no longer walk as far as the distance and it was too cumbersome to fit her into a litter. In fact, she could hardly stand at all and spent most of her time in her bed, arising only to relieve herself. She even took her meals in the bed and was so bored of the bed that she felt she would scream every waking moment of every day.

Belen gave her a light sedative from time to time to help her sleep as the constant movement of the babies kept her awake at all hours. She loved the days after taking the sedative the night before because she would continue to doze through the day, allowing the time to pass more quickly. She now had to have Maia and her attendant priestesses massage balms into her over-stretched skin because she was unable to reach the underside of her belly or her hips. When she sat up in bed, her arms extended outwards to her sides over the roundness of her enlarged abdomen. Her thighs had not met in months and when she did walk very short distances, she not so much waddled as lumbered.

As the four strong Druids lowered her chair to the floor, several in the room gasped audibly upon seeing her condition. Maia and Danu flanked her and assisted her in transferring to her large chair at the head of the table. A soft pillow cushioned her chair and carefully, she edged her massive body into the seat.

The room was silent as everyone at the table stared at her. At last, one of the elder Druids said uneasily, "You look well, My Lady."

Lillian gave him a look of icy disdain. "I look well?" she asked incredulously. "I look well? Father, your words are ill chosen. I am carrying within my body, this sacred vessel of the Great Goddess herself, a minimum of two babies…"

"Possibly more," Danu added.

"…and possibly more," Lillian continued. "I look like a fleshy house."

The older man looked cowed and Lillian immediately regretted her harsh words. "I apologize, Father Cleon," she offered. "My mood and my graciousness seem to have diminished exponentially to my waistline. I do not intend unkindness."

"It is fully understandable, My Lady," he said.

"I thank you, sir. Now fill me in."

They apprised her of the news, both encouraging and otherwise, and she realized that it felt good to be doing something that was remotely useful. She could no longer spin or weave because she could reach neither spindle nor shuttle. She could not embroider because her eyesight was blurring on close work, which Danu told her sometimes happened to women as their pregnancies progressed. She could not read for the same reason. She could no longer visit the House of Maidens to teach the young girls or the House of Mothers to share birth and pregnancy tales and play with the children or the House of Crones to listen to stories and hear their wise words. The walk was simply too far for her.

Now, here, her input was valued and she felt she could provide some sort of worthwhile service to her people. Due at first to the crippling nausea and then to the immense size and pressure of the babies, she had been unable to lead any of the major rituals since her coronation, instead having to delegate to Danu. Her counsel was often sought and she felt she led well when called upon to do so, but she was also painfully aware that many avoided asking for her advice and input because they were either concerned that they would trouble her needlessly or were fearful of encountering her irritable nature as of late.

Throughout the discourse regarding the most recent information, Danu eyed her carefully to make certain she was not tiring. Since the isolated incidence of bleeding and the news that there was a minimum of two babies inside (possibly more), the midwives monitored her more closely than ever. All agreed that it was encouraging that they had gleaned the pending support of four major kings, each of whom had substantial armies since they had not lent troops to Constantine's quest. Many of the Druids speculated that the armies were no doubt itching for action since the Saxons had slowed their campaigns into Britain, at least for the time being.

With the North in full support of Avalon, that left only the lower kingdoms, those right outside their

Southern door, intent on destroying Avalon and the common folks still honoring the Goddess. The troops would all arrive within two moons, some sooner than others. Ironically, their nearest neighboring kingdoms posed the greatest threat and marching armies of soldiers through The Summer Country or Gwent would no doubt constitute an act of war, even without overt hostility. To protect the South of Avalon and the villages on the mainland that bounded it, the soldiers would undoubtedly face potential combat.

Although this conflict was likely unavoidable, there was another issue of great concern. The soldiers need to eat. Lillian ordered that both the Druids and the priestesses immediately allocate large portions of Avalon's food holdings to feed the inbound troops for a sustained period. She tasked two of the elder priestesses with the job of architecting larger fields for their harvests in the coming year and asked the senior Druids to coordinate with the common people off island who kept Avalon's traditions and to provide them with seed and even labor assistance to grow more grains and vegetables in the coming year.

"Tell them that they are to keep half of whatever additional harvest they yield from your contributions to lay back for themselves or to sell. The other half is to be tithed to the soldiers who protect us."

All agreed that this was a generous, yet mutually beneficial solution. The previous harvest was extremely bountiful and many rumored that this was due to the auspicious and ultimately very fruitful joining of The Lady of the Lake and The Merlin of Britain. The fields yielded so much food that Avalon distributed much and more of it to the neighboring villages on the shores that bordered the Lake. They even left food as offerings to the Faerie people who lived between the worlds on the island. Many of the villagers lost their harvests to the torches of those who felt the crops profane from the blessings of the Goddess. Under the protection of the soldiers, the common people would be safe to grow their harvests in peace while also providing a surplus for themselves and food for the troops.

The Avalon reserves would feed the armies until the harvest came in the following year without difficulty. The northern kings also vowed supplies for their men; however, most of the men were far, far from home and support would take time to reach the area. The combination of food provisions from home and the increased harvests would allow the island and the villages to have healthy, well-fed men prepared to defend the area and its people.

No one dared speculate on when Bran might return home. He had made tremendous progress that exceeded everyone's expectations and the support he garnered for Avalon was of tremendous value. He also acquired enemies and his exposure in the world as The Merlin of Britain put him in immediate danger from those who wished to eradicate all who embraced magic in their lives, as if spells were different from the fervent and ego-driven prayers they offered up to their God. They had the support of most of Britain, but their neighbors were the ones who most wanted them destroyed.

Bran still had two kings to address, so the idea that he might return to Avalon soon was not a hope worth having. On this, the High Council of Avalon agreed.

Chapter 11

One day before the Vernal Equinox, Lillian's babies were born. No one believed she would carry them for so long, but carry them, she did. No one believed that a person's skin could stretch so very much, but by the time she delivered, her belly reached out to the sides of the bed that confined her for the previous three months. She was not restricted from leaving the bed by midwife's orders, but by the ability to do so. One morning, after a night of fitful sleeping, she realized she could not get out of the bed. The weight of the babies and pregnancy matter inside of her were just too heavy for her body to carry.

From that time on, her Sister Priestesses, the midwives, and the ever-present Maia attended her at all times. In the final month, she could not even manage to change position in the bed, so they brought pillows and blankets to prop her up in the bed. If she lay on her back, she could not breathe due to the weight of the babies on her lungs and a sick feeling of nausea and faint that would come over her. They moved her once a week to change the bedding which required five or even six people to accomplish and took the better part of an hour.

She had to use a modified chamber pot to relieve herself. It was flat and they could slide it under her in the bed while other attending priestesses helped her to lift herself up. Anytime she had to move, it was utterly exhausting for her.

A few hours before dawn, she awoke to a strange, pulling sensation in her lower abdomen. She sat with it and observed it for a bit, verifying that yes, it was a different feeling than her usual aches and tugs. The babies had moved little in the night and she had slept well for a change. Carefully and with some determination and a mighty dose of will power, she managed to ease her bottom further up the bed and arrange her pillows so that she was upright. She longed for a cup of tea, but did not wish to wake Maia, who slept in the chair beside her bed, or the priestesses in the next room. Everyone had been so attentive to her every whim, her every need, and she wanted to cherish this moment where she did not feel uncomfortable for the most part, where she was relatively alone, and where she did not need impose upon anyone, but oh my heavens, did she ever need to relieve herself.

Her pregnancy had been difficult for so many people and in many ways, the entire dynamic and business of Avalon had been pre-empted to center solely around her needs. The question on everyone's mind was, "When will the babies come?" The babies had stolen the thunder from the usual ponderous questions such as "When will The Merlin return?" and "How are the villagers faring with their additional harvest duties?" and "Are the Barbarians at our door?"

Lillian felt a slight *pop* inside of her and almost giggled at the sensation. Immediately, she felt the bedding under her receive warm, wet fluid and at first, she thought she had hesitated too long in waking Maia, but the very sudden increase of pressure in her lower body, coupled with the fact that the stream of fluid was showing no sign of slowing told her that her waters had broken. If there was any doubt in her mind previously, she now knew that her babies were about to arrive.

Gently, she rubbed her hands over her expansive belly and tried to connect once more to her babies inside.

They were enigmas, these little ones. Still, Belen and the other midwives were unable to determine how many were in there, despite much divining, scrying, touching and probing on both the inside and the outside. "Possibly more than two" had, at some unclear point, shifted into "likely three or more."

Lillian did not fear the birth. She had attended countless births in the House of Mothers and she knew that when a woman faced her own power with fear, the experiences of womanhood tended to be fraught with pain. Anything from a first sexual experience to Croning to birthing to nursing a baby could be painful if not approached with the full empowerment of the Goddess and of herself. Even as trained priestesses, there were times when a woman, in times of distress, would flinch away from her own power.

As she considered the actual mechanics of childbirth, she wondered how something as large as a baby could come out such a small opening in her body. Until now, the largest thing to pass through those sacred, fleshy gates had been Bran's cock on the night she conceived the babies. She had no point of reference as to whether his was average size, smaller, or larger, but regardless, a baby would be significantly bigger. She knew of girls who had experienced pain with their first joining with a man, but hers had been glorious. The sheer might a woman demonstrated when birthing was a remarkable sight and a profound rite of passage.

Watching a woman's birth passage open like a blossoming flower as the baby's head emerged was always awe-inspiring for her. The women who she had observed birthing became fierce during this part of the process. Whereas before, they were moving between the worlds and disjointed, riding on waves of sensation and surrender as their wombs opened to allow the child passage out of their bodies, once the womb passage released and the baby began to descend, the mothers were awake, aware, and fully engaged. Some roared with power as they pushed their children forth into the hands of the waiting midwife or even their own hands. She saw others find sexual release at that moment with waves of pleasure coming over them while still others gasped and grunted with effort. Childbirth seemed to be an individual experience for them that did not duplicate from woman to woman, other than the result of a newborn child.

She could not help but wonder what her passage from Maiden into Mother would entail, especially with the added complication of a multiple birth of proportions heretofore never managed on the island. Still, she refused to give over into fear and worry, which she knew bled the magic from all things. Fear, worry, and over thinking were the primary downfalls by legends that had gone before them. The cautionary tales of all that had befallen those of Camelot and Avalon in the decades past had done much to craft the magic of her time and served as strong warnings of the dangers of ego, closed-mindedness, and the rejection of the Goddess and one's own destiny. Clearly, the Goddess trusted her to carry these babies and she would trust herself at least as much and meet whatever their births entailed with dignity and courage.

Many of the island's leaders left extensive, self-aware, and frank accounts of their own actions during their reign, including what had motivated them, the ultimate result, and things they would have done differently. It was, in fact, the obligation of the Druid priests and the Avalon priestess leaders to document all they had learned in their current life and to identify and reconcile their own lessons in the self-awareness of advanced age. In retrospect, of course, it is always easier to identify places where ego, fear, and the drive for power took over. When a person is in the moment, however, it can be a challenge to identify and overcome. This task of objectifying what the Goddess taught them in life left a valuable and historical tool for the education of those who would come next in line.

She considered her own past lives and the information she accessed when she tapped into the birth memories of the women she had lived as before. The birth process was a rite of passage designed to expose a woman's greatest fears and insecurities so that she might work through them and further embrace her own empowerment. It was a dance of knowing when to surrender and when to take command; when to lead and when to follow.

Lillian had experienced little time to work with the power and prestige of her own position. So quickly did her pregnancy overtake her life that debilitation had encompassed very nearly her entire reign. At one point, she sought out Danu's advice, wondering plaintively if she was lacking in some moral or personal fortitude since the pregnancy was so difficult. Danu had smiled lovingly at her and assured her that the very self-awareness and taking herself to task that she was doing was a sign that she was a good and righteous leader. She then went on to say that surely the Goddess had a plan since these babies had been born of such a potent magical moment and at this very critical time in history.

Since the withdrawal of Roman forces from Britain, the country had seen no darker times and if ever a need for magic was strongest, she could not imagine when else that would be. Danu promised her that the Goddess never gives a person more than what they can bear. It is our own lack of faith in ourselves and unwillingness to endure adversity that short-changed our own abilities. Goddess always knows what we can effectively manage and has more faith in us than we do in ourselves. "Sometimes," she said, "We have to endure hardship for a greater cause."

Lillian clung to this wisdom as her own saving grace. If the Goddess believed she could do this, who was she to argue? She gave herself over into the full experience of carrying and birthing the babies; open to whatever came from that process. Her experience at the Sacred Well left her with the knowledge that her babies would somehow be instrumental in the salvation of Britain and of the work of the Goddess. She owed it to so very many to bring these babies into the world in good health and safety. What happened to her in the commencement of that was irrelevant. Her role was to give them life.

As a mother, however, she found she could not connect with the little lives growing inside of her. She had always imagined that when her time came to carry life within her that she would glow with motherly light and would bond with her baby intensely as it rolled inside of her. Instead, she only felt a mass of confusing energy patterns inside of her body. In fact, the rolling balls of life in her belly reminded her far too much of the chaos that had moved through her brain for the first eighteen years of her life until Bran had freed her from the ongoing chatter of other voices., so she found herself reflexively shrinking away from them.

When she tried to connect to her babies, they all sent out vibrations at once and she was utterly unable to separate one thread, one voice, from another, even to identify how many. She regretted that this caused her to distance herself from that connection, even with what was growing and thriving inside of her own belly. She felt as a vessel, nothing more, and prayed that when the babies arrived and were their own separate little beings, visible as individuals, then perhaps she could connect with them, each one, and feel bonded as she did not now.

That time was quickly arriving, she realized, as the tugs of pressure in her lower body became more urgent and frequent. As if on cue, Maia opened her eyes and was surprised to see Lillian awake and very focused.

"Is it time?" she asked excitedly.

Lillian nodded and said, "I need new bed clothes and I think we should get the midwives."

"Do you need the chamber pot?"

"Oh yes. So much so." She sighed with pleasure as Maia helped her slide the pot under her bottom and her bladder was relieved. Even so, the flow of urine seemed to encourage the birthing process even further and she was not surprised to see a trace of blood in the chamber pot as Maia took it away.

"I will be right back," Maia assured her and she went to wake the attendant priestesses to send them for Belen and her midwives.

Chapter 12

Bran slept fitfully in the servants' quarters of King Marcus of Cornwall. Normally, he slept like a rock, even under the most adverse of circumstances. Since leaving Avalon months before, he had slept in hollow logs, in prisons, in palatial beds covered in bedding of the finest silks, and on benches in taverns. His favorite sleeping quarters were the ones most familiar to him: the sparse priest quarters in the monastery at St. Francis. He considered himself fortunate to have visited the monastery during his recent travels for a blessed respite and to catch up on news he may have otherwise missed. Regardless of the accommodations, he always slept deeply and well when he could find the time to do so. Gretchen, his foster mother, had once laughed at him when he slept through a particularly intense thunderstorm and said that the Saxons could invade and burn the house around him and he would sleep through it.

Tonight, however, sleep was elusive and when it did come, was ragged and unfulfilling. King Marcus was entirely non-receptive to his attempted negotiations for peace between the people of the Old Ways and the ruling forces of Cornwall, much as Bran suspected he would be. Marcus was a good man, but it did not take the inheritance of one of the greatest minds of the time to know that the homeland of the High King would follow the lead of the High King. Bane to stand alone as a sole beacon of reform in the South, King Marcus apologetically explained to Bran that his armies were not strong enough to stand against Gwent and The Summer Country. Even with the backing of the North, he had no interest in angering the only kingdom to border his own country by land, not to mention incurring the disapproval of Carmeliard.

With the entire North allied with Avalon and those kings committed to bringing Britain together as a united force against their enemies, one would think that the other three kingdoms would follow suit. Carmeliard, Gwent, and The Summer Country, however, were the most populated, most militarized, and the most pious of the kingdoms. The Christian priests had commanded the consciences of the sitting kings for decades and were determined to rid the country of all those who practiced the old religions and continued their adoration of the Goddess.

Just before dawn, Bran pushed himself up from the pile of straw where he had spent the night tossing restlessly. He walked into the moonlight and breathed in the cool Spring air. The moon was full and rich, hanging in the dark sky like a bright coin. His thoughts strayed to Lillian; a pleasure he rarely allowed himself lest he come lost in his memory of her. When first he left Avalon, he had searched for her often with his mind, knowing well that he could call to her if he wished and that they could easily connect on the astral realm. They had done so with little effort when he had come to her on the afternoon before their ritual coupling to tell her that he must leave. Since his departure, however, it was as though a wall blocked their magical joining. He knew she was safe and well as of several weeks ago when he had met with one of the Druid priests from Avalon on the lower edge of North Wales. When he provided the priest with his update and what he had learned on his travels, he dared to ask the man how things were with the Lady of the Lake.

The man had looked askance, seeming to avoid Bran's eyes as he answered that Lillian was well and ruling Avalon to the best of her abilities. Bran wanted to press the man for further information as there was obviously more to this story, but Bran knew that if he was meant to know more, the priest would have told him. It took all of his will to allow the man to leave with the news untold to him, whatever it might be.

His heart longed for her, a feeling of encompassed passion and breathless need as he had never known existed. Most men of his age had long since lain with women and known their pleasures. Many were married with a brood of children already started. Although he was fully aware of attractions he felt to lovely women he had met in his life and had even been the target of aggressive seductions in the past, he had never felt inclined to share himself with any of them. His early years left him with an aversion to the company of other people and so intent had his study been of holy writings and laws of state that he rarely found time for social activity.

Before he came to live with the priesthood of St. Francis, he endured the jests of the other boys in Lord Seaton's court, who suggested that perhaps he preferred the company of other men or even the horses he tended, to female companionship. Even Duncan, his foster brother, gingerly questioned why he never took advantage of the attention given to him by the young servant girls in the court. He had no answer to give; only that the idea did not suit him.

Now, oh now… he knew he had kept his heart pure so that he could give it to Lillian untainted by the affection of another. Oh, how he had loved her, through oceans of time and across centuries of space, since human existence first began. He loved her as Lilith, as Bathsheba, as Ruth, as Mary, as Caillean, as Helena, as Eilan, as Nimue, and as Vivienne. He had loved her as his mother, his daughter, his obsession, his sister, his lover, his wife, his confidant, his student, and his mentor. He had loved her in every possible way for a man ever to love a woman. He had loved her in ways that were the purest, most blessed joy and ways that were the most destructively forbidden. Always, though, he had loved her profoundly, passionately, and always, they found one another.

None of this had he known until the words of power left her lips on the day they first met this time: "*Is it you?*"

He never thought to ask if she loved another, if she cared not for the affection of men, if she was taken under a vow of chastity to the Goddess, if she even felt what he did in that moment. He belonged to her, heart, body, and soul, and she to him and anything contrary to that never occurred to him.

She haunted his thoughts every day he spent away from her and he was weak with anticipation to return to her presence. He was self-aware enough to understand the vulnerability his feelings for Lillian created in both himself and in his obligations to the cause of Avalon. Rarely did he ever allow full indulgence of his emotions and his memories, both of this life and others gone before. His focus on the matter at hand of creating liaison with the seven kingdoms was strong and demanded more attention than he wished to give, if he were to be completely honest. His head still swam with the events of the past two years and more specifically, his coming to Avalon. So much had changed so quickly in his life. Two years before, he had been a scribe at the abbey and now he was negotiating for peace as the Merlin of Britain. He knew he could not give in to the enormity of all that had transpired or he would become lost in the thick of it.

Lillian was a delightful luxury thought that he embraced from time to time, most often as he drifted off to sleep. Regardless of the victories or challenges of the day, she was his last thought at night and his first thought in the morning. It vexed him that on the times when he dared to reach out to her with his thoughts, he could not find her. It was as if the very earth itself had swallowed her up and held her from him.

As if by habit, he found himself at the courtyard stables. The whickering and rustling of the horses was a familiar comfort to him, having spent his years from ages of nine to thirteen as a curry boy for Lord Seaton. King Marcus was proud of his collection of prize stallions and mares, all descendants from the breeds perfected by Leodegrance of Carmeliard. They were fine animals, that was for certain; strong and tall with backs that passed his own shoulders in height and he was an unusually tall man. No man of conventional height would be able to sit one of these fine creatures without using a stepping mount to boost him into the saddle.

Bran wandered outside and sat on a bench near the door to the stable. Moonlight bathed the path before him and reflected back to him from the watering trough at his side. He found himself gazing into the reflected moonlight, wishing that just once he could see Lillian's face again. He felt the weariness of the past months seep into his bones as never before. They were a long cry from safety and the threat of war loomed heavily over them; one that would take place right on Avalon's doorstep. He doubted that the villagers, so besieged by the royal soldiers, could withstand a war and, in fact, one he triggered by bringing defensive troops to their shores.

Not only was he courting war, but he was doing so in the back yard of Carmeliard and the court of the High King himself. The King was rarely in his own court, but the principle remained the same. He felt himself dozing as he sat, with his last vision of the full moon reflecting on the water behind his eyelids as he at last gave way to sleep.

He woke with a start, unsure of how long he had slept. His body was stiff and argued as he tried to rise. The moon was now low on the horizon and the sun was just starting to rise. The courtyard was quiet and he heard no sound of kitchen activity that would herald the start of the day, so it must be quite early yet. It was now, in fact, darker than it had been when he sat down with the moon ducked behind the trees and the sun easing dimly up in the East. The lighting effect was surreal and created shadows in odd places.

His skin prickled not only from the cold, but from the unshakable feeling that what awakened him was Lillian's voice. "*Ah!*" she had said. "*Ahhhhh!*" and those two syllables alone had been easily identifiable in his heart as her voice. As he awoke to the eerie silence of the pre-morning court, he mourned the slipping away of the last echo of her voice. He turned to the water trough, cupped his hands full of the brackish horse water, and rubbed it over his face to help him wake fully so he could begin his preparations to leave. He would attempt one further meeting not with Marcus specifically, but with his court advisors, including the priests. If he could find but one sympathetic ear, perhaps a few well-placed words could at least end the persecutions. Regardless, this would be his last day in Cornwall.

As the water trickled down his face, he pushed it aside with his hands and flicked it away. He opened his eyes and caught a reflection in the water that was not his own. As the ripples in the water settled, he saw Lillian there, her beautiful round face alight with love and her eyes bright and joyful. He watched with delight and awe as her hands reached out of the water and handed him a bouquet of seven flowers. He pressed the flowers to his face and breathed in their heady aromas, each different from the other. The bouquet turned to water in his hands and the vision was gone.

He stood stunned, wondering what the vision meant, but cherishing the brief moment when he felt her there. It had been so long since he felt any nearness at all from her. Her cry that woke him echoed in his mind and he gazed into the water's reflection again, desperate for any sign of her, for any connection. He saw only his own face looking back at him.

Sighing, he walked away toward the servants' quarters to prepare for the day, the scent of the flowers still heavy in the air. From all around him, all directions at the same moment, coming up from the ground and descending the sky, reverberating on all sides around him came the sudden cry of, "Brannnnnnn!!!" His walk broke into a run.

Chapter 13

Sweat rolled down Lillian's body as never before and her arms strained against the counter pressure of three priestesses holding her up. She was no slacker when it came to physical labor, but never in her life had she worked so hard and the exertion was tremendous.

Her labor itself went swiftly. It seemed like no time at all had passed between Maia leaving to tell the attending priestesses to get Belen and a huge crowd forming in her small bungalow. Quickly, she began to drift between the worlds as people shifted her position and put cool cloths on her forehead and warm ones on her back, which began to ache as the babies lowered into position. After an initial exam, Belen marveled at how far Lillian's labor had progressed.

She felt nothing she would call true pain. There was a moderate cramping in the lower part of her body and the pressure grew with tremendous, unbelievable force. Her breath began to come in shallow pants and sweat streamed from every pore of her body even before she started to push. At one point between the waves of contractions, she told Danu to get all of the observers out of her house. "This is not a show for their entertainment," she said firmly, trying to keep the seething she felt from contaminating her speech.

Danu smiled, "They are just excited, my sweet. You are giving birth to a royal family."

As the next contraction overtook her, Lillian said quickly, but intently, "That does not mean they all have to witness it. Get them out. Ahh… Ahhhhhhh!" She let the air flow through her to channel the energy her body was demanding, then continued to breathe in rapid, light breaths as it the power washed over her. She could feel her body giving way to the force inside of her. For a brief moment, she felt as though all time and distance were irrelevant and the veil between the worlds had come crashing down. She was at once back in the House of Maidens, running in the fields of flowers that grew in the Avalon gardens, taking her vows as a Priestess of the Goddess, feeling Bran's strong, warm arms around her, hearing the chants of the brothers and sisters and mothers and fathers around her, *"Lance to grail! Lance to grail!"* In her vision, she clung to him fiercely, breathing in his scent, savoring the taste of his mouth as his tongue wound round hers. Almost savagely, her body began to take over again, bringing her forcefully back to its processes. "No!" she thought desperately. "Don't take him from me again. Brannnnn!" she called out.

As guttural grunts began to pepper her breathing, Belen gently placed fingers inside of her to check her progress. "Very good, My Lady. I can feel the baby's head. Do you want to kneel? Sometimes that is more comfortable."

The thought of changing positions was odious to Lillian, but she knew that a change of position would shift pressure inside of her body and help her labor to progress. "The people are gone?" she asked.

"Over an hour ago," Danu assured her. Only the two of them, Belen, Maia, and three attending priestesses remained. How had time passed so quickly? She felt as though only one or maybe two contractions had passed since she had made her request. As she had seen happen so many times before in other laboring mothers, once she began to push, she was centered, cohesive, and focused.

All thought left her except to work in cooperation with the enormous task her body was undergoing.

Carefully, the women helped Lillian onto her knees, where she began to sway rhythmically, breathing softly and rapidly. They wiped her brow and continued to place warm towels against her back.

Her body began to push without her. Some part of her stood aside as silent witness, stunned at the involuntary force that took her over. She surrendered to it completely and found that when she would bear down forcefully, she felt complete relief from the pressure.

As was customary on the island, the room was silent as she went about her task, with every mind and spirit in the room concentrating on giving her their energy and support. Belen gently massaged Lillian's delicate birth opening around the baby's head as it began to emerge. The priestesses behind her helped to reposition her so that she was standing and squatting rather than kneeling with Belen kneeling in front of her. Danu was beside Belen, holding soft blankets warmed by the fire.

With the next push, she felt an intense, burning, stinging sensation and then a momentary rush of relief as the baby slid out into Belen's waiting, experienced hands. She barely had time to pass the baby off to Danu before another slipped out of Lillian's body. The midwives began working urgently to clear the mucous from the babies' mouths. One gave a furious yell at the intrusion and the other took a deep, ragged breath and then looked around in seeming amazement. Danu and Belen both laughed at once and then beamed up at Lillian who had all but collapsed against the three priestesses holding her up. "Avalon welcomes two new perfectly beautiful little priestesses," Danu said with tears in her eyes.

Lillian smiled gratefully and then gasped aloud as her body bore down again. Belen quickly passed the second baby to Danu. "You have more work to do, it appears, My Lady."

Chapter 14

Lillian, for the first time in weeks, carefully walked herself to the privy with a priestess on each side of her. Her legs shook from exhaustion and her womb ached for the effort it had exerted all through the morning. The skin that had been on her abdomen now hung loosely over her knees and down her sides. She had to pick it up in her arms through her thin breeding shift to walk with the priestesses weaving their arms into the crooks of her elbows. Still, she felt better and certainly lighter than she had the day before.

She had suckled each one of the babies, two at a time, before passing them off to wet nurses, which amounted to a little over two hours of tandem nursing. The afterbirths had passed without incident and although the final baby had at last arrived more than an hour after the one before it, all were well and alive. Belen and Danu had both wept with relief that so far, the birth had transpired with no loss of life for babies or their mother. No one aptly realized the degree of stress everyone had been under prior to the birth. It was not until now that the threat had all but passed that people acknowledged the fact that few really expected all the babies, however many there were, to survive. For that matter, most thought it unlikely that Lillian would birth so many babies and herself survive. The midwives would consider the danger mostly passed when the babies sustained life outside of Lillian's body for a day or two. Still, now they appeared healthy and strong with a mother who was understandably weak and exhausted, but alive and well. This was encouraging, a best-case outcome, really, and a collective sigh of relief went through the island.

As Lillian returned from relieving herself, Danu met her halfway to the bed and said to her, "You need to come see this, my lady." Curious, Lillian allowed the priestesses to lead her to Maia's room, which served as a temporary nursery. All of the babies lay sleeping in three baskets, two by two, with the exception of the last bed, which held the three smallest babies. They lay twined together, each in a warm embrace of another, content in blissful slumber. Behind the beds, a large window looked out onto the Avalon gardens. The day before, fresh, green shoots that would take months to develop into blossoms had peppered through the gardens. Now, weeks ahead of schedule, the garden was a sea of blooms of all kinds, bright and full of life. Lillian drew in a breath and let the magic of the moment wash over her.

She looked at her daughters, each one beautiful and perfect, and her heart overflowed with joy. Seven beautiful baby girls. Some of them were dark and olive-skinned like Bran. Some were as pink-cheeked and creamy white-skinned as she was herself. Some were blond, some had dark hair, and some had hair of flaming red. It was as though every life they had ever lived had been born into their children. No wonder she would only feel chaos when she tried to connect with them while they were in the womb. All those little minds so hard at work! "Possibly more" indeed! She looked with amazement at what her body had created and what had been born of her love for Bran and their place in the world. As she admired the magical garden that had suddenly bloomed, so alive with flowers; spring flowers, summer flowers, and late bloomers all joined in an orchestra of color, she said softly, "Danu, I know their names."

And so it was that the following day, the royal daughters were presented to the Druids and Priestesses of Avalon: Violet, Rose, Lily, Iris, Jasmine, Aster, and Dahlia.

Chapter 15

Lillian looked out over the Valley of Avalon where the Beltane fires burned high in bright patches in the darkness. She could still see shadows dancing around the fires, both Priestess and Druid indistinguishable in the play of dark and light. Many of the revelers who had gathered to share the celebration of life had already paired off for their own joining and would later perhaps re-couple in different configurations. Some still danced, with or without clothing, immersed in the magic of the night dedicated to the fertilization of the fields.

This was the first High Holiday ritual she had led since her coronation as Lady of the Lake. She ached to have Bran at her side for it, but as soon as the circle was sealed, she felt the power of the Goddess come upon her stronger than ever before. She knew that the ritual was powerful and filled with portent. Big magic was coming and Avalon would sit in its center.

She excused herself from the festivities and returned to the House of Mothers to find the babies all sleeping. The support provided since the birth of the girls was exemplary. She never had a moment to feel overwhelmed. From the very beginning, wet nurses and attending priestesses were present to cuddle, feed, soothe, and lull the babies as needed. She slept for many days and nights after the birth, waking only now and then as the attendants brought one baby or another to her to suckle. She loved nursing the babies and feeling their individual little personalities come forth as she spent time with them. Someone would come in and remove the baby from the cradle of her arms as she slept and two, maybe three hours later, would bring another one to her.

So fractured was her sleep during the pregnancy that exhaustion overtook her as soon as the birth was done. She slept deeply and restoratively. The broken sleep from feeding the babies barely bothered her at all as her cumulative sleep kicked in and she became more rested with each passing day. On the third day, she started walking outside again and enjoyed breathing in the fresh Spring air. Between the tinctures, pfilters, and salves provided to her by the midwives, a diet of fresh fruits and good meat, and her daily walks, the skin on her body finally started the long creep back up onto her torso. Just before Beltane, she found that she could again wear her old tunics, which had always been a little loose on her for comfort. One of the priestesses in the House of Mothers helped her to craft nursing slits in the folds of her clothing so that she could easily access her breasts for feeding the babies. Her post-birth bleeding stopped around the same time and she no longer felt the twinge of pain in her womb when she nursed. Belen said that the bleeding stopped early because of the ongoing nursing of seven babies.

People of the island, both priestess and Druid, stopped by all through the day to visit with the new princesses. There were times when Lillian did not even know where all her children were because some were in arms in the House of Maidens as the younger priestesses cooed and sighed over them, inhaling the scent of their soft, fine hair and touching their tiny fingers and toes. Some were in the House of Crones where the older women would kiss and preen over the babies. Some were in the House of Mothers where experienced hands nursed and diapered and cared for them along with the other babies. By twilight of each day, however, all seven babies nestled into their beds in the bungalow nursery with Maia, Lillian, and several wet nurses and attendant priestesses to soothe and comfort them. They were babies raised within an abundance of love and magic. Daily, the midwives marveled that all the babies had survived and that the birth had transpired without incident. The only marker that made it different from any other birth they attended was that there were seven babies instead of one. They wore the success of her pregnancy and birth like a badge of honor. Life began to piece itself back together again.

As she watched the dancers below reveling in the power of the night, she thought back to the Beltane of the previous year when she craved the fires with a white-hot passion. Danu denied her request to stay, which meant she had to leave as soon as the ritual completed, much as she had done tonight. Angrily, she had sulked her way back to the House of Maidens and contented herself eating honeycakes and drinking cider with the other girls, most of whom were much younger than she was. Maia and the other girls of her age attended the fires that year and even two or even three years before. THEY were in the valley making love, laughing, and raising energy with everyone else while she remained behind with the children, frustrated and angry, feeling the life tides flow through her with no means of release.

She smiled now as she saw the sense of the wisdom of the choices made on her behalf. She was thrilled that she had been able to contribute the power of her maidenhead to the coronation ceremony and equally delighted that it had been Bran's first encounter as well.

Normally, she would not place so much attention onto who was intimate with whom on what occasion. Unlike the very restricted and parochial beliefs in the world beyond, on Avalon, she grew up with the idea that sexuality is a very natural part of life and that it was perfectly reasonable to share her bed with whosoever she should choose when she felt that energy rise. All acts of love, pleasure, and joy belonged to the Goddess, but that first moment of the male to female, lance to grail, joining was especially potent. She was even more certain that events had transpired exactly as they should when she considered the seven sacred and beautiful little lives created by that one act.

Was that not the very essence of magic: something that had not previous existed in the world suddenly did so by the grace of the Goddess manifesting through humans? The very thought made her smile broadly and, she had to admit, proudly.

As she watched the joining of couples together in the valley here and there and there, with body melding into shadows created by the fire and the play of the moon, she felt her own energy gather in her loins for the first time since she gave birth to the babies. Her sexuality was the last thing on her mind for a very, very long time given the complications of pregnancy. It had been months and months since she had found her pleasure with Maia or any of the other women and the thought of joining with another man when Bran filled her thoughts and her heart was unthinkable. All the energy that would have fed her life tides had gone to sustaining life for her and the babies for so long she began to doubt she would ever feel the tides rise again.

Still, as she watched the joyful unions developing below, she felt the familiar tingle in her breasts and throughout her body as her blood began to race and her life tides rose within her. She felt a trickle of milk ease down her front as her breasts filled with milk and it squeezed out from her nipples. She breathed in deeply of the night, grateful that she had only worn her lightest sleeping tunic into the night air. Its soft, gauze-like cloth brushed against her naked flesh in the light wind, heightening her arousal. She brushed her fingertips against her nipples and felt the dampness there, which instantly cooled in the night air. Her hands lingered, giving each nipple a tight squeeze and pressing against the fullness of each breast, warm and tight. Her breasts were now significantly larger and she had not been a small-bosomed woman before. Although the nipples were slightly less sensitive from the breastfeeding, the sensitivity had increased in other areas of her breasts.

Lillian leaned back against a stone statue of the Goddess that stood in the garden with her as she watched the festivities below. The arms of the Goddess reached outward and seemed to embrace her as she eased backward more fully toward their support and slipped the back of her knee into one of the outstretched stone hands. The spring breeze stirred again and carried on it the scent of the fragrant island flowers and the heady aroma of sage and cedar from the fire below. She smiled as someone cried out in pleasure below and rested further into the embrace of the stone Goddess behind her. A man ran across the field below and jumped wildly over the fire, the antlers of a stag mounted on his head. A cry of raw power erupted from him as he leapt and a woman dressed in feathers and fur ran into his arms as he landed.

Laughing with joy, she pulled him to a nearby stump, turned around, and bent over it as he grasped her hips and took her enthusiastically from behind, each of them crying out with pleasure.

Other couples writhed together on the grass, reveling in the primal magic of fertility and lusty mirth that permeated the air. It was exciting to Lillian to watch from above the experience that life and circumstances rightfully denied her before. Easily ten, fifteen, maybe twenty couples came together below within her scope of vision and who knew how many had chosen to take their celebrations into the orchards, onto the Tor, or by the lakeside. The very wind was electric with passion and enthusiasm. Lillian found her fingers beginning to wander first across her wild thatch of pubic hair, then into the soft, wetness below. Her awakening passion felt good and alive, as though she was now a woman in a way far different from when she fed babies and babies and more babies through the day. Now, she was her own woman, individual and ripe, detached from the bounds of motherhood for a few moments. The wetness around her fingers increased as they moved faster and she let her head fall back into an ecstatic moan.

No, she was not completely individual. She was bound to Bran in a way she could never fully understand or describe. Thinking of him only increased her desire and she flashed back to the few moments they had spent together in this life. As her mind and her passion deepened, she thought of her first eye contact with him, when he had seen into her very soul and had known her, loved her, and accepted her without hesitation. She thought of the awkward time they shared on the Tor later that night, interrupted by Danu as they had been moments from consummating, then the thunderous orgasms that had rocked her body and his later when at last they consummated their union.

For the first time since he left, she allowed her mind, her spirit, to travel and reach out to him, wherever he might be, and rode a wave of lusty desire as she searched for his mind in the ether beyond. A soft, urgent mouth suddenly moved her fingers aside and drank hungrily from the juices of her passions and she shrieked in shock. She grasped the head, now firmly planted between her legs, and tried to push it away. The light was dim, but she could feel her fingers twining into thick, black hair and she gasped not only from surprise, but also from the sensations she was feeling. The life force energy of her assailant slammed into her and she reeled. "Bran?"

"Busy now," he said and did not miss a beat in his focus on the task at hand...and at mouth... as he began to use both to her pleasure. Lillian lost all control of her legs and he pushed his shoulder against her right thigh to effectively pin her against statue, again, never shifting his attention or losing rhythm. Every thought that did not involve his mouth, his fingers, or this moment completely left her and she was awash in ecstasy.

Her fingers twined through his hair, tugging and pulling as she moaned with pleasure. It was as though the whole world came crashing down on her as a floodtide of release swept over her, wave after wave of power and delicious tremors pounded through her body. She could not stop the primitive cries of erotic rapture that tore from her throat.

He stood, wiped his mouth roughly against his cloak, then kissed her deeply, drinking in the taste as though he could never quench his thirst for her mouth.

He broke away only to say, "I must have you this very moment or I fear I will die." His voice was raspy and hoarse. "If you have any hesitancy, tell me now."

In response, she pulled him to her and he thrust himself into her, hard and urgent. He roared his pleasure as she tightened around him and they moved together in a desperate frenzy. Somewhere in the back of her mind, she knew that the deep penetration hurt and the soreness from her recent birth was very real, but those thoughts were quickly subdued by the tides of their desire. The ferocity of their joining rocked them both to the core as they began to find their release. It was as if they were joined together in a molten flow of consuming passion.

Loud, fierce, intense cries of unbridled pleasure rang into the night as he came and came and came within her. So loud were their expressions of love and passion that the sounds below temporarily quelled in surprise.

Afterward, they clung to one another, afraid to let go. Finally, she said, "Are you really here? Is this happening? If this is a sending, I never want to let it go."

Bran traced her features, remembering every curve of her face and the feel of her soft skin under his touch, reconciling what he could feel with the image he held in his mind for the past months.

"I am here," he said, "and I am not going far away again for a very long time if I have any say in it."

This caused her to hold him to her more tightly than before. She felt tears of relief sting her eyes. *Now,* she thought. *Now my life can begin.*

He drew back from her and touched his chest. "Why is my front so wet?" he asked. "Did I drool that much or were you simply that pleased?"

She laughed. "I am sure it was the latter, Lord Merlin, but there are things you need to know. A lot has happened while you were away." She lifted his hand moved it across the front of her bare breast. Her nipple stiffened and squirted a spray of milk onto his hand.

She could not see the expression on his face in the darkness, but she could hear it in his voice. "What? Is it supposed to do that?"

Lillian laughed. "It is when you are a mother."

She heard his breath catch in his throat. "A... a mother. Lillian...Lillian, you had a child?"

"You could definitely say that," she laughed.

His voice was suddenly fraught with concern. "You gave birth. My Beloved, did I hurt you? Was it OK that we...just now...?"

She put her fingers to his lips. "It's fine. I am fine. Come, I will show you...if I can walk." Laughing, he scooped her as effortlessly into his arms as if she herself were an infant and carried her down the hill and into the bungalow.

Chapter 16

Bran looked down at the sleeping babies. Rose, Violet, Dahlia, and Jasmine lay bundled in the portable sleeping baskets in the nursery. "There are four babies here," he said confused. "Is this where the babies of the mothers at the Beltane fires are staying?"

Maia and Lillian looked at one another and smiled. "No. This is where our babies stay," she replied.

"Babies? Wait. *Our* babies? We have *babies?* All four of these are…our babies?" His dark eyes widened in shock.

"But wait!" Maia said with a mischievous twinkle in her eye. "There's more."

"More?" he looked to Lillian for confirmation. She nodded.

"You have seven healthy, beautiful daughters, Lord Merlin."

Bran swooned and looked as though he might collapse. Maia quickly brought a chair and he sank down into it. His jaw simply would not close and hung limply agape.

"Seven?" he gasped in nothing short of wonderment. *"Seven?"*

"I cannot believe you made it through the Druid priests without one of them telling you," Maia said. "Our girl, Lillian, and her wee ones have been the talk of the island…and we never heard of the barge being summoned."

Bran sipped at the cup of healing Avalon water that somehow found its way into his hands. "I have not spoken to the priests. I knew it was the time of the

Beltane rite, so I came onto the island through the marshes and went at once to look for My Lady." He gave her hand a squeeze. "The Druids could wait. I could not."

"Surprise!" Maia said with a flourish of her hand. "You're a papa."

"May I touch them?" he asked softly.

Lillian smiled, "Of course, you can. They're yours."

Gently, he reached a shaking hand to the light, silken hair of Jasmine and stroked it lovingly. The baby stirred briefly and made a sucking movement with her rosebud lips. Startled, he jerked back his hand.

"It's fine," Lillian said and guided his hand back to the baby's head. He stroked her tiny head, feeling the skin beneath his fingers that felt so soft and fragile. Tears welled in his eyes.

"What are their names?" he asked, his voice breaking slightly. "I have missed so much."

"These are Rose, Violet, Dahlia, and Jasmine," she said, indicating each one. "Lily, Aster, and Iris are in the House of Mothers. They will come back here to sleep after the priestesses know I have returned from the Beltane fires."

"A bouquet of seven flowers," Bran said softly. "All of this from our one joining at the coronation rite?"

Lillian felt her heart lurch. "Bran, I assure you, that was the only time I ever…"

His face reflected the clench of alarm that gripped him, "Oh, beloved, no, never. It never came into my mind for a moment… This is just all so much to absorb. I was merely marveling that from that one incredible, magical time that all of this…" He took her face in his hands. "Of course, I never doubted you, although you would be within all rights to do so with me gone for so long. I had not considered…"

"Then don't," Lillian said, placing her hands over his and cradling them more closely to her face. "I am devoted to you and no other."

"And I you," he said.

Maia cleared her throat, "If you don't need me for anything more, I believe I will go take a turn through the fires myself."

Lillian broke away from Bran's loving gaze. "Of course," she said. "I apologize for keeping you for so long. Thank you, dear sister, for your help tonight."

"Tra la," Maia wiggled her fingers in a playful goodbye. "I will not likely be back until tomorrow mid-day. The attending priestesses are on notice."

Lillian laughed, "I hope you have as much fun as I did!"

"No doubt," Maia's musical voice trailed after her.

Chapter 17

Bran pulled Lillian close to him, wrapping his long arms around her and pressing his face into her hair, breathing deeply. "Oh, how I have missed you. I could not feel you or find you while I was away. You were just *gone*."

"I could not have you worrying about me and the babies, my love. If you had known about the pregnancy, you could not have focused on what you had to do."

He laughed into her hair and kissed the top of her head. "You are so right. I would have been a man obsessed had I known you were carrying our child..." he smiled again as he corrected himself, "...our *children*. Still," his tone grew serious, "You had to go through all this alone. When I left, you were a young maiden. Now, you are a mother."

"Not as young as all that," Lillian said. "I know women who have two or three children by the time they are my age."

"Seven daughters. He shook his head in wonderment. "You are an over-achiever, aren't you?"

"That joining was powerful," she said with a more serious tone.

"And productive," he added, not quite as serious as she did. "I want to see you and be with you and hold you forever and tell you how much I love you, but first...I want to see the rest of our babies."

Minutes later, all seven babies were in place in their sleeping baskets, two by two except for the last one, which contained three. Lillian noted that as quickly as they were growing, they would soon all need larger accommodations. As usual, they had escaped their swaddling clothes to embrace one another as they slept: two with a fine cap of blond hair, three with dark hair, and two with flaming red hair.

Bran gazed at them in abject awe. "How do you tell them apart?" he asked.

Lillian leaned in, terrified that anyone other than Bran would overhear what she was about to say. "I cannot," she said under her breath. "They say that mothers can see differences in twins. You know, subtleties that others cannot see or they can tell the difference in their cries or their scent. They all look so much alike that I swear to you, I cannot tell one from the other. I just call them 'sweetling,' or 'precious child.'" She shrugged. "I hope eventually I can tell them apart and if I cannot, I will have to embroider their names on everything. Honestly, I am not convinced anyone else knows one from another.

"I know that Violet, Aster, and Iris have dark hair. Lily, and Jasmine have blond hair, and Dahlia and Rose have red hair. That's…as far as it goes."

"How old are they?"

"Coming upon two moons. They were born just before Spring Equinox."

"How long did it take? To have them, I mean?"

"Oh…," she thought back. "About half a day, I guess, from start to finish."

"Did it hurt?"

"At times."

"Does it hurt when they suckle?"

"Not anymore."

"May I watch sometime as you feed them?"

"Of course," she said and laughed. "You will have ample opportunity for that if you are here for any length of time."

He looked at her and said, his voice heavy with intent, "Lillian, I have to be honest. It very nearly killed me to be away from you. Now, with the babies here and coming back to Avalon to find that I have a family, I do not know that I can ever leave again. If that hinders my work as The Merlin of Britain, then so be it. I refuse to believe that this miracle of our bonding and our babies was brought to me for me to shun in favor of diplomatic travels."

He pulled her into his arms. "My mother died as I was born," he said softly. "My foster mother loved me dearly, but she died when I was but twelve-years-old. In this life, Lillian, I have never had a family and I have never known what it was like to love someone with my whole heart, my whole being. It is so damned blindingly intoxicating and I am terrified that I will fail at this in some way. That would devastate me."

"I know," she replied. "My mother also died giving birth to me and I was raised by the priestesses here on Avalon. As such, I had many mothers and now, I have many daughters." She smiled. "It allows me to give back the love that was given to me." She lowered her eyes and said softly, "Bran, I have loved you for many lifetimes and always we find one another and always, every time, it feels as though we did not have *enough* time. I do not want to lose another single second with you. We will both fail as parents from time to time, but we have all these wise people to help us. Surely we will fail no worse than anyone else."

They held one another for a long time, looking at their sleeping children. "Do you remember," He asked, "the night before I left when we spent the night just holding one another by the lake?"

"Of course," she smiled. "It is one of my favorite memories."

"Mine as well. As much as I love what little lovemaking we have enjoyed together, to me that was even more intimate. You have my heart, Lillian. You always have and always will."

"And you mine," she murmured. "I have loved you forever and will love you forever more."

"It has been a night of surprises," Bran said, laughing.

"Indeed," she agreed. "I was going to watch the Beltane celebration and come home alone, aching for you again…and here you are."

"My Lady," he asked. "May I escort you to your bed and hold you again, all night long?"

She lifted his big hand to her lips and kissed it, feeling the warmth of a love she could not have previously imagined course through her. "Nothing would please me more, My Lord."

And so he did…for many, many years.

Ophelia

Chapter 18

Around the time that Bran learned that he was the father of a bouquet of seven flowers, King Constantine took an injury in his crusade to rid the land of the Sons of Mordred, none of which were actually the sons of the real Mordred anymore. Mordred was long dead; just as long as Arthur was, in fact. King Constantine killed Mordred's two Saxon sons early on in his quest, and the remaining avenging marauders continued their rampages until the interest simply bred out of them. Most of them forgot why they were fighting so hard and the nature of their actual cause. By the time Constantine was injured, there were but a scant handful of rebels actively engaged in the attempt to overthrow the sovereign kingdoms of Britain.

Constantine truly felt that the years he invested as an avenging angel against these rebels was in the best interest of Britain and there were many who agreed. One cannot simply have one's lesser kings picked off like so many chess pieces on a board and not do something about it. To that end, he had a point, but there came a time when he was doing little more but chasing shadows and avoiding larger matters of state and it was at that point when the seven kingdoms really started to get antsy.

This was all resolved when he cornered a small band of those who still called themselves the Sons of Mordred on the shores of Anglia, as far as one could go into Saxon lands. It is left to victors to write history and by the account provided by King Constantine and his modest army, an assassination squad aimed for King Lucia of The Summer Country was surrounded by the crown's army and slaughtered on the Western shores. Although all the rebels met their deaths, one managed to cleave a sword into King Constantine's right arm and in doing so, mortally wounded the High King's horse. The horse reared wildly and threw the King who landed to the side of the horse moments before the beast collapsed directly on top of him.

Bleeding from his wound and pinned under hundreds of pounds of dying horseflesh that struggled to get up and refused to accept that its days of "getting up" were now forever past, the King was repeatedly crushed under the thrashing weight of the dying horse. The soldiers put the beast out of its misery and used strong saplings as pry bars to raise the horse's body enough to pull out the King. So bathed the animal's blood was the monarch that it was impossible to tell his degree of injury.

The soldiers carried him between them, forming a chair with their arms, to the freezing ocean water and submerged the King into the frigid ocean waters. When they returned to Carmeliard, the court physician said that the cold water had done more to save his life than anything had as the freezing cold slowed the blood flow and the salt water helped stave off the infection that may have developed in their long travel home.

Another thing the cold water did was to revive the unconscious king, who began screaming and thrashing in a most magnificent fashion. In the end, the soldiers bound wound on his arm and his ribs, which were undoubtedly broken. As loudly as he screamed, it was quickly determined that he had not suffered a lung puncture, which was always a primary concern with fractured ribs. His arms and legs all flailed about well, which was a good sign. The only true concern was the aggressive flow of blood from the arm that had met the sword.

After the King was calmed and bandaged, the army of royal vigilantes built a litter and dutifully and most carefully transported the King back to Carmeliard. After decades of crusading against the Sons of Mordred, the quest ended with more of a whimper – or I supposed you would call it several loud shrieks – than a bang. There were no more instances of lesser kings killed for the revenge of Mordred, a long-dead traitor to the crown. The last battle had ended and the King and his men returned home and if the truth be told of it, the King's heart was not much in the chase anymore.

Already of advancing age for his time, King Constantine took to his bed for a few weeks to heal under the care of his latest wife, Queen Ophelia. Since Ophelia was only in her early twenties when she married King Constantine as he passed through Carmeliard on his way to his ill-fated battle in Anglia, she herself lingered in bed only for resting and for pleasing moments with her spouse. Aside from this, she did what she had done for the past many months during his absence: she efficiently and most conservatively ran the royal household like a well-oiled machine and, for the most part, the country as well.

Ophelia barely knew the King when he took her as his wife. His previous four wives had all died within a short time of marrying him and some said that Queen Morgawse of Orkney had cursed the title of High Queen when was denied to her. Queen Guinevere had fallen to ruin and every queen since her had died early.

Ophelia did not subscribe to any such nonsense. She was beyond all other things, a practical woman. She knew the King had not been beguiled into marriage by her beauty. Her beauty was not particularly beguiling in the first place. She was a comely young woman, but there were fairer women aplenty in the kingdom and many from noble birth where she was not.

It was certainly not her father's estate or wealth the King sought for her father was merely a common miller who barely made enough to put bread on their own table, much less to sell at the market.

No, she and her father stood before the King that fine autumn day because her father was a drunkard and a blowhard. Not that the King specifically sought to wed into a family of drunkards and blowhards rather than, say, the daughter of a lesser king with whom he could align himself in a politically advantageous union. Since he spent so much of his ruling time away from Carmeliard, most of the lesser kings had no clue what Constantine looked like or held any degree of affection for him or fealty to him. They ran their own kingdoms independently from the High King, for so long that they largely forgot what it was like having a High King. It was doubtful that any of the seven lesser kings could even pick King Constantine out of a small crowd.

Would it have been better for Constantine to elevate the status of one of the lesser kings to "in-law of the High King?" Most assuredly, it would have been.

Context, however, is important, and by this time, King Constantine was not only without an heir to the throne, but by that time had also buried four wives, or rather, had other people bury them. He did not engage wives or potential wives with any degree of permanence assigned to the arrangement, so her lack of suitability by family or by training to act as High Queen was not of issue or concern to him. His interest lied in other areas where she was concerned, perpetrated by the previously stated fact that her father was a drunkard and a blowhard.

Since she was a child of twelve, Ophelia had worked in the tavern serving ale and dodging the hands of the men of her village. She could carry more in her strong hands and generous reach than could most grown women and she learned quickly. The landlord of the tavern, Forrest, was a good sort, although it was far less than a princely sum that he could afford to pay her for her hard work in his establishment. The title of "miller" was more of a formality bestowed upon her father for the fact that *his father* had been an *actual* miller of some prosperity and upon his death, the mill had been bequeathed to *her father*. With the mill had come the title and although Mills knew exactly how to use the mill, the mill was never used.

The less than regal sum that Forrest paid Ophelia afforded a little meat to their table and a few scraps of cloth to make serving dresses for herself. She was handy with a needle and thread and very fine-handed. Forrest was good to her and would often pass along leftovers from the evening meal for her to take home and store.

The lion's share of her meager wages paid for her father's ongoing drinking in the tavern. After sleeping away most of the day, he would stumble in around dusk when she had been working for several hours already.

Her father's name was Henry, but everyone called him "Mills." She had never heard him called otherwise except by his father, who was long dead and used to call him Henry. "Mills!" the other drunkards in the tavern would yell out his name in greeting and he would raise his hands high in the hair in salute to them. He would take his usual seat at the table in the center of the room where he held court for the night, still a little drunk from the night before. Over time, "sleeping it off" was something that did not happen for Mills. He would sleep, but the drunken state never really left him. Ophelia would have his supper plate ready and would bring it to him with his first large tankard of the evening. To her knowledge, supper was the only food he ate in a day and he ate it with great gusto.

As she worked through the night, the stories would unwind. Her father was a magnificent storyteller and she often thought that he would have made a wonderful court jester or even a bard. He could weave a story like no other she had ever known and the people who knew him held him in great affection for that very talent despite his obvious personal flaws.

She had no idea who her mother had been and each time she had asked her father over the years, he had told her a different story. They had no friends in the village that seemed to have known her mother and, being such a reasonably minded young woman, Ophelia had pushed the thoughts of her aside as a fruitless pursuit.

Often her father would pull her over onto his knee and encourage her to sing for him and his friends. It was certain that she had no fine voice. It was brassy and hearty like a sailor's and nothing like the tinkling, sweet voices she heard from other girls in the village. Still, she loved her father for all his faults and usually humored him with a bawdy song or two. Her favorite was called "The Landlord's Daughter" and was about a randy girl who served ale in a tavern belonging to her own father.

It was as different from her as night and day, but it made everyone laugh and the tavern patrons would always join in for the chorus.

On the night that ultimately landed her in front of the High King, some of the soldiers from the Sons of Mordred crusades had come in to drink and wager on dice. They heard her father loudly braying about some nonsense or another and before long, were at his table laughing along with his friends. Ophelia stopped by to bring him another tankard and as she did, one of the soldiers caught her hand and asked with an odd accent she could not place, "Is it true then, girl?"

Ophelia looked confused and tried to extract her hand from his grasp. "Is what true?" she asked.

Her father interrupted her and slurred, "Of COURSE it's true! Do I look like a liar to you? Go on, sweet'eart, tell'em."

"Oh, it's true," Ophelia said, having no idea to what she was agreeing. "My father never lies."

The tavern broke up at those words, with men spraying mouthfuls of ale and holding their sides as they laughed uproariously.

The soldier, however, studied her face carefully, "You're saying that you can spin regular old flax straw into gold. Really?"

Ophelia beamed. "Oh, aye! My mum, you see, was one of the faerie women from Avalon, priestess trained, she was. In fact, the Lady Morgan knew her personally and taught her the arts. Yes. Then she passed it down to me."

The soldier's eyes widened. "You know that spell crafting is outlawed in Britain. Are you a witch, woman?"

Ophelia laughed. "Silly man. If I were a witch, would I be spending my time serving ale to this lot? No, I would be living in a castle of my own with grand towers and servants waiting on me hand and foot. That's the life I would live."

She thought nothing more of the interchange and went on with her evening as usual, cleaning up a bit more upchuck than usual from the increased traffic the soldiers created. Forrest even passed her a higher payment than usual because the house take was greater than on most nights. "Someday, Fee," he said with a smile, "This will be all yours."

"I can only aspire to such greatness," she laughed, slipping the coins into her pocket. He gave her a hug around the shoulders and offered to help her walk her father home.

"I can manage," she said, slinging her father's arm over her shoulder and shifting his sleeping weight onto her hip and looping her fingers through is belt. Years of practice had taught her well how to move her father's deadweight with speed and efficiency. "Come on, Mills. Let's get you home."

Automatically, as they did every night, his feet began to move. It was no soldier's march, that is for certain, but they moved enough that she could propel him forward. When they arrived at the mill house, she struggled the door open and pushed her father onto his bed, which was near the door for just such nightly events as these. She helped him off with his boots and drew the cover up to his chin. He turned over to his side and muttered, "You're a good girl, Fee" without even waking. Within moments, his snores resounded through the tiny house fit to shake the walls.

The mill house had two other rooms: the kitchen and Ophelia's bedroom. When she was fifteen-years-old, she took over the only bedroom without bothering to ask her father's permission. He had offered no protest. She took off her serving dress and used a cloth and water from the bed stand to wash away the stains of meat juices, spilt ale, vomit, and dirt. She then hung the dress in the closet with her two others and slipped into her nightclothes.

The room was chilly, but she was too tired to make a fire and knew they could not spare the wood anyway. Once under the bed covers, she was warmer anyway and soon fell into a dreamless sleep.

Chapter 19

She awoke the next morning to an incessant pounding on the door of the millhouse. Her father reached the door before she did, but not by much. He let loose with a slew of swearing but came up silent when he saw the King's entourage at the door. He blinked repeatedly and she was unsure whether it was because he was actually unfamiliar with seeing the light of day or if he was trying to make sense of the royal brigade before him. Ophelia could see at least five, possibly more, of the royal guard across the threshold of the millhouse.

The one in front was reading a proclamation that required that the two of them present to court immediately. Ophelia was given a moment to dress but was admonished to "make haste."

She chose the nicer of her serving dresses, ran a comb through her hair and pinned it up, then hurried outside where a finely dressed man of the court was pouring water over her father's upturned face.

"It won't do any good," she said. "He is as sober as he is going to get for the foreseeable future."

The man snorted and pushed Mills up onto the back of a patient horse and handed him the reins. "Can you manage to ride?" he asked impatiently, holding a kerchief to his nose.

"Like a prince," Mills slurred and then promptly slid off the other side of the horse. Several sets of hands pushed him back up onto the horse, where he was secured with ropes, his belly stretched across the horse's back with his head on one side and his feet on the other. Almost immediately, his snores rang through the early morning air. The man looked at Ophelia and she shrugged one shoulder.

The King's guardsman who had read the proclamation aloud helped Ophelia onto his own horse and before she knew it, she was standing before Constantine, the High King of all of Britain.

At first, Ophelia laughed aloud at the idea that she was addressing the King. "Begging your pardon, Your Highness, but I can assure you that you do NOT have the right person. There has been some mistake."

"Do you know why you have been brought before me?" he asked, "Or are you merely presuming that I do not know what I am doing?"

Ophelia stumbled over these thoughts. "Well, no Your Highness," she said. "It's just that I am no one of any importance."

"Are you not Ophelia of the Miller?" he asked his voice firm and strong.

"I am," she replied.

"And do you not serve ale at Forrest's Tavern?"

"I do," she said, becoming increasingly uncomfortable.

"And can you not spin straw into gold, as taught to you by the faerie folk of Avalon?"

"Oh," Ophelia said, feeling the air rush from her body in something between laughter and hysteria. "Oh, no, Your Highness, I am neither a witch nor a sorceress! That was merely a jest for the drunkards in the tavern, I…"

"She CAN!" Mills bellowed, suddenly awake and alert at the most inopportune time possible. "Like none I have ever seen before! We have run out of straw ourselves, or else we'd be ssssilly with gold right now."

Ophelia turned and glared at her father, feeling that a noose and a burning pyre were not far off in her future. "Sir, I mean, My King, assure you I...*please do not kill me."*

The King looked at her for a very long moment and while she trembled under his gaze, she forced herself to look him squarely in the eye, praying it was more difficult to order the execution of a woman who could look at him unflinching than one who subjugated herself fully. Or would he want to kill her more for her impudence?

"Young woman," he said. "I have no intention of *killing* you. If what you say is true, I intend to marry you."

Mills cheered as though he was a maiden in the stands at a fete and his favorite knight had just won the joust. "Fee, do you hear that?" His laughter roared throughout the large hall. "You're going to be High Queen, girl!" He laughed so hard that he soon turned and vomited onto the boots of the King's guardsman next to him, and then snorted laughter to the point that even more came out of his nose.

All attempts at maintaining any degree of dignity abandoned Ophelia and she buried her face in her hands, attempting to compose herself and becoming more certain by the moment that this was some bizarre nightmare. No one made a sound except for the hearty chuckles of her father, which now sounded obstructed by phlegm. She took a breath and lowered her hands to find the king and, in fact everyone in the room, looking at her intently.

"It's not true," she said. "I am nothing more than a serving wench and a miller's daughter. My father, he is given to drink and spins wild tales just for fun. He loves a good story and gets, well, *caught up*."

The King continued to stare at her without notice of her father. His expression was completely unreadable to her, which was an unusual situation for her to experience. She was an excellent judge of character and could read faces quite well but found his intent impossible to decipher. At last, he said, "There is only one way I can know if what you say is true or if you simply do not wish to show me this magic that you can do. Here is what is going to happen."

He went on to explain that the guards would take her to a room in the castle. For now, the room would have a bed and a bed stand, but by nightfall, it would also contain a spinning wheel and a large quantity of straw. The faster she could spin the straw into gold, the faster she could leave. Until the straw became gold, there she would stay.

Ophelia protested to no avail. By mid-day, she sat on a stool in front of a spinning wheel, surrounded by more straw than she had ever seen in her life. "Oh Mills," she said aloud to no one in particular. "Look at what you and your stories have gotten me into."

She imagined that the day could not possibly bring more madness than it had already.

The room was very large, larger even than their entire millhouse. The castle was built with heavy Roman stone long before time of King Arthur. This room had seven windows, very high up on the outside wall, even higher than she could reach and she was an unusually tall woman. Even if she could get *to* the windows, she would be unable to get *through* the windows because they were very tiny. The height was no more than the breadth of her hand and the width as far as her two hands' breadths. They let sunlight and air in the room but were not good for much else and certainly unsuitable for escape.

And what good would that do?

No one would be willing to hide her from the High King and she would not know where to run anyway.

She sat down on the bed and had she been another type of woman, would have wept. She could not remember ever having cried and was not sure she would know how to do so. Certainly, the inclination was there somewhere inside of her, but it seemed like such a waste of energy that she did not bother to attempt it.

She heard the outside bar lifted from the door and steeled herself. An ancient, toothless woman with a kind face and bright blue eyes waddled into the room. She balanced a tray of food on one hand and closed the door behind her. "Are you hungry, Dearie?" she asked, her raspy voice not much over a whisper.

"No," Ophelia said, clipping her words, and determined not to like anyone involved with her captivity, least of all her troublesome father.

The old woman placed the tray on the bed. "Look," she said, "I've a nice loaf of bread 'ere for you and some cheese and a good cup o' warm wine and some lovely grapes. Won' you eat a bit, Love?"

Ophelia's stomach growled despite her fury.

The old woman cackled. "Is a shame when our bellies go rogue and belie our intention, eh? Come on, then, Sweetling, 'ave a bite." She pushed the plate of food across the tray to Ophelia.

Ophelia sighed and picked up the piece of bread and nibbled on it, then smiled her approval. "This is very, very good."

The old woman beamed. "Thank ye. I made it myself this morning, I did. Try the cheese. I made that myself as well."

Ophelia nibbled at the edge of the small block of cheese and then took a larger bite. "This is amazing!" she said, temporarily forgetting her outrage. "But you are…"

"…so old?" The woman laughed heartily. "Yes, I am," she said. "I met my crone years before you were even birthed. I'm not infirm, though. I can still see as well as ever I could and I can still move around. I can damn certain still cook. I've my uses." She puffed herself up like a proud hen.

Ophelia smiled a genuine smile.

"They call me Ducky," the old woman said, patting Ophelia's hand. "I will be the one taking care o' you while you're here. You just tell me if you want anything."

The reality of her situation again flooded her mind. "I am being held captive against my will," she said. "What I want is to *go home*."

The old woman's smile faded. "Y'know," she said, "sometime, the best stories begin this way. Why don' you just take a day or two and think about it. Is it really so bad? Is your own life so wonderful that you canna wait to return to it?"

"But I cannot spin straw into gold!" she shouted. "That's ludicrous! My father was drunk and told a tall tale and some fool believed it and told the King!"

"So?" Ducky asked. "Do y'think he'd be the first t'find big talk at the bottom of a tankard? Pshaw." She waved her hand as if dismissing something ludicrous.

"Surely he is the first to get his daughter held captive to spin straw into gold just by running his drunken mouth!"

"You so sure about that?" Ducky eyed her. "And how do you know you canna spin straw into gold. Did you ever try?"

The laugh that escaped her took her by surprise. "I cannot even SPIN WOOL! I have no idea what to do with that contraption!"

Ducky clucked. "Aw, luv, did yer mum never teach you to spin?"

"I never knew my mother and my father was not given to spinning," she said, biting back sarcasm.

"Well, I can spin an' spin well," the old woman said, beaming with pride. "Would you like for me to teach you? I learnt it as a young girl. Tell me, dear, are you neat handed by nature or do you know?"

"I can sew well," Ophelia said.

"Then we start tonight," Ducky said. "I will be back with the wool after I serve the evenin' meal. But truly, girl. Do consider staying. You will have good food, good rest, and a change of your scenery. Everyone can use that from time to time, don' you think?"

True to her word, Ducky arrived at her door at sunset with a tray with a large bowl of stew, a cup of cold milk, and a hunk of bread. She carried on her back a large sling that was full of wool.

After they ate, Ducky told her the history of the spinning wheel and how the first ones came from Avalon and that people thought they were magical because they could transform one thing into another. "Like alchemy," she said softly. "Only the richest houses had them, didn't they? It honors us to have one here. The spinning wheels were destroyed in the purge that started under King Arthur's rule 'cause people thought them a gateway to visions and other magical works. This very one, though, belonged to the Lady Morgan and she showed the women of the court how to use it. We were all drop-jawed that it moved so much faster than hand spinning and she showed how it wasn't magics, but just mechanics and nothing more.

Ducky showed Ophelia how to mount the spindle in the proper position so that she could rotate it by the cord that encircled the large wheel. "You put the wool on the spindle like so. The spindle is sharp at the tip, so mind yerself. Hold the spindle wool in your left hand," she said, "and give it a bit of an angle as you feed in the strands of wool, overlappin' each other, then turn the big wheel with your right hand. Careful now…not too fast! When the wool is spun, you wind it up back up onto the spindle like so…"

Ophelia was a quick study and soon, they two were laughing and admiring her handiwork. "This is incredible!" Ophelia said with delight. "I had no idea I could do this!"

Ducky placed a gnarled hand on her shoulder. "Girl," she said solemnly. "We dunna know what we can accomplish until we try. N'er limit yerself. Don' say 'I canna' when you have not even tried."

She picked up the tray of now empty supper dishes and left as Ophelia turned her attention to her newly discovered talent.

Chapter 20

The coming days were a blur to Ophelia. She would wake as the sun began to creep into the tiny windows at the top of the room, wash herself, and dress. On the second day, Ducky brought with her several fine dresses that had been left in the castle by previous ladies of the court. They were the perfect size, if slightly short. Ophelia reminded herself that no one was likely to see her anyway.

Ducky brought her a comb and fine copper mirror and even some kidskin boots and warm stockings to keep her feet warm. Ducky would always arrive mid-morning with some splendid feast she had served the court to break their fast. Ophelia was certain that she had never tasted food as delicious as this.

They would practice spinning for hours until the sun began to creep to the other side of the building. When the room darkened, Ducky would leave to prepare the evening meal for the court, returning in a short while with another fine meal for Ophelia.

The guards of the night would bring in torches and place them in the wall mounts to provide light in the room. Before the week was done, Ducky began bringing her own evening meal in with Ophelia's so they could eat together. She shared stories of her time in the court and Ophelia found herself drawn into the elaborate stories about King Arthur. Yes, Ducky had known him well and, in fact, and worked in his court when she was a young girl.

Ophelia was stunned to hear these stories unwind and said, "Ducky, Arthur has been dead for more than forty years. You knew him and Lady Morgan, so you must be…"

"I am sixty and three years," she said proudly. "and those days are as fresh to me as if they happened yesterday."

"And you have been here ever since?"

"I have. My dear husband was the King's chamberlain for a while and a fine one he was. When Arthur died, he continued to care for the place until the elder King Constantine was crowned. Then he carried on for him as well until he died of the influenza, God rest his sweet soul."

"Did you remarry?"

"Oh no," she laughed. "There was none for me but my sweet Bors from the time I first laid my eyes on him. He was my whole world, he was."

"Did you have children?"

Ducky's face darkened. "No," she said, and Ophelia noted a bit of sadness in her voice. "God dinna see fit to bless us with babes. I was breedin' three, maybe four times, but they never did stay inside long enough. I used to think 'twas the curse on this place." She looked around as though the walls would argue with the notion. "Queen Guinevere, now there was a piece of work that one, she could never bear a child either, but soon, the babies were coming again to the ladies of the court, just not to me and my Bors. Do you have any babes, my dear?"

"Oh no, I never… Work keeps me busy," Ophelia said simply.

Ducky would empty her chamber pot, bring her fresh bedding, and keep wine and water at her bedside. They would chat and spin into the night and the next day would go on unchanged from the previous one. The only thing that was ever different was the food brought to her. Some days, Ophelia even forgot she was a prisoner.

One morning, how far into her captivity she had no idea as she had completely lost track of days, Ophelia heard the door open and turned, expecting to see Ducky wrangling a tray onto the bed stand. Instead, she saw the King himself, looking around at the room that was still filled with straw with a degree of consternation.

"My King," she said, dropping into a curtsey.

"Madam," he said in return. "I cannot help but notice that there is considerably more straw in here than gold. That is to say, all straw and no gold."

"Your Highness," Ophelia said, trying to keep her voice steady. "As I tried to tell you when last I saw you, I do not possess the ability to spin straw into gold. It was merely a careless boast by a drunken man."

"Did you not confess to my captain while in the tavern that you could indeed do so?" he asked.

"Only in jest, My King," she said. "I was certain he understood that…"

"He seemed rather convinced when I spoke with him," Constantine said dourly.

"If I may be so bold, Your Highness," she began, "as to ask about my father…"

"Your father has returned to the mill," he said simply. He began to go into, shall we say, a degree of physical distress without his drink. I had him returned."

"But there is no one there to care for him!" she said without the formality the situation demanded.

Constantine arched his eyebrows. "Good woman, I am certain that he can manage to stumble to the tavern on his own, he is a grown man."

Ophelia lowered her eyes. "My apologies, Your Highness," she said softly.

Constantine crossed the room and his stature seemed even more imposing that usual when he stood close to her. He was taller than she was and that was unusual, even in a man. His dark curls, threaded with white here and there, were carefully coifed in a way that showed a vanity she had not expected. He was clean shaved in the Roman fashion and close enough to her that she could smell his scent of cloves and, she thought, lavender.

"Ophelia," he said, as though testing the feel of her name in his mouth. "I am going to tell you something that very few people know and I need to believe that I can trust your confidence." He looked with great intensity until she raised her eyes to his. She nodded slowly. "The kingdom, at least Carmeliard which includes Gwent, is bankrupt...and it is my fault." She drew in a quick breath and it did not pass unnoticed by him.

"The other lesser kingdoms all have their own industries, whether it's furriers or meat or crops of the fields or artisans or even fishing. All that Carmeliard does is collect taxes and support, well, me." He looked abashed. "My crusade to keep the lesser kingdoms safe all these years has jeopardized my own homeland. Taxes have not been collected for...well, I will admit that I have no idea. I have neglected my throne in what I thought was a higher cause. Now, I'm just not so sure."

Ophelia listened, fascinated, as he drew in a breath and continued. She had the distinct feeling that these were possibly the most words he had put together in a very long time.

"I do not claim to be a wise man, but I do try to be a good man. I am a Christian man and I have no interest in witchcraft or magic. I am, however, a desperate man and quite frankly, all of the praying I have done to my own God seems to have availed me little and nothing."

His eyes met hers as if evaluating her, and then he said, "Ophelia, I need you to do this. If there is one spark of magic inside of you, I need you to do this incredible task, not just for me, but for our country. When Donovan told me what you had said, he laughed and yes, we all knew it was a jest. But if there was one chance, one ounce of truth, we had to try."

"I cannot..."

"Try. Please. That is all I am asking. I will marry you and you will have a good life. I swear it. Every need and want that crosses your mind I will meet. I will respect you and honor you as my wife for as long as we live. I will make certain that your father is cared for in a manner that is far greater than what he deserves. Neither of you will ever want for a thing."

His eyes pleaded with her. "Please do not refuse me this."

"Your Highness," she said choosing her words with care and locking her eyes with his for emphasis. "I have no such magic. I am nothing more than a miller's daughter." She was acutely aware that this was the closest she had ever been to a man who did not reek of ale. As frightened as she was, she could not help but feel a pulse of attraction run through her, which intensified when he took her hand in his.

"Just try," he entreated. "I know how ridiculous it sounds, but for your country, I am only asking that you try. I give you my word as a gentleman and as King, I will never, ever bring harm to you. The worst that will ever befall you by my hand or at my order is that you will return to your home, safe and sound, with adequate compensation for the time you have spent here. Just…try, please."

"I will try," she said, the words flying out unbidden. *Too late.* She fought back the urge to clap her hand over her fickle mouth.

He nodded curtly and dropped her hand. "Have your accommodations been adequate? Are you well cared for here? Is there anything you need?"

"I *need*," she said matching the tone of her voice to his, "fresh air and sunshine. I *need* to be able to walk outside and breathe the air that is not stuffed up in this room night and day. I *need* to be able to look out at the land for which you wish me to do this monumental task and I *need* to not have armed guards stationed outside of my door as if I am a prisoner."

"The guards are not armed," he said softly.

She stared at him…hard.

He sighed. "May I have your word, please, that you will not leave the court without telling me and that you will at least try to do what I have asked?"

"You have my word, Your Majesty. You have asked me to try and try I shall."

"Then the things you have requested will be provided to you this very day." He nodded formally to her. This time, she did not curtsey, but merely tilted her head in his direction with a wry look on her face.

Chapter 21

Later that day, two of the King's guard assisted Ophelia in relocating to a much larger room on the other side of the castle. The room was airy and spacious and both the windows and the bed were bigger. She had not imagined there could be a room larger than her previously one that was for personal use and not a dining hall or some other public room, but here was proof to the contrary. A large mirror dominated one wall of the room and a generous vanity was stationed in front of it. Off to one side, a smaller anteroom held even more straw than had been in the first room. The ever-present spinning wheel stood in a position of prominence and she was pleased to find a small table with two chairs in a little alcove near a shuttered window. No more eating meals on her bed!

One of the King's guardsmen walked her through the castle and showed her how to get to the courtyard and into the gardens. When they returned to the room, he nodded politely toward her and left the door open behind him in a pointed display of non-captivity.

She tested the theory by stepping out into the corridor and found that she was, indeed, quite alone. She took a few tentative steps in the direction of the gardens to see if anyone would stop her and no one seemed to notice her footfalls. Back in the room, she opened a huge armoire that stood in the corner of the room and found it to be full of dresses of all level of formality.

"Oh my, 'e done right by you, 'e did," Ducky cackled from the door. "'e's put you up in the Queen's chambers, big as anything." The old woman made her way into the room and sat the evening meal down on the table. "'is Majesty must be fairly certain you are going to do as 'e asked if 'e already put you into the royal quarters."

"Well, that's the trick, isn't it?" Ophelia said. "Now all I have to do is spin that room full of straw into gold. No problem."

"Little Luv," Ducky said, taking the girl's hands in her own. "Our King is not by anyone's measure the sharpest tool in th' box, but 'e's a good sort and 'e'd not make a bad husband given the chance. 'e's locked up and just needs someone with a kind heart and the right key. Would it be so bad to stay 'ere?"

Ophelia sighed. "I don't know anymore," she admitted. "But what I do know is that I cannot… or rather," she said correcting herself, "I *do not know how to* spin straw into gold and I have trouble imagining that it is even possible."

Ducky's eyes twinkled, "My girl, there are so many more things on heaven and earth than e'r you knew about. Why a singular person alone canna know it all. Now drink your wine an' we will talk about it more."

Ophelia did feel better after drinking the warm, potent wine. They did not speak during the meal, but her head began to feel comfortably warm and a little fuzzy. She did not often drink strong wine, but at the same time, she did not imagine herself to be such a lightweight.

At last, Ducky said, looking around the room, "This is a good thing, you bein' 'ere an' all. You will be more comfortable than in the other room. 'e did you right, 'e did." Ophelia began to nod and worked to hold her eyes open.

"Oh, look at you, Sweetling," Ducky cooed. "You're drowsing like a babe. 'ere, let's be gettin' you into bed."

The sun was just going down and Ophelia was shocked by how exhausted she felt. Why in her old life, her father would only just now be stumbling into the pub to be fed and her night would not even have yet begun! Still, her eyes would not stay open. She allowed Ducky to undress her, put her nightclothes on her, and ease her into the bed covers. The bed was more comfortable than any she had ever felt before.

"Sleep well, my little queen," Ducky cooed in her ear. "Happy dreams to ye."

Chapter 22

Ophelia did dream.

She was dancing with King Constantine in a formal ballroom. She knew it was a dream because in "real" life, she had no idea how to dance, but in her dream, she floated effortlessly in his arms. He smiled down at her, his eyes full of pride and satisfaction, plus something else she could not quite place. Could it be...affection?

"I knew you would do it, Ophelia. You have saved the kingdom," his voice caught in his throat, "and you have saved me." He pulled her closer and she could smell his scent, cloves and lavender. She felt her heart leap a bit and just then, he twirled her in an elaborate spin and dipped her so that her hair almost grazed the floor. From far away, she heard soft applause. She caught her breath as he raised her again, even closer then she was to him before.

She could feel the warmth of his skin through his clothes as he pressed her body to his. Her blood pulsed through her like liquid fire as he leaned closer to her and whispered into her ear, "I can barely wait for tonight. Truly, you test my every reserve as a man."

She felt the color rise to her cheeks and smiled to herself with secret delight. The dream shifted and she was at the head of a large banquet table spread with an elaborate feast. All around her were people she did not know, laughing and drinking and making merry. Far down the table, she saw Forrest smile at her and raise his cup appreciatively. His was the only familiar face.

As she looked down at her food, and began to cut the meat, the meat became hard and gilded. It had turned to gold. Constantine leaned over to whisper something in her ear and when she reached for him, he too turned to gold. "See?" Ducky said at her shoulder. "You can do it. You just have to know how."

Next, she was sitting in her new room at the spinning wheel and here she again knew it wsa a dream and not reality because the tears came hot and fast, streaming down her hands and into her lap. "It is useless," she thought with dismay. She pushed piece after piece of straw into the wheel and all she accomplished was to cause the wheel to spin in an uneven fashion and twisted straw to shoot out the other side. The pile of rejected attempts became larger and larger. Her fingers bled from trying and she knew her efforts were for naught.

"You just have to know how," Ducky said, suddenly materializing in front of the wheel. "Do you want me to show you? I can show you. You have the magic in you, you do, Fee. You just have to unlock it."

"Show me!" Ophelia begged. "Please show me what to do!"

"Ah ah ah!" Ducky said with a smile, waggling her long, bony finger at Ophelia. "Such knowledge does not come for free! All magic 'as a cost!"

"I have nothing," Ophelia wept. "There is nothing I can offer you."

"You have nothin'…yet," Ducky corrected her. "Once this is accomplished, you will 'ave much an' more."

"Anything," she begged. "Name your price."

"Your child," Ducky said, her voice suddenly quite serious, more refined, and with no trace of her common accent. "I want your baby when he comes."

"I am not pregnant!" Ophelia cried. "I have no baby!"

"But you will!" Ducky said firmly with a voice that seemed stronger and more vibrant than her years, "and when he comes, you will give him to me with no argument, no resistance, and no debate. I spent tens of years catching the babies of others and I want one of my own. That is my price."

In the intensity of her dream, Ophelia had no qualm about bartering away a child that did not even exist. So fraught was she with frustration and fear that she shouted out her agreement. "Yes! Fine! You can have my first-born son that does not exist. This, however, I have to do now."

Ducky's broad, toothless smile seemed to reach from one ear to the other. "Do you swear?" she asked in that misplaced, regal voice.

"I swear," Ophelia said, and on a whim, pushed her finger down onto the sharp edge of the spindle. "Here," she said, "take my blood oath."

The old woman reached out her hand and caught the drops of Ophelia's blood on a linen cloth and tucked them into the folds of her robe. "What is done cannot be undone," she said.

Although there were no more dreams, Ophelia was restless throughout the night and found herself coasting on the very edge of sleep without moving into its embrace. Something was very wrong and she knew it.

Chapter 23

She was slow to leave the warmth of the bed covers and was still drowsing when Ducky brought in the late morning meal.

"Look at you, still abed!" she clucked. "Are you not feeling well, dearie?"

"I feel odd," Ophelia admitted, "But there is still no excuse for languishing." She reluctantly pushed herself up out of bed and began to dress. She did feel odd. She had rarely been ill in her life and usually had a fair amount of energy. Today, she felt as bleary and disoriented as her father looked on a good day and had the eerie feeling of wrongness as though a goose had walked over her grave. Her head throbbed mercilessly and she had a dull ache running up her arm. Her bones felt made of iron and she had trouble sorting out her fuzzy thoughts.

"Here," Ducky said, pushing a warm cup of herb tea into her hands. "Drink this. It will put you right in no time."

Ophelia smiled and welcomed the cup, drinking deeply. The warm liquid seemed to carry new life as it moved through her body and she felt herself becoming more awake and focused. The porridge and bannock that Ducky brought for her was delicious and she ate heartily.

"Feeling more yourself now, dear?" she asked.

"Definitely," Ophelia replied, stifling a burp. She did feel better, although her arm ached as though she'd slept on it and her stomach still gave a vital lurch now and again.

"Then let's see what you can do with the wheel today, shall we?" the older woman's bones creaked and cracked as she pushed up off the chair. Ophelia shrugged, remembering her promise to the King to "try."

She took her seat at the wheel and looked at it helplessly. "I really cannot imagine where to begin," she said after a few minutes.

"Well then," Ducky said thoughtfully. "Let's start at the beginning, shall we? She pulled her chair from the breakfast table to the opposite side of the wheel. "Have you ever seen gold?"

Ophelia thought for a moment. "I have," she answered. "A patron who came into our tavern had a bit of gold that he showed to me. It was lovely."

"Tell me what you remember of it."

"It was bright, even though he had carried it in his pocket for a while, I am sure. When he handed it to me, it felt warm to the touch. It was the color of the sun."

"Very good," Ducky cooed. "*Very* good. Now what else is the color of the sun?"

"Flowers, sometimes," Ophelia thought for a moment. "Corn."

"And what is the same about flowers and corn?"

Thinking this hard was pushing the patience of a pending headache. "They are both plants?" Ophelia offered.

Ducky beamed. "They are both plants," Ducky agreed. "Now, think of other plants, maybe even something in this very room that was once a plant."

"Straw was a plant before the grain and the chaff were removed."

"Well *done*, my girl. Well done. And what color is straw?"

"Yellow, the color of the sun," Ophelia answered.

"So we aren't really that far away, now are we?"

"I suppose not," Ophelia said, although she was starting to feel a little disoriented again and rubbed at her temples.

"If a lady has a gold ring, where will she wear it?"

"Where would she wear it?" Ophelia repeated, confused.

"Where would she wear it?" For the first time, Ducky's voice took on a cross edge. "Think, child! Where would she wear a gold ring?"

"On her finger, of course," Ophelia replied.

"Can you wear a ring on any of your fingers?"

"If it fits, I suppose."

"So where does gold belong then?"

"On your fingers?"

"On your fingers, through your fingers, around your fingers…"

"On your fingers, through your fingers, around your fingers…" Ophelia repeated softly.

Ducky ambled over to the anteroom and gathered up a pile of straw in her arms, then deposited it next to Ophelia. "Pick up the straw," she said, simply.

Ophelia picked up several blades of straw and began to move them through her fingers. The straw protested at being bent and strained as she looped it around and through each individual finger, then gently pulled it through, then wound it around again. Each time she did so, the straw became more pliant and agreeable. She found herself mesmerized by the motion. Why, the straw seemed to become positively fluid after a time! As she did this, Ducky's lilting voiced slipped into her ear, "Remember, now, that gold is made in rock and gold flows through rock in veins, just like the blood in your body flows through you. Gold flows. Gold grows. Gold must be pulled from its source material. Gold flows. Gold grows."

Ducky continued to hand her pieces of straw, which she conditioned through her fingers. "Gold flows. Gold grows." As the softened straw flew between her fingers, Ducky would pick it up and wind it onto the spindle.

"Now," Ducky said after a while. "Feed it through the wheel, just as you did the wool."

Ophelia found that the conditioned straw fed effortlessly into the wheel. Although her hands turned the wheel, after a while, Ophelia often felt that it was turning itself. Her movements became rhythmic and automated as the wheel spun and she fed more straw into the wheel. Soon, she found that the warmth of her hands was enough to prepare the straw and the conditioning, feeding, and turning of the wheel became one fluid motion. Her hands moved so rapidly she could barely see them and thought was beyond her capacity. On some level, she knew that her fingers were bleeding, but her only concern was that the blood would contaminate the straw.

As if reading her mind, Ducky said, "Oh no, Pet, the blood will make the gold stronger. Keep spinning, my sweet. Keep spinning."

Ophelia had no idea how long she worked, but she knew that at some point, Ducky left and returned with torches so that she could see in the darkness. She also knew that Ducky extinguished the torches some time later when sunlight began to pour into the room. She was aware of very little around her until she reached out her hand for more straw from Ducky and found there was none.

Instead, Ducky beamed at her and said simply, "It is done." With those words, Ophelia became fully aware that her back was screaming in pain, that her hands ached, and that she had neither eaten nor relieved herself since she started the process. How long ago had that been? She had no idea. The wheel continued to turn on its own for a while, still hungry to work, until it finally slowed and stopped. She tried to stand, but found she was so sore and stiff that it was an effort. She pressed her hand against the wall behind her to brace herself so that she could rise and when she pulled it away, a harsh, bloodied handprint remained on the wall.

She could barely walk but managed to work past the pain in her protesting muscles and make her way around to the front of the spinning wheel. She was stunned to see piles and piles of gleaming, golden...puddles. It was as if liquid gold had poured out of the spinning wheel and solidified into pie-shaped rounds. Hysteria began to take her over and she thought, "Golden cow pies. I have made golden cow pies." Laughter overtook her and she found that tears were streaming down her face. Then, she collapsed and knew no more.

Chapter 24

When she awoke, an old man with a long beard was leaning over her, pulling one of her eyes open and passing a candle before it.

"She seems to have no brain injury as nearly as I can tell," he said in a voice that was like a soft breeze. "Her reactions are good. I have salved and bandaged her hands and I believe that after a day of broth and rest, she will be right as rain. Oh...*hello*," he said, noticing that Ophelia was awake. "Welcome back to us, young miss."

She felt disoriented and tried to rise, but he pressed her back down onto the bed with one hand. The strength he exerted with one hand surprised her. "Oh no," he said. "You had best stay put for now until your body has recovered. You have sustained some injuries to your hands and you are suffering from exhaustion as I have not seen in years. I will have the kitchen women bring up some meat broth and wine for you and I want you to finish both, do you understand?"

She nodded and relaxed back into the pillow, too weak to do otherwise. Soon, she was sleeping again.

When she awoke again, a young woman was setting a tray on the small table. She brought a bowl of broth and a cup of wine to Ophelia and offered to help her with it. Ophelia shook her head and wrapped her bandaged hands around the warm cup. It tasted good and the heat felt nice on her injured hands. It was not as good as the food and drink that Ducky brought to her before, but still, was nourishing and palatable. The kitchen woman left as soon as Ophelia declined her help and Ophelia was alone. She tried to piece together memories from recent days, but they fell and tumbled as if from a dream. At last, she stopped trying and allowed herself to relish the hearty broth and rich wine.

After eating and drinking, Ophelia slowly worked her way out of bed and relieved herself at the chamber pot. Her legs were weak and she felt as if all of the strength had drained from her body. She pushed open the shutters on the window and felt the cool air bless and refresh her face. Scattered memories came back to her but were still in mighty disarray. She looked around the room and was surprised to find that except for the bed, the vanity, and the breakfast table and chairs, the room was empty. Where was the wheel? Where was the gold?

Still weak and shaky, she made her way into the anteroom and there stood the spinning wheel with the stool, again looking like no more than a piece of furniture, a tool. Had she dreamt? What happened to the gold? Was she truly mad? If so, where was the straw that she knew had been there?

Her head was reeling and she stumbled from the anteroom. In a powerful and sudden wave, she felt darkness start to come over her again and she pitched forward. The last thing she remembered was falling into an embrace that smelled of cloves and lavender.

When she awoke, the lighting in the room gave no indication as to how long she had been asleep or unconscious this time. It could have been twilight or dusk. A lamp on the vanity gave off a soft glow and she could see the High King sitting in one of the breakfast chairs at her bedside with his forehead resting on his hands, which were on the bed itself. She could see only the top of his head and thought that he looked surprisingly vulnerable like this. Was he sleeping? She shifted in the bed and he raised his head and met her eyes.

"You are awake," he said, relief showing on his face

"So it seems," she said and pushed herself to a seated position. Her head began to clear, more quickly this time than before. "I owe you an apology, Your Highness. I tried, but honestly, I am not sure what happened."

"What do you mean?" he asked.

"The spinning," she said. "The straw is gone. I don't know what happened to it. I, well, I guess I had a dream and..." she struggled for words to explain herself without sounding vapid. "I apparently have failed you. I must have been ill because what I thought was so does not appear to be."

He looked confused. "Ophelia," he said with barely concealed jubilance. "Ophelia, you have saved our country and then some. You have saved my reputation as a High King. Without that gold, I would go down in history as a folly...a joke. Now, I have a fighting chance to establish some measure of dignity in my reign."

"The gold?" she said. "It is real?"

"Oh, it is very real, Ophelia. It is in my vault right now. I had it moved while you were recovering."

"Is it...Is it enough?" she asked timidly?

A broad smile broke across his face and suddenly, she felt he was the most handsome man she had ever seen. "Oh, it is more than enough, Ophelia. The lesser kings may not be excited that taxation will begin again, but everyone should contribute to the upkeep of the country and that is simply the way of it. They profited wildly during their years of not contributing and so they can bear the burden now of fair taxation when the time comes. For now, there is plenty to sustain us, thanks to you.

"I have been negligent in my own responsibilities to the common weal and it is my greatest shame that so many know that is the case. There are reasons why I chose not to stay here in this place and fraternize with its many ghosts and memories. The quest I have been on was honorable, or at least I convinced myself it was, but it was also an excuse."

Instinctively, Ophelia reached out and squeezed his hand, then winced at the pain. He jerked his hand away from her.

"Your Majesty," she said, her cheeks reddening. "I apologize for my forwardness. I should not have…"

"Oh no!" he said quickly. "No. I was afraid I would hurt you." His brow furrowed. "Am I as formidable as all that?"

She smiled in spite of herself at his insecurity. "No, but you are the High King. It can be challenging to forget such a thing."

"Shall I send the court physician up to salve and redress your hands?" he asked, rising to leave.

"I think that would be good," she said, flexing her hands in front of her. They were tender and stiff, but the pain was not extreme.

"It has been quite some time since you had the broth and wine this morning. Shall I have the kitchen staff bring up some more?"

Her stomach rumbled at the thought. "That would be nice," she smiled. "I'm actually quite hungry."

"I will see to it right away," he said. He paused at the door and said without looking at her. "Ophelia, my men and I will ride out in a matter of a few days. I do not know how long I will be gone. I would appreciate it very much if you were amenable to our marriage taking place before I leave."

Ophelia blinked. "Your Highness, I in no way would hold you to such a promise. I am happy to have been of service and I will be perfectly content to return to my own life as you vowed. You owe me nothing."

"How can you say that?" he asked with a look of genuine confusion on his face. "You've been wounded. You have not been home in a long time. You worked so hard. You deserve compensation."

"My Lord, I do not intend for my marriage bed to be provided to me as compensation or barter for a job well done. I would like to believe that I am worth more than that."

"Is it the curse?" He asked, his expression darkening. "Are you afraid you will meet the fate of my other wives?"

"What?" she asked stunned. "No! I don't believe in such foolishness."

He smiled and said, "I believe I already knew that about you," then stopped, appearing to collect his thoughts for a moment.

"Ophelia, I am going confide in you even more so than I have already done because it is important to me that when you make this choice, you know exactly where I stand." He continued, a seriousness weighing on his voice. "I have not been given to emotional investment in women for a very long time. My first wife died attempting to give birth to our son, who died with her. My second wife died of a lung illness. She drowned in her own body fluids. My third wife hemorrhaged to death after a miscarriage and my last wife suffered from tremendous depression and, well, she chose to end her own life." He sighed heavily. "There is no curse here. There is nothing more than just life and death and all that entails in these times."

"Always in the past, I have followed the advice of my counselors and have married women of noble blood. What many people do not understand is that it is rare that women of noble blood are sturdy, healthy, and strong. They are fragile, needy, and frail or at least this has been my own experience. I cared for all of my wives, but I found myself distancing from them more and more."

"My Lord..."

"Please," he urged her. "Please just hear me out." She nodded and he continued.

"For years now, wives have meant little to me, Ophelia. They are a matter of state much as the signing of declarations and the collection of taxes. I am not a man of strong carnal needs and I have spent so much of my adult life on the battleground that I am likely no fit companion for a woman, I will admit. I have no heir and I am not a young man. I cannot seem to keep a wife living for long enough to produce a lineage to inherit my throne. I am an only surviving child and there is no down line after me, nor is there even a sideways lunge such as I was. I am, in fact, the last known living legitimate relative of the Pendragon line. When I die, there will be chaos in Britain as every lesser king competes for the crown. They will likely, kill each other.

"You, Ophelia, are strong and vibrant and alive and when you were brought before me with the claim that you could spin straw into gold, it seemed to be a brilliant way that I could do the impossible and hit two targets with one arrow. How could I *not* marry a woman who could perform such a task? Even my staunchest counselors would not dispute my marriage to a woman who saved the country from financial ruin. This is, above all, an opportunity for me to legitimately marry a woman who actually *interests me* and yes, I will say it, *excites me.*"

She began to speak, but again he interrupted, holding up one hand.

"If I do not say this now," he said, "I fear it will not be said. I will not trouble you or inconvenience you in anyway unless you desire me to do so. I will ask that you consider the idea of helping me to create an heir for this kingdom so that the lineage of the Pendragon family continues. If you wish not to be with me in that fashion, we will allow everyone who is not in this room to presume you to be barren. I would give up an heir before I would put hands upon you in any way you do not desire."

"I will make certain that you and your father are cared for in such a way that you never want for a thing. All I ask is that you marry me now while I am here in court and then get to know me later. If, after you have come to know me for the man I am, you wish to part ways, I would make certain that our separation is clean and without encumbrance upon you and I would continue to provide for you and your father throughout your lifetimes. This I swear."

Ophelia waited a few moments to make certain he was finished, then said with a wry tone to her voice, "That is the most you have ever said to a woman in your life, I will wager, is it not?

He looked both surprised and sheepish. "Most likely. No," he corrected himself, "most assuredly."

"Little wonder then that you do not value them over much," she observed. "I am very hungry. Could I get more of that delicious broth and wine now and could you please send the court physician around to tend my hands?"

"Certainly," he said. "Of course. I am remiss to stand here speaking endlessly of my own interests and concerns while you are hungry and in pain. I beg My Lady's pardon for my…"

This time, she held her up hand to stop him, "…and would you be so kind as to join me for the evening meal, Your Highness?"

His efforts to suppress his smile were ineffectual. "I will be here," he said, looking for the entire world like a besotted man a third of his age.

Chapter 25

The court physician returned before dinner arrived and carefully removed her bandages. He remarked at the rapid healing and asked her to move her fingers and her wrists. She even managed to convince him to leave off the bandages after promising to keep the area scrupulously clean and to avoid doing anything to stress the area, such as making more gold from straw. He gave her salve to use several times a day to promote healing and reduce the chance of infection. As to the exhaustion, he told her she could begin walking a bit the next day and urged her to go into the garden for fresh air if she could make it that far.

As he was leaving, the King himself arrived with her evening meal on a tray, which he placed on the table. "How is our patient?" he asked.

"Not very patient," the old doctor chuckled. "She seems eager to push the natural course of healing beyond my own comfort."

Ophelia smiled at him. "If I see any signs at all of a problem, I will ask for you right away," she assured him.

The doctor gave the King a knowing look and shook his head. "She's all yours, Your Highness."

"I hope that is true," Constantine said with a meaningful look to Ophelia. "I brought meat, cheese, and a bit of bread in case you are able to eat more than broth."

Ophelia's appetite surprised both of them and she ate of the food he provided with great enthusiasm. She could feel life returning to her with every bite and her strength improving as her body welcomed the nourishment. Constantine tried to control his anxiety and impatience as they spoke of unimportant matters and ate in comfortable companionship.

At last, with a hint of regret in his voice, he began to collect the used dishes and put them on the tray to return to the kitchen. "I will take your leave now so that you may rest. Thank you for your company this night, Ophelia."

She smiled up at him and said, "Thank you for the lovely meal and yes, for your company."

He turned to go, but she stopped him, "Your Highness," she said softly.

He looked back trying to control the expectation in his voice, unaware that he was holding his breath. "Yes?" he said.

"I accept." He felt the strength go out of his knees and he leaned against the door to stabilize himself. "Are you talking about what I think you are talking about?" he asked.

Her eyes sparkled. "You picked up the dishes yourself and carried them away. This tells me you are neither spoilt nor arrogant. I told myself that if you could get through the entire meal without pressing me for an answer that I would say yes to your proposal. You did so and this tells me that you are patient and respectful. So this me saying yes."

"My dear," he said. "Are you sure?"

She looked at him with mirth and growing affection. "I will not profess love for you because I do not know you. I will not profess desire for you because I will confess that I am uncertain of what that is or how it feels. Before this time, my life has afforded me little opportunity to experience love or desire, so my frame of reference is limited. I will, however, say that I find you to be an appealing man and I know that there is something that shifts inside me when I am near you that I wish to further explore." She forced herself not to look away from him. "I believe you when you say that you would not hurt me and I suspect I could do worse in life than to be your queen. I accept."

Chapter 26

She thought that with such short notice, the wedding would be a small, intimate, and simple affair of family and diplomats. She thought wrong. The following morning, she was up and dressed when a young woman brought breakfast in to her.

"Would you care for anything else, My Lady?" she asked.

Ophelia smiled at the formality and replied, "No, this is lovely, thank you." The girl curtseyed to her and left. It was difficult to process that a month ago, she served ale and fire roasted potatoes to the bawdy men in Forrest's tavern and now she was betrothed to the High King. She had, on that last night, laughed with Forrest over the idea that she might one day be the barkeeper of the tavern and now, it appeared she would be High Queen. No matter how she tried, she could not take the idea seriously. Certainly, men had caught her eye before, but never had she been courted or experienced anything remotely resembling romance in her life. She neither craved it nor expected it. To her mind, she was to spend her entire life caring for her father until the self-destructive path he chose to follow finally took him to his grave. The idea of what to pursue after that never occurred to her.

Marriage? Children? Those things had not been an option to her before, even though they were what every young woman seemed to crave. She was not highborn and brought with her no dowry. The idea that anyone, much less a man of nobility, and certainly not the High

King, would ask her hand in marriage was laughable to her.

But a king? Did her father know? Did he wonder what happened to her after she went behind castle walls and he was deposited back into the millhouse, which was little more than a rough shanty with a mill wheel attached? Would anyone even miss her? Forrest, perhaps, but he himself was husband to a woman who adored him. Ophelia had no friends to speak of and, in fact, could count the number of women who she knew by first name on one hand.

She never realized how empty and downright pathetic her life had been until that point. Since her first memories, her father had been her only priority and his care her daily task for her waking hours. She had not bothered to create a life for herself because it had not dawned on her that she might want one. And why would she? Wanting a life beyond caring for Mills would have availed her nothing except for a hole in her heart that she could not hope to fill. She released that expectation in much the same way as she released the idea that she might know something of her mother.

No, a practical girl like Ophelia knew better than to long for anything that was not right before her face and to keep her thoughts focused on the here and now rather than some distant possibility in the future. She did not dream and she did not want.

By some bizarre twist of fate and through, of all things, the drunken ramblings of Mills, she now slept in the High Queen's quarters and was eating the High Queen's food to break her fast. "What a funny old world," she mused to herself.

A brusk knock on the door interrupted her thoughts. She did not bother to rise, but bid her visitor to enter, thinking that it must be Ducky, come at last to check on her. Instead, a woman with a kind face and wheat colored hair wound in a braid around her head looked around the door and smiled at her. "Ophelia?" she asked.

"Yes?" Ophelia said cordially. She automatically extended her hand, but then withdrew it. "I would offer to shake hands," she said, "but unfortunately…" she showed the woman her palm, "I am still healing a bit and I am not sure I want to incur the wrath of the court physician."

The woman laughed. "Druston? He's a lamb. His bark is worse than his bite, especially since he has no teeth." She nodded to Ophelia. "My name is Nuala. I am the King's aunt and I have come not only to introduce myself since we are to be related soon, but to start the preparations for your wedding."

"You are his aunt?" Ophelia asked. "You look so young!"

Nuala smiled. "Why thank you, dear. I appreciate the sentiment. May I?" She gestured to the chair opposite Ophelia.

"Certainly," Ophelia said. "I wish I had refreshment to offer to you, but I am sadly lacking."

"Thank you, but I have just taken the morning meal," Nuala assured her. "My older sister, Adella, was the King's mother. She died when the King was a very young man. I have had the charge of running the household since my nephew became High King. I am his chamberlain."

"That is quite a job."

"Oh, not normally," Nuala said. "The court is not huge, not like it used to be. There is a rhythm and flow that we find around here. The King is gone so much that a great deal of our life is one day much as the other, just like any other household. In times past, there were tournaments and grand festivals to manage. Now, almost never…well, until now." She smiled at Ophelia.

"I have no idea where to begin," the younger woman admitted. "My mind is still reeling over the idea that it is happening at all."

"Do you have any special desire? Anything you have always wanted for your wedding, my dear?"

Ophelia shook her head.

"Friends you want to invite? Extended family?"

"Only my father and perhaps my employer and his wife. I am not close to many people."

"How about your dress, then? What colors do you like?"

Ophelia thought about her serving dresses, which were all undyed cloth. "I…I don't know," she said, looking down at her hands in her lap. "I am so very sorry. I just really have not been blessed with choices in my life." She looked up at Nuala and took in a breath. "I have to learn how to manage them when they come, but I have not yet done so. This is all a bit overwhelming."

"I see," Nuala said with great patience. "What about foods? Are there any special ones that you enjoy?"

"I am not a picky eater," she said. "I like most things."

"Dear, do you want to be involved with this? I feel as though I am dragging you through the process." Her voice sounded more resigned than irritated.

"I know," Ophelia said. "I can see what a task this must be for you and I cannot imagine what all is involved with this sort of thing, truly. If it is acceptable to you, I would like to defer all decisions regarding the wedding to you and to the King. I have never witnessed one moment of a royal event and never imagined I would do so. I have no past impression upon which to draw for what should happen. The thought of trying to be an important part of this process beyond getting there is more than I can muster just now."

Nuala smiled again. "No worries." She patted Ophelia's knee. "In a way, this makes it easier. The others before you all had lifelong ideas for how their weddings should be. One wanted doves released. Another insisted on a cake that involved a set of spices that took half a year to locate and get to the kitchen. Another wanted her dress in a specially dyed fabric that is only available in Spain from one elusive merchant. Your expectations are so low that I do not have to worry that you will be disappointed."

"Oh, heavens no!" Ophelia laughed. "I am sure that whatever is planned will be lovely and if there is anything I can do to help, please let me know. I am very neat-handed and I sew quite well. I am a hard worker and I learn quickly."

"What you need to learn," Nuala said firmly, "is how to let others handle the work. As High Queen, your days of toil are ended."

"Hmm." Ophelia thought aloud. "You know, I am not certain I want them to be. I enjoy busy work and I have never been good with idle hands. What exactly is it that a queen does other than breed?"

Nuala laughed at her candor. "If you figure that one out, let me know. I have sat with four High Queens and two lesser ones so far and none of them did a thing beyond that and a good bit of preening."

"You have no danger of preening with me," Ophelia assured her.

"Not so," Nuala corrected her. "Your attendants will be here later to measure you for your dress, work with your hair to find the finest arrangement for it, treat your skin, and teach you how to make yourself up a bit."

Ophelia cringed. "Is that completely necessary? And, wait, I have attendants?"

Nuala surveyed her critically. "Completely necessary and yes, you do," she said. "You are a lovely girl, that is for certain, but it is going to take some work to get you to High Queen material. I want you to focus on what they are saying and to put that quick learning to work on how to tend to your hair and your skin. Let that be enough for today."

"Nuala, is there no dress of the previous queens' that might be able to be altered to serve as a wedding dress? Would that not be easier to manage than creating a whole new one?"

Nuala smiled. "I do appreciate how you think and thriftiness of resources and energy is a fine, fine quality in a queen; one I have yet to see. Let me think about it. You have likely seen the collection in the armoire there?"

Ophelia nodded. "That is only a sampling that I thought might fit you after seeing you from a distance. There are two rooms of this castle filled with gowns. If you would like, I will look through them and see if what you suggest is possible."

"Thank you," Ophelia said. "Not just for that, but for everything. I don't know what I would do without you."

"Just relax and listen to what the girls tell you. I will handle the rest."

Chapter 27

"Ow!" Ophelia complained as one of the young women, Clara, she thought she was called, aggressively rubbed her forehead with what felt like a scythe and smelled like unkept animals. "How can something so small cause so much pain?"

"Be STILL," Clara fussed. "You aren't High Queen yet and you aren't going to be until we get these eyebrows tamed into two instead of one."

"I LIKE my eyebrows how they are," Ophelia protested.

"Did you or did you not agree to do whatever the Lady Nuala told you to do?"

"Yes, but I did not expect that the removal of body parts would be involved," Ophelia grumbled.

"Have you SEEN the Roman woman?" the girl who was rubbing oils into her feet and legs asked. Bess, Ophelia thought they called her. "Their eyebrows are *completely off* and they draw them on with soot and dyes. It's horrible."

"Why would you scrape them off and draw them back on?" Ophelia asked, followed by another "Ow!" as Clara resumed her scraping.

"I heard it was because of the lice," Faith said as she massaged Ophelia's hands. "They cannot keep the lice at bay, so they shave off their hair. I heard that they even shave *down there*!"

"Like this? Oh that is most certainly not going to happen," Ophelia said. "Don't even imagine for a minute." The girls all three laughed at once. "And what is that awful smell? It smells like…stables or something."

"It is the special paste they use in Egypt," Clara told her. "It keeps the eyebrows from growing back so fast."

"Why does it stink so?" Ophelia wrinkled her nose.

"Well, I am told it is made from… well, the excretions of animals they have there."

"Wonderful," Ophelia said. "That is just wonderful. To be High Queen, you must have animal shit smeared onto your face?" The other two girls gasped, but Clara smiled.

"Mostly just urine," she shrugged, "and maybe some local herbs. Do they have herbs in Egypt? Is their soil only sand? Can herbs grow in sand?"

"You know," Ophelia said. "In all my years on this earth, I have never stopped to notice whether or not the High Queen had any eyebrows or to what degree she had eyebrows. Does anyone do that?"

"Nuala does," Faith offered. "And if Nuala says the eyebrows go, off they go."

"All of them?" Ophelia asked.

"Oh no," Clara said. "We're done. Look." She held up a mirror so that Ophelia could admire her handiwork.

Her brows were red and puffy, but significantly reduced. She did like the way it made her forehead look larger and smoother. "Hmm," she said. "How often does this have to be done?"

"The other queens were done every moon," Clara said.

"Let's not do that," Ophelia said.

Clara shrugged. "By the next moon, you will be High Queen and you can do as you like. No doubt King Constantine will be off on another of his quests before long and you will be free to live as you choose, with or without eyebrows."

"Is he gone often?" Ophelia asked.

"Oh always," Bess (she thought it was perhaps Bess) answered. "He has been here longer this time than in so many years. Some say it is because of you."

"Me?" Ophelia was truly startled. "Why would it be because of me?"

All three girls stopped what they were doing and looked at her, tremendously perplexed, then looked at one another.

"My Lady," Clara said carefully. "The whole court knows that he is completely smitten by you. Why, he never took the other queens to marry so quickly. We all thought, well…"

"Thought what?" Ophelia asked sternly.

"Well," Faith said. "We thought you must be breeding and him eager to not have his only heir be born a bastard while he was away, begging My Lady's pardon for saying so."

"Ssssh," Clara hissed at Faith. "Do NOT speak so in the company of our next High Queen."

Ophelia laughed. "I am not breeding, I swear to you."

Their eyes got bigger. "Then he must be completely taken with you, My Lady," The one who was perhaps Bess said, "to plan the marriage so soon."

Ophelia's head reeled. She understood in a flash her extreme disadvantage not only in having little to no experience in friendly banter among women, but also in having no idea what public story Constantine wished to present. She had a stunning realization that she had just thought of him by his first name rather than his title as though he were actually her betrothed, which, she realized in an even more stunning realization than the one just prior to it, he was. *She was to be married to this High King of Britain.* The thought caused her to let out a quick bray of laughter that she quickly squelched. The young women looked at her in quiet amusement.

"That's it," Clara announced. "You're all done. The dressmakers will be up to see you as soon as we tell them you are ready."

"Dressmakers?" Ophelia looked confused.

"For your wedding dress, silly," Perhaps Bess said, "You have to be measured and fitted so the sewing women can bet busy on it."

"I see," Ophelia said. *So much for remaking one of the other queens' dresses,* she thought to herself.

She welcomed the quiet of her room once the giggling ladies left. She could not fathom their ages. She would guess somewhere between seventeen and twenty, most likely. Her head still rang with the timbre of their voices. She spent so much of her life around Mills and the men at the tavern that she had no clue how to act around women of her own age or women at all, really. The entire process made her feel tired. She was not skilled in the delicacies of how to carry on small talk or interact casually. Suddenly, she found herself missing Ducky profoundly. She had not seen the older woman since she woke up after spinning the gold. Young women from the kitchen now brought all of her meals. Had she somehow offered offense?

Before she could further that thought, a team of sewing ladies arrived and in short time, she was pinned up, propped up, measured, stuck a few times, had the breath pushed out of her by some kind of waist cinching contraption that she enthusiastically and firmly rejected, and had her feet measured for new shoes. Unlike the dallying approach of the young women who had worked on her face and skin, these ladies were not only all business, but were gone practically before she knew they had arrived. It was a whirlwind of activity during which, true to Nuala's word, she was never once consulted about what type of fabric would be used or how the dress and veil would be designed. That suited her just fine.

Chapter 28

They came to get her at sunrise three days later. She did not have any idea whether the dress she wore was newly made or an altered version of an existing dress, nor did she care. It was breathtaking. Never in all her life had she dreamed of wearing such a beautiful creation. The primary color was deepest gold and was reflected in both silk and velvet with dark green accents. A veil, dyed the same gold, covered her face and had tiny dark green leaves embroidered along the edges. She prayed silently that the veil had already existed in some armoire or chest of drawers somewhere in the court and not painstakingly created in a matter of days. The detail was exquisite. The sleeves of her dress were so long that she was assigned a child to accompany her on either side as she walked down the aisle so that they would not be soiled dragging the ground. Four children would carry her veil; two in the back and two midway between the end of the veil and, well, *her.*

Beneath the veil, her brown hair had been washed, rubbed with sweetly scented oils and intricately braided so that it not only spilled down her back in a cascade of curls, but also was twined around her hair in a lovely crown. Tiny flowers were woven throughout the braid and the curls and were pinned in place with the tiniest fasteners she had ever seen.

Her skin was again conditioned and was soft and radiant so that she kept touching her face and her arms, mesmerized by the smoothness. Tints brightened the pink in her cheeks and kohl framed her eyes, enhancing their depth and creating an exotic, mysterious appearance. She fought the urge to rub her eyes and knew the powder was causing her to tear up.

Her fingernails were oiled and picked and buffed and the calluses had been filed until her hands were soft as a baby's. Her feet had received the same treatment. She might not be a princess by birth, and certainly not a queen, but she was starting to feel closer to it than she ever had.

One month to the day after she was first presented to the High King Constantine of Britain, Ophelia walked down the aisle and married him. As part of the same ceremony, the Archbishop placed a crown on her head and proclaimed her High Queen of Britain. Of all the things that could go through her mind as this happened, her thought was, again, "Funny old world, isn't it?"

She saw Mills twice at the wedding. Both times, he was very joyful, very drunk, and very friendly with the serving women. His absence in walking her down the aisle was unnoticed as far as she could tell, not that he would be sober enough to make the trek from one end of the cathedral to the other without falling or vomiting. He barely seemed to notice her but waved at her with the same fondness that he did everyone else.

Nuala had carefully prepped Ophelia to the point that she knew every move to make and what to expect at any moment. By the time that the feasting portion of the celebrations began, Ophelia found herself anxiously seeking out Nuala's expression to see if she had successfully navigated the proceedings thus far. She was rewarded with Nuala's kindly smile, nod of approval, and a raising of her cup. She could ask for no more validation than that.

The degree of affection Constantine showed Ophelia surprised her, intermittently holding her hand, stroking her cheek, and sharing her plate at the meal. She thought it likely a ruse to establish a publically perceived intimacy where none actually existed. She brushed the thought away and realized that it really did not really matter. She would learn the true nature of how things were soon enough. For now, the King and Queen must present a united front and show the country that they were sovereign leaders. She also felt it did not matter because she enjoyed it very much.

At last, several of Constantine's royal guard carried the couple to their bedchambers. A crowd watched as the newlyweds entered the royal suite and then firmly closed the royal doors behind them.

Once inside, Constantine relaxed visibly and put his hand out to her. "I do not think we have been properly introduced. My name is Phillippus Constantinius Dominicus of Cornwall."

The formality of it broke through her nervousness and made her smile. She took his hand. "I am the Lady Ophelia of…the Mill and Tavern and late of the Gold Spinning Room. I am honored to make your acquaintance." It occurred to her that she had not seen him at all since she had accepted his proposal many nights before.

Her response coaxed a more relaxed smile out of him and he held her hand between his two. "I am sure you have questions that have not yet been answered to your satisfaction and I applaud and appreciate your patience. I thought that perhaps this would be a good time to get to know one another better."

"Don't we have to, um, do that…" her eyes shifted to the bed and then back to his face.

He released her hand and placed his hands on her shoulders. "Lady Ophelia of the Mill and Tavern and late of the Gold Spinning Room, I am certain that you saw that the door closed firmly behind us two. What happens within this chamber is for no other than the two of us to know. We are under no obligation to hang our marriage sheets out for display. If you find, in the course of the evening, or any other time that you are with me that you are desirous of such activities, then and only then will 'doing that' take place. You will never be asked to do anything in that capacity that you do not want to do so long as you are with me."

His kindness warmed her heart and she smiled as he led her out of the bedchamber and over to a sitting area with comfortable chairs. They both sat and he offered her warm wine that was waiting there, which she gladly accepted. "Now, Queen Ophelia," he said softly, "What would you like to know?"

"Anything?" she asked.

"Anything," he affirmed.

"Phillippus? That is your name? How…Roman."

"Phillippus Constantinius Dominicus. My father, the Duke of Cornwall, was deeply immersed in the Roman culture and credited them fully for the success of Britain. He named me for two of his favorite Roman officers and for King Constantine…I mean the real one," he stammered.

She laughed. "'The real one?'"

"Well, the first one, at least. My father was a devout Christian and the avid conversion of all people to the

Christian faith was paramount in his world view, in his politics, and most importantly, in his home."

"And you?" she asked.

He made a dismissive sound. "I could not care less about how a man comes to God. I am more interested in who he is in this world than where he is going in the next."

"And your mother?"

"My mother was quiet and passive, very nearly invisible." He smiled almost bashfully. "Nothing like you."

"Is that good or not?" she asked before she could stop the words from coming.

"That is delightful," he assured her. "I cannot abide an insipid woman. Mother died when I was nine. My Aunt Nuala raised me from then on. I rarely saw my father. He was always at battle and then later, died here while on the throne."

"Do you have brothers or sisters?"

"I did, but only two of us survived to adulthood. My brother also died while High King."

"The positing seems dangerous to your family as well as your wives," Ophelia observed.

Constantine winced visibly. "It is a position not without danger," he agreed.

"What should I call you?"

He blinked for a moment. "Call me?"

"How do I refer to you in public or privately?"

"In public, the standard form of address is 'My Lord,' 'My Husband," or 'My King.' In private, I would prefer that you never use a title for me. I have heard more titles than I care to recall and at the end of the day, I crave being with someone with whom I can just be myself. It would please me greatly if you would simply call me Phillip."

"And what will you call me?"

"In public, you will be called 'My Queen' or 'My Lady.' In private, I will call you whatever you wish to be called."

"Ophelia is fine. It is all anyone has called me other than Fee. Have you any bastard children, a preference for male intimacy, or other potential social waters that may be difficult to navigate if I am not given warning?"

He thought for a moment. "Only the four dead wives, really. That tends to carry some stigma, but you said that issue does not really concern you."

"No," she confirmed. "Not at all."

"I have never had intimacies with a woman to whom I was not wedded, so no, there are no bastard children. My desires are exclusive to women and I have no male lovers stowed away. I believe in fidelity and will never betray you in that or any other respect. I cannot imagine any embarrassment that could befall you on my account."

She blushed. "Truly, Your Highness, I meant no disrespect."

"And I took none. It was a perfectly reasonable question." He leaned out the door and asked the king's guardsmen who stood there to fetch more warm wine and she was grateful that he did.

"What is our story to the people?" she asked.

"Our story?"

"It seemed to me that the compromised fiduciary state of the kingdom was not widespread knowledge."

"No," he agreed.

"So you cannot confess the actual reason why you married a miller's daughter and a tavern wench. I have to be able to back your story, so I have to know the story."

He shifted uncomfortably. "My advisors all know the truth and are nearly all supportive of the marriage. Beyond that, there has been no story given. You are simply the High Queen, Ophelia. I would never ask your father or friends to misrepresent their relation to you. It will fall as it does. All anyone needs to know is that I married you because I enjoy your company and feel tremendous affection for you. I have no interest in distributing anything but the truth, but admittedly, I would prefer not to have all of the truth exposed if that is avoidable. I also fear," he lowered his voice, "that if the truth were known about your ability, your life could be in danger. There are many who would take advantage of what you can do and exploit it."

She looked down at her hands, "About that…"

"Yes?"

"Will you need for me to do it again?"

"No," he said quickly. "I saw the toll it took on you on all levels and I will never again subject you to that. You have provided amply for our kingdom and the taxation has already begun again. My lesser kings were able to flourish without my taxation. I am not requiring recompense for those years; only that they begin to pay now. The taxes are reasonable and with all of the lesser kingdoms contributing, we will thrive."

"Your Majesty…Phillip," she found she could not meet his eyes. "I have never done that before. I am not completely certain how I did it this time. I am honestly quite eager to put the whole experience behind me."

"Then that is how it will be. Ophelia," he said with hesitancy in his voice. "Now that you know more about me, do you regret our marriage? Are you having second thoughts?"

She studied his face thoughtfully and did not answer for several heartbeats. "No," she smiled. "I think I quite like it."

He returned her smile warmly. "I am glad."

"Do you regret it?" she asked.

"On the contrary," he said. "I look forward to the future now more than I ever have before."

"Another question...You were very sweet during the day today. I am not accustomed to such displays of affection. Was that purely a show for the masses?"

Now it was his turn to look at his hands uncomfortably. "No," he answered after a while. "None of it was for them. It was all for me. I supposed I did not realize how lonely I have been and I was a bit taken in by the excitement of the day. Did...did it make you uncomfortable?"

"No, I quite liked it," she smiled. "I suppose I was lonely as well and did not realize it. The opportunities this marriage opens up for me are dreams I did not ever think to have. I do not mean wealth or status, but simply a husband who cares for me and children and a life that is not one of servitude and hopelessness. I was content to spend my days and nights as I had done for many years. Just these few days I have spent here have made me dare to want more. It will take some getting used to," she admitted.

There was silence between them for the first time in many hours.

"May I ask you some questions?" he looked at her expectantly.

"Of course," she said.

"Where is your mother?"

"She died when I was a baby. A fever took her."

"Do you love your father?"

She smiled. "There is no one who meets Mills who does not love him, so yes, I love him."

"Do you want him here with you?"

"I want him to be where he is happiest. That seems to be where he is and now with a tale as big as his daughter being High Queen, I am sure he is holding court in a way I never will even manage with my fine new title."

He glanced down at his cup as though composing his next question carefully. "Ophelia, I have noticed that you do not speak… as a low-born person. From what you have confided to me previously and tonight, your life has been fairly limited to caring for your father and working in the tavern."

"That is true," she agreed.

"…yet your speech is more refined than I would expect of a person of your limited experience."

"Are you saying you are surprised that I do not speak in grunts and slurs?" she smiled.

He grinned back, almost bashfully. "I suppose so."

"There was a man who roomed with us for a while. He was a priest from an abbey in a village some distance from the mill. In exchange for the use of my room, he taught me to read and left several books in my care. The books changed my life in many ways. They took me outside of my life as I knew it. They taught me new ways of speaking and of seeing the world, even though I never left the millhouse and tavern."

He looked surprised. "Books are a very expensive and generous gift. You are quite fortunate."

"I am," she said. "He taught me Latin and then how to translate it in my head as I read. Mills slept through the day and I did not work until the evening, so he and I had many hours together while he stayed in the village."

"Where are the books now?" he asked.

"I hope they are still in the trunk in my room at the millhouse. Other than a few serving dresses I made for myself, the trunk has all my possessions in it. I have a comb that belonged to my mother…it is the only thing I have of hers. The rest of the items are worth little. I am not given to placing value in material objects."

"Would you like for me to send for your trunk?"

"I would like that very much," she said, her eyes dancing with joy.

"Do you know that the castle has its own library?" he asked.

She was in the process of taking a sip of wine from her cup and she peered at him from over its brim. "Is that so?" she said.

"We have some books from Egypt, Paris, the works of the last Merlin of Britain, and some other scholars. You are welcome to see. My scribes and priests will be happy to help you get through them."

She smiled delightedly. "That idea is certainly seductive."

He lowered his eyes, surprised at how her choice of words affected him. "Do you want children?" he asked.

"Yes," she said quickly. "As I mentioned, I never gave much thought to the idea until speaking with you. I have not been around babies and would have no idea what to do with one, but I think would like to have the experience."

"We are at no loss of mothers here to share their help and wisdom," he assured her. "How old are you?"

"I am twenty and two," she answered. "How old are you?"

"Forty and two years. Did the purity examination offend you?" He looked away as he asked.

"No, not really," she said. "I understand the necessity of it and yes, I am virgin. I guess you know that already or I would not be here."

"I would have taken you regardless," he said and met her eyes. "I mean," He said quickly, "I would have married you regardless." She noted color creeping into his cheeks and found it endearing.

"I did bring a substantial dowry," she smiled.

"Yes," he agreed, "Yes, you did. Next question: do you want your own sleeping chamber? I am rarely here in court, so you would normally have these quarters all to yourself, but when I am here, the court expects that we would share a room. If this is not acceptable to you, I am happy to make other accommodations."

Ophelia looked around the opulent room, decorated with richly died velvets and silks. "This is absolutely lovely," she said. "It will do nicely whether you are here or not. I never imagined living in such a place."

"There is," he said with a tone of unease, "Well, there is only one bed. I could take the chair if you like. It is quite comfortable."

She arose, feeling the fatigue of the long day and night working its way through her. She walked over to him and stood beside him, close enough that had he tilted his head, it would have rested on her breasts. Gently, she reached down and took his hand. "You are my husband. When I spoke my vows to you, I meant them and it is my thought to continue being your wife for as long as we live provided you treat me well and do not find a time in your life where you are unhappy being wedded to me. I believe I should like to see where that path takes me. My husband, High King or not, shall not sleep in a chair in his own home unless he has well and truly earned banishment from our bed."

Then, he did lean his head against her breasts and closed his eyes. It felt very natural that she should cup her hand to his forehead and begin to stroke his ebony curls, laced with white here and there, and so she did this with very little thought about the intimacy of the action. She leaned over, kissed the top of his head, and let her lips rest against the scent of his hair. Cloves and lavender. She smiled, recognizing that already, this scent combination was dear to her. She could see daylight starting to creep through the windows of the room. They had talked for the entire night.

"Shall we go to bed now, Husband?" she asked, giving his hand a tug.

He patted her hand and before rising, caught her eye and said, "Thank you, Queen Ophelia."

They did go to bed and they did eventually "do that", and as she began to fall asleep, nestled into the crook of the arm of a husband she had not known a month before, she asked sleepily, "Phillip, may I ask one more question?"

He pulled her a little closer to him, enjoying the feel of her warm, strong body against his own. "Of course, you may, Queen Ophelia."

"Why did Ducky not come to the wedding party? I was sure I saw other servants there. Were all not welcome? Is she perhaps ill?"

"The entire kingdom was welcome," he said, sleepily. "What was the name again?"

"Ducky. She was married to Bors, a man who was a chamberlain here at one time. A crone-like woman, heavy, stooped over, works in the kitchen? She took care of me when I first arrived."

"My sweet girl," he said, kissing her forehead. "There's no one here like that."

"Are you certain, Husband?" she asked, confused.

He stroked her hair and said quietly, "There was a man named Bors many, many years ago with a wife called Ducky, but this was far before my time as King and she died years ago, Ophelia. Drowned herself in the lake in the West yard after he died, mad with grief. Some said she was carrying their child when she did herself in. Tragic, really. The servants still believe that she haunts the castle and the courtyard and tell stories to the children that Ducky will come for them if they misbehave. No, Love, the kitchen girls were the ones who fed and cared for you and none of them are more than three-quarters grown."

Breathless, she stared into the darkness and felt his arms encircle her protectively. "Don't worry," he said, yawning. "I won't let Ducky get you. Sleep, my dear. You are exhausted. I feel that tonight, I will sleep the sleep of the righteous."

She was exhausted, but as she listened to his breaths slow down and deepen and felt his hold on her relax, she knew that no sleep would come for her that night or perhaps, for some time to come.

Chapter 29

After a generous breakfast the next day, King Constantine personally escorted her to the court library and introduced her to the scribes and priests. They promised her, after the King's urging, free access and any translation assistance she needed. Her fingers slipped over the carefully printed vellum, the parchment pages, and the elaborately tooled leather covers with reverence. Even as they toured, several priests were working as copyists to recreate books borrowed from other libraries. Her heartbeat quickened a bit at the prospect of reading the words contained in those carefully wrought pages.

Following the library introductions, Constantine himself took her on a tour of the court, from servant quarters to the grand hall that had hosted their wedding feast to the great chapel which was unmatched throughout the land for craftsmanship. The opulent colored glass in the windows astounded her and the altar cloth the current priest in command was using was one Queen Guinevere herself embroidered. Ophelia again met Archbishop Augustine, who had officiated at the ceremony. He was painfully gracious to her in front of Constantine, but she sensed and underlying hostility in him.

"My Queen," he bowed to her. She nodded her head to him in greeting. "I was not asked to hear your wife's confession before the marriage took place." He looked sternly at Constantine. "Am I to presume she will not be joining us for mass?"

"My wife knows her own conscience," King Constantine said firmly. "I suggest you ask her directly."

The Archbishop looked stunned at the reprisal, but quickly composed himself, "My Lady," he said with a note of contrition to his tone. "I do apologize."

"Thank you," Ophelia said. "I can assure you that you will see me on a regular basis."

As they walked away from the chapel, Ophelia asked, "Are you a pious man, Phillip?"

The king laughed at her directness. "I am about as far from that as you can imagine," he said, catching her hand and slipping it into the crook of his arm with an affectionate pat. She gave his arm a squeeze and walked closer to him. "My father was pious to the extreme and it seemed my every moment was spent in prayer or contrition until he died. I had more than my fill and it never really took off with me. Augustine was his bishop and he stayed at Carmeliard after my father and brother died. I am here so rarely that it does not really affect me much for him to be around and I have yet to hear the servants or people of the court complain about him. Should he ever impose upon you to act beyond your own interests, you are at liberty to dismiss him completely."

Ophelia stopped in her tracks and he looked at her, confused. "Is something wrong?"

Ophelia's eyes were wide. "I am 'at liberty to dismiss' the Archbishop of the kingdom and spiritual counselor to the High King, a man who has served your family for years?"

Constantine looked surprised. "Of course, you are. You are High Queen. You have my complete proxy in my absence. We have a staff of advisors who can help us to examine potential pitfalls of decisions we make, but ultimately, we rule exclusively and our word is law."

"You would accept the word of a tavern serving wench in matters of state?" she said, her eyebrows furrowed. "I find that hard to believe."

He smiled at her. "Ophelia, have you any idea what complete dolts men of state actually are? Look at me, for instance. I am not here because I am a great leader or pulled a magical sword from a stone as did Arthur. There is no embellished tale of my own birth about how some wizard bewitched an entire court so my father could slip into my mother and plant a future king in her womb. No. I sit on this throne because of I happened to be a distant cousin however many times removed to a man who used to be king. Clearly, my need for you and your special skill in the first place demonstrates I have no right to be here, yet here I am. Here, watch this…"

He called out to an elderly man who was carrying no less than four buckets of water across the courtyard toward the kitchen area. "Here, Gwydion. Let me help you with those." He began walking toward the man, his arms outstretched to take half of the buckets.

The dirtied man dropped the buckets he was carrying and fell to his knees. "Your Highness," he said, bowing forward to Constantine from his position on his knees. "My King, I would never allow you to do my work for me. How may I serve you?"

"You may let me carry a bucket, Gwydion. Just one bucket. I assure you, I am more than capable."

The man was clearly aghast. "My Liege, I am honored you would ask and you are most gracious and kind to do so, but never, oh never…"

"Fine then, Gwydion," Constantine said. "Thank you for all you do."

"It is my honor to serve you, My King," the man said, still bowing.

"Stand up now, Gwydion," Constantine said patiently.

"As you wish, My King," and the man shuffled to his feet, his head lowered, and resumed carrying the buckets to the kitchen.

"Do you see?" He asked Ophelia. "It's ridiculous. I serve no earthly purpose, yet good and capable people who are likely far more intelligent than I am bow and scrape and genuflect. It is maddening, truly. If I were a good king, do you think I would have neglected to collect the taxes? My advisors asked me countless times to sign the orders and I never remembered to do so. Then out of the blue, an old man makes a tavern boast and here I am with my problem solved and a clever new queen on my arm."

Ophelia smiled, "It is good to be king?"

He laughed aloud and then looked at her with a more serious expression. Tenderly, he reached up and pushed aside a part of her hair that had escaped the grasp of the many pins she had used to secure it into a clumsy bun early in the day. "It is now," he said.

"My point is," he continued as they began to walk again, "that no one is these days any more or less qualified to lead this kingdom or really any kingdom. None of the lesser kings nor I were schooled in the princely arts as children. All of us grew up in our fathers' courts as spares, not as heirs. We had older brothers meant for the thrones we hold. Our fathers intended to be kings and not give up their thrones for decades. By all rights, I should be the Duke of Cornwall holed up in

Tintagel right now." He stopped walking again and looked at her.

"That is why I crusade with my guard against the Sons of Mordred, Ophelia." He looked down as though shamed. "Because I have nothing better to do to show my worth to the kingdom and because the Sons of Mordred are the murdering dogs who put all of us in the position of leading kingdoms when we have no skill or right to do so."

Such a thing had never occurred to her. *A king with "nothing better to do?"* Not knowing what to do herself, she smiled at him and said, "Then perhaps we should work on finding you something better to do because I am not certain I will want you gone from your home quite so much."

His face brightened and she felt sad for him that it seemed he had never before had a reason to be home or had anyone who would miss him when he was away. Could that possibly be?

As if reading her mind, he said, "My other wives did not want me. They wanted the title of High Queen. I needed a wife in place to produce an heir. Honestly, I have spent as much time with you in the past twenty-four hours as I did with any of my four wives in the entire length of our marriages. Ophelia," he brought her hand to his lips and kissed it gently. "You are the first wife I have ever chosen for myself. Advisors handpicked the others for me according to who had the best dowry or family lineage or who would make the best match in the interest of the kingdoms. You, I selected for myself. Do you know why?"

She smiled wryly. "The whole, 'spins straw into gold' thing?"

"That helped," he laughed, "but no. When you stood before me in court, I told you straight out that if you could do such a thing, that I would marry you. Still, you denied you could do it. Do you know how many women would have immediately begun hatching a plan to deceive me so they could become High Queen? My dear, you do not have a deceitful bone in your body. You had never seen me before, but you met my eyes when you spoke to me and were entirely honest, regardless of what I offered in return. It came to me then how much I needed someone, anyone in my life who I could trust and, in that moment, I knew I liked you and would marry you."

"Well, how about that?" she said. "And here I thought you only wanted to marry me to get closer to Mills."

They both laughed over that and shared a comfortable silence for several steps. "I have done two things you should know about," he said.

"Oh?"

"I have sent Falia, one of the kitchen women that your father was admiring at the wedding, to the millhouse to care for him. She will be visited twice a week by one of my guardsmen who will provide her with any food or supplies she needs to cook and clean for him. She will also take over your duties at the tavern."

"Oh dear," Ophelia said.

"Is that not good?" he asked, suddenly concerned.

"I just hate to ask that of anyone," She said, "and I truly hate to order it."

"I did so in a round-about way," he said. "I spoke with Celia, my woman who runs the kitchen, and asked her if she thought Falia would be comfortable doing so. She told me that Falia had spoken of enjoying your father's company and was looking for a new adventure. She has never been happy in the kitchen and I thought the change would do her good. So did Celia. She said Falia jumped at the chance to do something different. She will receive a more generous salary than for the work she did here. I believe it will work well for everyone."

"That is very kind of you," Ophelia observed. "I never imagined a king would be concerned about how his servants feel or what they want. 'Celia,' 'Falia,' 'Gwydion,' you even know them by name."

"As I mentioned, I have very little I can offer as a king. I can at least show my court kindness and consideration. They have suffered much during the times when I was gone and the ability to keep food and supplies in the court was at times neglected. The number of people in court is not even a quarter of what it was when I came to the throne, mostly because people became unhappy and left. It is these few who remained with me and I owe them for that. My hope is that together, you and I can rebuild this kingdom into a good and sovereign structure again."

"I will do whatever you need," she said.

"The other thing you should know is that I have sent for your trunk. It will arrive by nightfall. Please look through it and make certain nothing is missing. In that thought, also please do not hesitate to let me know if there is anything at all you require to be comfortable. Nuala will be here to guide you if you need counsel and the advisors will assist you with any matters of state."

"You are leaving soon then?"

"I ride out tomorrow," he said.

"Tomorrow?" her stomach rolled at the thought of him going so soon. "Must you?"

He smiled, moved by her dismay. "I assure you, My Lady, that I will be back as soon as I possibly can be. I will confess that the idea of leaving does not hold the appeal to me that it normally does. Most times, I cannot wait to be shed of these walls and out in the forests and cities again. Now...already I feel the pull to return. There is now so much life for me to live here, in Carmeliard with you."

Still unaccustomed not only to attention, but to affection, particularly words spoken aloud, Ophelia again felt her cheeks color and a she felt a smile play across her face. "I trust you will return quickly, Phillip," she said softly.

For the first time in her marriage, he leaned over and kissed her fully, deeply on the mouth, pulling her to him with a warmth and enthusiasm he had never in his life felt for another person. She returned his kiss passionately, enjoying the play of his tongue against hers and the feel of his hands on her back and in her hair. For a moment, both could have sworn there was no one else in the world except for the two of them. She felt as if her body was tingling in every cell, alive, ripe, and vital. He felt his desire rise and his heart pounded with such fervor that he thought it would break through his chest. With regret, he pulled away from the kiss and breathed in the scent of her hair, memorizing her in every way. Ophelia felt her blood racing and her pulse thumping in her ears. If they had each known the thoughts of the other, they would know their thought was the same, "Could this be what true love is?"

Chapter 30

Ophelia was a good queen and that is not just to say that she was good to the people in her court, which she was, but also that she was good at *being* a queen. Under the instructions of King Constantine IV before he left to ride against the Sons of Mordred, his council of advisors began instructing Ophelia every day on the government of state. Although at first, they did little to hide their condescending placation of her, in no time at all she impressed them by being a bright student and a quick study. Her common sense and problem-solving acumen intrigued many of the advisors. Within a fortnight of Constantine's departure, the older men - almost reluctantly at first - began to look forward to Ophelia's lessons as much as did she.

Soon, intense and lively conversations streamed from the Council Hall where the advisors would meet to discuss current issues of state that had to be resolved. Quickly, the process of hearing petitions, managing taxation issues, coordinating the defense of the kingdoms against the Saxons, and bringing the lesser kings into greater alliance fell into focus after years of inactivity while no king was in court. Of the twelve advisors, Ophelia felt confidence in all but Archbishop Augustine who scowled at her from across the room and rarely contributed to the lessons or discussions except to argue or complain. She tried several tactics to connect with the older man, including attending mass with the rest of court on a regular basis and offering him her confession each week. She found very little to confess and wondered if she should make up some sins to liven up the experience for him. She confessed to impatience over things such as her husband's return and "the intolerances of others." She confessed to sloth after she slept in an extra hour one morning when she was exhausted from another night without sleep. She confessed to gluttony when the kitchen women made a good batch of honeycakes that reminded her of Ducky's delicious meals. Always, she did whatever penance he assigned her without complaint, even though they often felt unreasonably harsh to her.

One day, after a productive meeting with the advisors, she asked the advice of her favorites, a severe looking man named Master Solomon who she quickly learned had a scathing wit and straightforward manner she deeply appreciated. After the other advisors left she asked, "With all due respect, what have I done to incur the wrath of Archbishop Augustine? No matter what I say or do, he holds me in such a position of revulsion that I cannot make headway with him. Do you have any suggestions?"

Master Solomon worked the handle of his staff for a moment and rubbed his long beard thoughtfully. Unlike many of the advisors, he was bearded, and she found comfort in his scruffy looks. At last, he shook his head. "There is nothing you can do, My Lady. I have taken time myself to speak with Augustine about his attitude and he is unyielding. He has his ways and when it comes to matters of the church, he does not leave room for compromise."

"Matters of the church?" Ophelia asked, stunned. "How have I threatened the church? I have done everything he has asked. I go to mass without fail. I confess to him each week, even to the point of nearly contriving sins to confess so that he is not left wanting."

He patted her shoulder fondly. "You cannot atone for the sin of being born female," he said. "Men of the church do not look well on women being included in matters of state. Their holy scriptures teach that women are to subjugate to their husbands and to be silent in matters of church and state. The fact that the King has given you so much power in his proxy does not sit well with the Archbishop."

"Is that all?" she asked. "My husband and king left me with this task and I have no interest in letting him down. Is this then unable to be resolved?"

"I fear so," the old man said. "But then there is the other, which is an even more treacherous issue than your gender."

"The other?"

"The means by which you came to be queen." He explained this to her as he did most things; presuming that she knew nothing and speaking slowly and clearly, a tactic that she would find irritating were it not so damned helpful. "You were accepted by the advisors as queen because of an act of magic. As you well know, all magic is forbidden in this, a Christian land. The Archbishop will never sit well with a woman he considers to be a sorceress having so much power."

She blinked at him. "Master Solomon, I honestly have no idea how that happened. I am not a person given to matters of spirit by nature and I am assuredly no sorceress. It had never happened before and this time it did. I know no more than this."

"I believe you," he said. "And truly, it does not matter to me in the least where the gold came from and I would gladly do some soul swapping with any manner of imps and demons if it meant saving this kingdom. However it came to be, I and the majority of my peers are very grateful. For your ability and willingness to listen to our guidance and make wise decisions, I am just as grateful. For the first time in many years, I have hope for our country. It also does my heart good to see the way my king was smiling in the days before he left us again. I, however, am not your problem. I feel Archbishop Augustine will not be content sitting on his laurels as you become increasingly involved in the running of the country. Already, he has attempted to undermine you to the rest of the advisors and when none offered support to his resistance, he was not pleased. He is a proud man and a determined one. He will bear watching."

Ophelia's mind reeled. "What can I do?"

"Nothing at this point," the old man said gently. "To anyone else, I would say that you should be beyond reproach in all things, but as nearly as I can tell, you already are. Augustine will look for any vulnerability, any mistake, and will exploit it. He will still have to deal with the rest of us, but if given a foothold, he will be relentless. I would prefer it if you would have the king's guardsmen, at least two, with you at all times when you are out of your quarters. As Augustine goes, I trust him not and I like him not. There is little I would put past him."

"Thank you for your candor," she said, her head reeling with the impact of his words. "I knew I needed to seek your counsel on this and you have given me much to consider. Tell me, how did my predecessors manage when they had to cope with the sin of being female when discussing matters of state?"

"I'm sorry, dear," he said, perplexed. "I don't understand."

"The other four queens," she explained. "Did the Archbishop hate them as much as he hates me or is it all about the spinning wheel?"

"Oh, my Lady," he said, chuckling. "The other queens never sat in counsel. They never had the king's proxy nor had any interest in matters of state. They...sewed."

"Sewed?"

"Yes, My Queen. I rarely saw them at all. With respect for the departed, I am not certain I would trust any of the four with the running of a game of knucklebones, much less of a kingdom."

"I see," she said, and with stunning clarity, she did. The other queens were not a threat to a way of life Augustine wanted to create and protect. To his mind, she was and was therefore, a target.

"Do the other advisors feel as you do?" she asked, mentally checking off each one in her mind.

"Aye," Master Solomon said. "It has been often discussed of late. Had we known it would have been such an issue before the king departed, I suspect we would not be having this conversation right now."

Ophelia thought about this and agreed. The more she saw her husband through the eyes of others, the more she valued him.

"I believe he suspected there might be a problem," she confessed. "The day before he left, he informed me that I could dismiss the Archbishop in his proxy if it became necessary. It is not something I am eager to do."

"Nor do I advise it," he said. "It is far better to have an enemy like Augustine in plain sight than hidden out of view."

"I agree," she said. "I am fortunate to have people like you to come to, Master Solomon. Thank you."

"It is we who are fortunate to have you, My Queen," he smiled.

"Will you do me the honor of calling me Ophelia?" she asked.

"It would be my esteemed honor."

"Master Solomon, I am not one given to paranoia, but given the fates of the four queens before me, all of which I realize have a rational explanation, I would appreciate it if you could hand select four to six good men from the king's guardsmen to act as my personal entourage. I do not wish to over-burden one or two, but I feel I need champions, perhaps two at all times. Can you do this?"

He nodded. "I believe it is wise to keep this conversation between us, but it is fitting that as you become more involved in rulership you would increase the guard around you. This is regretful, but wise."

"I have another suggestion," she said, "and I am open to your advice on this."

"Yes?" he asked, looking intrigued.

"I would like to begin having council meetings in the great room again around Arthur's table which sits there. I need for everyone on my High Council to know that their opinion is of equal value to me...even Augustine."

"I will see to it right away," he said. "That is a fine idea and will certainly encourage unity. I will have servants clear and clean the area today to begin tomorrow."

She nodded, "Thank you. Please leave a position next to me for my husband and make certain to place Augustine across from you, not from me. I want your eyes on him and if he is across from me, it may increase adversarial feelings."

The old man chuckled. "Are you quite certain you are not a war strategist, Ophelia?"

She looked at him in all seriousness. "I have witnessed the beginning of every kind of confrontation that can happen between two people. I have listened to the problems of more men than this courtyard will ever hold and given them all advice. I am more than a war strategist, Master Solomon. I am a tavern wench."

Chapter 31

Two months later, Ophelia woke in the night to what sounded like a rather loud argument outside the door of her bedchamber. She wrapped herself in a heavy cloak from the armoire and opened the door a crack. Seeing her, the two King's guardsmen stationed outside the door bowed to her.

"Your Majesty."

"Your Highness."

"What is the problem?" she asked sleepily, and then caught sight of an anxious looking young woman who was cowering behind them. She recognized her from the set of servants responsible for cleaning the castle. "Neve?" she asked. "What's wrong?"

"She insists on speaking to you," Gahren said, not attempting to conceal the irritation in his voice. "We told her you were abed and not to be disturbed."

"We did," Felix agreed.

"Well, I am awake now, am I not? Thank you for your diligence, brave knights," she smiled. "Neve, inside." She jerked her head toward the room.

The young woman slipped quietly inside. "What is on your mind?" Ophelia asked, trying to conceal her impatience.

"A prisoner, My Queen" Neve whispered intensely. "He is asking to speak to you and will not stop. It is driving me mad. Every time I bring food to him, he begs me to have you see him." Her eyes were wide and tormented.

Ophelia was stunned. "We have prisoners? And why are we whispering?"

Neve looked at her puzzled. "Of course, we do," she said in a more conversational volume. "All kingdoms have prisoners."

"Many?"

"A few… maybe as many as eight or ten."

"Hunh," Ophelia said. "This had never occurred to me."

"And one wants to see you," Neve reminded her."

"Why me?"

"I have no idea. He just keeps asking."

"And you could not tell me this when the sun was up?" Ophelia asked. "Riddle me this, Neve. Why in the middle of the night are you making a commotion outside of my door?"

"Because before, My Lady, he would ask me as I delivered his food only. I told him prisoners have no need to see the Queen and he persisted, but now… it is as if he is in my head. I have not slept for two nights for him clamoring on and on about seeing the Queen *in my head without being with me.* I can bear it no longer, truly."

Ophelia would have thought the girl was addled if not for the tears slipping silently down her cheeks. She exhaled and asked, suspecting she would regret her decision. "Where are these prisoners?"

"Beneath the castle," the girl said, looking hopeful. "In the dungeons."

"We have dungeons?" Ophelia asked.

The girl nodded and sniffed through her tears.

"Well, then off we go. Keep Gahren and Felix company while I dress."

She changed with haste and pulled the cloak back over her clothing to ward off the freezing cold, then stepped outside, lifting a torch from the torch holder near the door. "Gahren," she said, making a point to catch the guardsmen's eye. "You stay here and keep things safe. Felix, you are with me. Stay sharp." Something about this entire situation felt off to her and she was not eager for any trouble when she already felt compromised in her half-awake state.

The girl led her to an area away from the castle proper and indicated a heavy, hinged door that was flush with the ground. "I cannot lift it by myself," she said. Fortunately, it had not snowed within the past week, so they would not have to dig out the door, but it did look exceptionally heavy.

"Felix?" Ophelia asked

"Yes, My Queen." She indicated with her eyes and said, "Door?"

"Yes, My Queen." With tremendous effort, Felix tugged the door open, which at last pulled open on frozen hinges, revealing a dark staircase that descended into the earth and blackness.

"Really?' Ophelia asked. Neve nodded, her eyes brimming with tears again. Sighing, Ophelia said, "Felix, you first," wishing she had brought more than one man with her.

Holding her skirts tightly at her waist, Ophelia edged her way down the narrow steps, which were no more than indentations dug into the hard-pressed earth. "What do you do when it rains?" she asked.

"Mostly fall a lot, My Lady" Felix said from in front of her.

"Marvelous," she replied. At last, they reached the bottom and she found that without the torch, the area in which they stood would be completely dark. "Where now?" she asked. "Good heavens, it is freezing down here."

"There are cells this way and that," Neve said. "He's in the row down there," she gestured to the left.

"Are there no guards here?" she asked.

"Don't need any," Felix said. "No one ever gets out of here. We just send food and water down to them twice day."

Ophelia was stunned. "What if one is ill or one of our servants is injured bringing the food?"

"Then I expect we would find them when it was time to feed them again," Felix said simply. Ophelia made a note to herself to address this with the council.

As they walked through the narrow passageway, she felt prickles rise on her skin as she realized that there was nothing she could do to get out of harm's way should a prisoner decide to reach for her. She could hear rustling in some of the cells and now and then, the torch would illuminate a dark moving shape in the back of a cell. Her teeth chattered from the cold. When they came to the end of passageway, Neve pointed toward one of the cells. "He's in there," she whispered.

"Torch," Ophelia said impatiently, reaching out her hand to Felix who passed the torch to her. She lifted it high and in the play of light and shadow created by the torch, she saw a very tall, muscular man with odd markings on his face sitting on a bench in the far corner of the cell. She could not determine his age.

"Your Highness," he said. Although his voice had such a strong timbre that it echoed throughout the dungeon, it was soft and almost dulcet.

"And who has summoned this command performance?" she asked.

"I am your salvation," he said. "You just do not know it yet."

Chapter 32

“Am I to understand that you have somehow influenced my servant by magic to force her to bring me to you?”

The man chuckled. “Well, not much. A little, perhaps, but I assure you, My Queen, it was all for a good cause.”

“And what cause is that?” she asked.

“Allow me to speak to you in private,” he said, “and I will tell you. I swear to you I mean you no harm.”

She considered this for a moment, warring the desire to be wise against the urge to be bold. “Felix, take Neve to the break between passageways,” she said at last.

“My Queen…” Felix protested.

She cut him an icy look. “Felix. Go. And I am keeping the torch.” She waved her hand dismissively toward them and they left without further question.

“This is as alone as we will be,” she assured him. “Now, tell me who you are and why you have called me here in the middle of the night.”

He untwined his legs from beneath him on the bench and ambled to the front of the cell, closer to her, as casually as if he strolled in the castle garden. “When I asked for you, it was daylight I believe,” he said, smiling. “It is your servant who took her time and required me to take more drastic measure.”

“All things happen in their due time,” Ophelia said dryly. “Now who are you and what do you want?”

He handed her a folded scrap of parchment, no larger than half the width of her palm. “Keep this,” he said. “You will need it.”

As he passed off the parchment, his fingers brushed her palm and she felt an odd sense of familiarity about him and brushed it aside. She could fool herself that he was a man who had drifted into the tavern while she worked, but she felt she would remember this one if she saw him. He was not the typical tavern patron.

She could not read the paper in the torchlight, so she tucked it into the bodice of her dress. "I see," she said.

As if he knew her thoughts, he said, "No need for you to read it now. It will mean nothing to you until the time when you need it."

"Ah," she said. "This becomes more mysterious by the moment. I suppose you are not going to tell me what is written on it then?"

"It is the name of the woman who cut me from my mother's dead body the day I was born. I will not be able to be here to tell you this on the day when you need it most."

"Well," Ophelia said, "of all of the answers you could have given me, I will admit I did not foresee that one. And what do you want in return for this bit of information that I do not yet need?"

"Oh, you will need it," the prisoner said. "You will need it more than you have ever needed anything before, Queen Ophelia."

She pulled back at his use of her first name. "Again, you have me at a disadvantage, sir. Who are you and what do you want from me?"

The odd exchange made her uncomfortable, but she could not help but like the man. "What I want from you is my freedom," he said. "There may come a time when I ask more from you, but I will never ask for more than you are willing to give, this I swear. For now, I need to leave. I have been a guest in these fine quarters for more than a fortnight and I have work to do that requires I make a safe and hasty retreat from Carmeliard. I cannot do so, alas, while I remain your guest here."

"And what was it you did," Ophelia asked, genuinely curious at this point, "to take up residence in my guest room?"

"Oh, I had audience with your delightful Archbishop Augustine to negotiate peace between Carmeliard and Avalon. His response was to have me locked in here. I have two more kingdoms to visit to attempt to form alliance and I cannot do so from here. Truly, I need to take leave of your fine kingdom and you are the only one at this point who can help me."

She gasped at the mention of Avalon and her mind burned at the thought that Augustine would imprison a man for nothing more than proposing a peaceful alliance. Although she was a formidable judge of character and could feel the truth in what the man was telling her, after a moment she still asked, "Do you swear that what you say is true?"

"I swear, Sister" He said intently, "I give you my oath as the Merlin of Britain."

"There is no Merlin of Britain," she said, skepticism coming over her in a wave. "There has been no true Merlin since Taliesin passed from this life."

The man arched one eyebrow appreciatively. "You are well learned, My Queen," the man said. "I could take the time to discuss all of this with you at length and later, when the time comes that I ask you for more than I do now, perhaps we can do exactly that and I guarantee you, it will be in more hospitable chambers. For now, I will have to ask you to take the valuable token I have given to you in trade for your help and allow me to take my leave before the sun rises. I am the Merlin Reborn and I know you feel the truth in what I am saying. Time," he explained with urgency, "is at a premium for me, so I beg you my leave if you will *just get me out of here.*"

He practically hissed his last words at her and his fingers wrapped around the iron bars of his cell. She could clearly see his eyes and there was no missing the intensity in his voice. "Felix," she called without taking her eyes off the prisoner.

There was a stirring in several of the cells at the sound of her raised voice. The knight hurried back to her in the darkness. "Yes, My Queen."

"Get this man out of this cell right away."

"My Lady!" Felix protested.

"Do it," she said.

Within minutes, the cell door was open. To her surprise, the prisoner hugged her tightly and even picked her up and spun her around, planting a kiss on her cheek. Felix bristled at the personal contact, but relaxed when he heard her laugh. "You," the Merlin said, "I will never forget, Queen Ophelia. Keep that parchment close. It will mean the world to you one day. Now, however I have other miracles to create!" He blew a kiss to her and was gone before she could offer him an escort to the border of Carmeliard.

"Where is Neve?" Ophelia asked.

"She left," Felix told her. "Said she was going back to her bed to sleep, My Lady."

"A brilliant idea," she said. "Shall we?" She handed him the torch and followed him out of the dungeon.

"An odd evening indeed," she thought.

Chapter 33

When King Constantine returned home from his latest crusade injured, the entire court seemed to fold around his recovery. Ophelia was thrilled to see him – even more than she expected to be - but held her breath with fear as the court physician did a complete examination. "My King," he said, with some trepidation, "You have broken ribs, although I cannot tell for certain how many. Several of your internal organs feel enlarged, which could indicate ongoing internal bleeding or could simply be bruising from the trauma. You have a severe cut to your upper right arm and it is unlikely that you will regain full use of it ever again. There is significant nerve damage and the muscle itself damaged. I have repaired it as best as I can, but you will likely always have some stiffening in your right hand and weakness in your arm overall.

"Your men got you into cold salt water right away which probably saved your life. It slowed down the blood flow and helped to disinfect the wound. Whoever tied off the wound also helped to slow the bleeding, but you are lucky I did not have to amputate the arm as a result."

"They released the ties several times a day to let it bleed and massaged the arm to keep the blood active." Constantine said.

"That is what saved your arm," the physician agreed. "The broken ribs will be sore for several weeks and the trauma to your lungs will cause you to be short of breath for a long while. You were lucky moreover that there was no puncture to the lungs from the break, however, it is my belief that the jagged bone ends have caused some minor damage to the lungs which should heal on its own. In this case, it is good your men took their time in coming home so the trip was gentler for you or you would likely not be with us now."

"We have been fortunate," Constantine said, "That over the years, we have suffered so few major injuries in our battles. I am grateful that it was I who took the worst of it."

"You can show your gratitude by not taking those men out on this quest again, if I may be so bold to say so, Your Highness."

Constantine smiled. "You may, Master Druston, and your wisdom is taken to heart. This quest is ended, for reasons you have specified as well as others." He smiled at Ophelia and squeezed her hand.

"I would like permission," the doctor said, packing his equipment back into his small bag, "to use leaches to draw out some of the blood from the bruising on your belly so I can better see where the extent of damage lies. After the leaching, I will bind your ribs again so they can continue to heal."

Constantine looked up at Ophelia, who nodded to him. The King gave his consent and the old man hobbled off to prepare for the leaching.

"Leave us," Constantine said to the King's guardsmen who hovered around his bed like worried hens. "I appreciate your concern, but I wish some time alone with my wife. Go spend time with your families and your ladies and eat of the fine feast the kitchen has prepared for your return. Drink and celebrate that we have ended this quest alive and well, my good men. You served me well and entertained my own pursuits for long enough. We have seen and done much together and now it is time for you to rest and celebrate." Each of the guardsmen bowed to him in turn as they left the room. Some came to clasp his hand affectionately and nodded to Ophelia. The admiration for him and devotion to their King was clear.

"I am happy you are home again," Ophelia said when the last had left and they were alone in their bedchambers.

"It is odd to think of this place as home," he said, "but truly, Ophelia, all I could think about the entire time I was gone was coming 'home' to you. It makes no sense, My Queen. I know that you and I barely know one another, but you make me smile. You help me to feel good about myself. You make me feel alive. Have you any idea how intoxicating that is to me?"

Ophelia smiled and squeezed his hand. "Phillip, my entire life, as long as I can remember, was nothing more than taking care of Mills or working in the pub. That was all I did and that was all I was. In my head, I could not even let myself dream of seeing other places or living a different life. I never thought about falling in love, having a husband, or bearing children and I certainly never thought about being High Queen and helping to run the country when my husband was away crusading. You are the one who opened my life to something new and different. I quite like it, actually."

She leaned over and kissed him gently on the lips and he cupped his hand around her cheek with tremendous affection and pulled her closer for a deeper kiss that they both relished. "How would you feel, Queen Ophelia," he asked tentatively as their mouths separated, "about sharing my bed tonight? I would like to feel close to you."

"As far as I know, My King, your bed is my bed and I have no interest in making other arrangements." At that moment, their midday meal arrived and they ate together, sharing comfortable companionship. He told her about experiences that had happened in the months he had been away, places he had seen, and people he had met. She told him about the efforts she and the advising council had made to get the kingdom back on its feet again and connecting with the lesser kings to shore up the borders and defend themselves from the invading Saxons. He told her about the accident and admitted his sorrow over losing his favorite horse. She told him about releasing Archbishop Augustine's prisoner a handful of months before.

"Who else have you told about this," he asked her with a serious tone to his voice that she found concerning.

"Only Master Solomon," she said. "I honestly did not know who else I could fully trust, so I chose to err on what I hoped was the side of caution."

He nodded. "That was very wise, my dear. You chose well in placing your confidence. What did Master Solomon advise you to do?"

"He agreed that given our goal to bring the kingdoms into alliance, it would be a poor move politically to keep the Merlin of Britain detained in our dungeon. He feels as I do that anything that could bring unity to the seven kingdoms should be encouraged. There was a time when Avalon was a strong voice in our politics and I do not believe that distancing ourselves from them is wise. We need to create a cohesive kingdom, not encourage greater division. Avalon wants what we want – a united Britain capable of defending its shores."

"My father was an avid and enthusiastic enemy of Avalon," Constantine said. "He abhorred magic of all kinds and would not take the advice of witches and sorcerers."

"I understand this is true," she said. "But as we know, you are not your father and it is clear what a country divided has cost us. Husband, it was an unadvised and independent decision I made to release The Merlin. Fault falls to no one but me and me alone if this was in error."

He squeezed her hand. "It was a very wise move and one I would have made myself with the perspective you have gained," he agreed. "Augustine was my father's advisor and was at the root of much and more of the politics he created. Have you heard from him on this action you took?"

"Not a word," Ophelia said. "It was not discussed in counsel and he never confronted me about my action against him. In many ways, that is more disturbing than if he had accused me directly."

"I understand. It is good I am home now. I want you by my side in ruling because in these past months, you have already surpassed me in knowledge of how to run the kingdom. As a united force, the two of us can make necessary changes to bring Britain back to the glory it enjoyed under Roman rule. This will not happen without making enemies, some of them powerful, but it can happen. I believe that now."

"I do not think you should make a move against the Archbishop unless you know that he is himself becoming aggressive. He has been quite cooperative in the past few weeks; unusually so, even."

"Yes," he agreed. "That could be good or not. It bears watching." He smiled at her. "You have done well. I am proud of you. You are a better ruler than I am and you make me look good."

"It is nothing more than common sense," she said. "There is little more to running a kingdom than there is to running a tavern. It is about bringing in more money than you spend, listening to everyone who has a problem, and making the best choices and compromises you can."

He stared at her, feeling unbelievable sweetness and admiration in his heart for her. "You are an amazing woman, Queen Ophelia."

"And you are a gracious and generous man, King Constantine. Now eat your broth before the oldest man on earth gets back up here with his little blood suckers to feast upon your belly."

Not long after that, Master Druston did arrive and significantly reduced the bruising on the King's body. After binding his broken ribs and reminding him to remain in bed for a few days, he left with a promise to return on the morrow to check on his progress.

Later that night, Ophelia and Constantine very carefully and with a bit of extra physical prowess on Ophelia's part, enjoyed the company of one another even more than they had done earlier in the day and in doing so, made a baby.

Ophelia did not tell her husband about the slip of parchment The Merlin had given her, not because she felt uncomfortable about sharing this part of the story and not because she consciously omitted the information, but simply because she forgot about it. After returning to her chambers nestled between her breast and her bodice that night, it fluttered to the floor when she dressed the next day. Seeing it laying there, she absently picked it up and slipped it in between the pages of the book she earlier took from the court library for further reading. Interestingly, the book was entitled, *A Treatise on Interfaith Government* by Taliesin, The Merlin of Britain, a plea for cooperative rulership among individual kingdoms with a universal acceptance and honoring of the faiths of all concerned.

Chapter 34

"Push, Ophelia," Nuala urged her. "I can see the head. Push!"

Ophelia bore down with all of her strength, then caught her breath and did it again. Her grip tightened on the leather strap looped over the rafters of the room and provided counter-pressure for her efforts. "What an ingenious idea," she thought in some far recess of her mind, then she pulled mightily against it and pushed with all her strength.

She felt a burning and then a sudden pressure release. Her legs began to shake uncontrollably just as Nuala laughed, "The baby's head is out. Look at all that hair, my goodness."

Ophelia reached between her legs just as another contraction took hold of her body. She did not even have to push. As she touched her baby's head, the little body twisted and then shot out into her hands and Nuala's.

"You eager little beaver," Nuala said, wiping a bit of mucus from the baby's nose and mouth. "Here, Fee, lay back so you can nurse your babe."

Ophelia could not stop laughing as she looked at the red, wrinkled little face that blinked up at her. "Well, is it a prince or a princess?" Nuala asked.

Startled, Ophelia realized she had not even bothered to look. She felt a rush of warm fluid on her chest and said, "Whatever it is, the water is flowing!" She turned the baby over and was greeted by a spray in her eye. "It's a boy!" she said and wiped her face on her tunic.

Ophelia's entire body began to shudder violently and she lay back on the fresh straw while Nuala pushed in on her abdomen with great gusto. "OW!" she complained.

"Put the baby to suckle now, Fee," Nuala said. Where moments before, she had felt like she could move mountains, Ophelia suddenly felt all the strength leave her body in a concerted wave. "Now, Fee," Nuala urged. "Right now."

Only the two of them – now three – were in the room for security precautions. Ophelia insisted that given the unfortunate fates of the other four queens that Nuala be the only one to attend her, much to Constantine's dismay. He campaigned for a room of midwives and attendants to keep his wife and child safe should they need extra hands. Opelia held firm to this decision and Nuala agreed. The women prevailed. Her head swimming, she lay back on softly covered fresh straw and teased the baby's mouth with her nipple. He latched on with great enthusiasm and that is the last thing Ophelia remembered for a bit.

She woke up to Nuala slapping her across the face. "Wake UP, Ophelia."

"Ow!" Ophelia said. "Stop hitting me."

"Are you with me, Fee?" Nuala asked, worry apparent on her face. "You fainted."

"I'm here."

"Keep him suckling. You've lost a lot of blood with the afterbirth."

There seemed to be no danger in the baby not suckling. He was chugging away mightily at her breast. She smiled down at him and he looked back at her with intense, dark eyes. "Get Phillip," she said.

"In time," Nuala said. "The last thing I want is for him to see you pass out again. It would devastate him. Here, drink this."

She passed a cup to Ophelia, who drank it down and then grimaced, "Agh, that is bitter. What is it?"

"It will help you to stop bleeding, along with the nursing," she replied. "Did you drink it all?"

"Unfortunately, yes."

"Then let's get some nourishment into you. BETH!" she called.

The door creaked open. "Yes, My Lady?"

"Get the Queen some chicken broth from the kitchen, a great deal of it. Also, a cup of warm wine."

"Yes, My Lady, right away."

Nuala continued to knead her fists into Ophelia's abdomen, which was painful to the extreme. "How to do you feel, Fee?" she asked.

"Tired," Ophelia grumbled, "and I feel well when you are not crushing my insides. Look at him, Sister. Isn't he beautiful?"

Nuala sighed and stopped her ministrations. Smiling, she put her arm around Ophelia and gently touched the baby's cheek. The baby was warm, pink, and perfect. "He's amazing," she agreed.

The two women had bonded closely over the past year since Ophelia had become High Queen. For the younger woman who had never had a close female confidant, the relationship was uneasy at first, but soon became indispensable. Nuala, on the other hand, found that she valued Ophelia's wisdom and loved talking with a sensible, funny woman her nephew had chosen as his queen. At first, she had doubted his wisdom in choosing a commoner as his bride and even more so when he gave her the power to lead the country in his absence. Time and again, Ophelia rose to the challenge and impressed Nuala with her good common sense and shrewd leadership. The pregnancy brought them even closer and found herself feeling tremendous kinship with her sister-in-law. After the troubled pregnancies of the previous queens, she was relieved to find that Ophelia's was remarkably uncomplicated and, in fact, one of the easiest that Nuala had seen.

Nuala pushed in on Ophelia's belly again. "That's good. Now you're clamping down. The bleeding will slow." Beth arrived with the broth and wine and Ophelia drank it down.

"Easy," Nuala said. "Your body has been through a lot. Drink slowly."

"It didn't take long, did it? Not like I thought," Ophelia said.

"No, not long at all. Only a few hours. I have seen it take days."

"How can they stand it? That was no small task!" Ophelia had never so much as witnessed a birth and only knew what to expect from the stories and descriptions Nuala and some of her attendants had provided. What she experienced had not seemed nearly as challenging as what was described to her, but still, it was the most enormous task she had ever undertaken.

"It's not easy, but our bodies know what we can do, usually. You did well, my girl," she said, patting Ophelia on the thigh. "Now let's get you cleaned up and show the King his son."

Nuala helped Ophelia change from her soiled smock and into a loose-fitting shift and told Beth to take away the bloodied, wet straw. She used a wet cloth warmed by water heated by the fire to carefully wipe the blood away from her thighs and abdomen, then wiped the baby off a bit, much to his dismay. He howled when she the nipple pulled away from his mouth, but delightedly accepted the other breast and was soon happy again. "There," Nuala said. "What a fine young man you are."

Beth returned from discarding the straw and Nuala told her, "Go and fetch the King."

"Won't be hard," Beth said. "He's all but pacing outside the door."

Moments later, Constantine burst into the room, his anxious and fraught expression changing to wonder and delight as he saw Ophelia nursing their son. "You're alive," he said, his voice cracking slightly. "You are alive."

"Very much so," Nuala assured him. "She is well, nephew. So is your son."

"Son?" he said. Ophelia saw his eyes well with tears that spilled down his cheeks. "I have a son. We? We have a son?"

Ophelia laughed. "We have a son," she said. "Come and see, Husband." Like a child himself, he crept onto the bed next to her and touched the baby's fingers, which were curled into a tight fist.

"It's a baby," he said and sounded as though there was no breath left in his body.

"Do you want to hold him?" Ophelia asked.

"Hold me? Me?" Constantine looked puzzled and excited at the same time. "May I? Can I?"

"He's your son," Ophelia chuckled. "Let me see if he will let go." She slipped her finger into his mouth to break the suction. The baby shifted his attention to look at Constantine. Nuala gathered the baby up from

Ophelia's arms and wrapped him in a soft blanket, then handed him to the King, who was mesmerized.

"A baby," he said. "We made a baby. There's a baby."

The two women looked at one another and laughed.

Chapter 35

Ophelia slept deeply and dreamlessly. The baby curled beside her in a tight bundle, also sleeping. Constantine refused to leave their sides and slept in a chair next to the bed. None of the three stirred when the air in the room began to shift.

Sometime later, Ophelia stretched and woke to a darkened room. She eased herself off the bed, mindful of the bruised, displaced feeling deep inside her body, and lit the lamp that was on the dresser. She smiled at Phillip, who was still fast asleep in the chair. A persistent, low cramping sensation reminded her that she likely needed to change the dressings between her legs and get some more broth from the kitchen to keep her up strength. She had no idea how far into the night it was, but it was very late. As powerfully as her son nursed, she would need to be prepared to produce milk in abundance. Nuala had suggested a wet nurse and while she might consider that later, for the time being, she wanted to feed her own child.

She opened the door, careful to make no more noise than necessary, and whispered to one of the king's guardsman outside to send to the kitchen for broth for her and a meal for the King. She doubted her husband had eaten anything since midday the previous day. She tiptoed back into the room and slipped under the warm covers again, eager to feel the warm bundle of baby pressed against her once again.

Except that the baby was not there.

It took Ophelia several seconds before the grip of panic built in her throat. At first, she moved covers, thinking the baby had simply worked his way further into the bed as he slept. Feeling foolish, she looked beside and under the bed, supposing he may have rolled off as she slept. Her movements woke Constantine, who was immediately on guard. "What is it, Ophelia? What's wrong?"

"He's not here," she hissed. "The baby. He's not here." She again threw the covers aside, moving the pillows. "Phillip, where is he?"

The king jumped to his feet and pulled open the door. "Gahren, who came into this room tonight?"

"No one," the startled knight said. "Since Lady Nuala left late this afternoon, there has been no one except you and the Queen. The Queen came out a moment ago and asked for food. Otherwise, it has been quiet."

"Did you sleep, man? Tell me true, did you and Felix sleep?"

Gahren looked shocked by the question. "In no way, Your Highness! I assure you we were awake and guarding the door the entire time!"

"Where is Felix now?" the King demanded.

"The Queen just sent him to the kitchen," Gahren replied, confused.

"Get Lady Nuala immediately," he said. "And get my Captain of the Guard."

With his heart in his throat, Constantine went to Ophelia and put his arms around her. She clung to him, frantic and breathless. "Where IS he, Phillip?" she demanded. "What could have happened to him?"

Nuala had arranged a room closer to the royal bedchamber than usual so she would be available if Ophelia developed any complications. She was in the room in a matter of minutes. "What is it?" she asked.

"The baby," Constantine said. "He's...he's gone. Did you take him?"

"No," Nuala answered. "I did not take him. What do you mean gone?"

"He's GONE," Ophelia shrieked, now on the edge of hysteria. "I slept and when I woke he was not here."

"Ophelia, he cannot just be gone," Nuala said. "You spoke to Gahren and Felix?"

"Right away. He said no one came into the room," Constantine said. "How can this be, Nuala? Why is this happening?"

"I do not know," she said, putting her arms around Ophelia, "but we will find out."

Chapter 36

T
he following day, there was still no sign of the baby anywhere. Ophelia kept thinking she would hear him cry out to her and that she had somehow just misplaced him in her sleep. Had she been sleepwalking, as she had known some people to do? She barely remembered sending Felix for food. Had she done more than this in her disorientation between sleep and wakefulness? She lost a great deal of blood with the birth. Had that influence her mental stability somehow? She questioned herself repeatedly. As wretched as she felt, Constantine was even worse, berating himself for falling asleep and forcing the Captain of the Guard to question each person in the castle and search every room.

The painful engorgement of Ophelia's breasts and the blood that flowed from her body was the only evidence that the baby ever existed at all. She continued to bleed to excess and Nuala forced the bitter herb drink on her frequently. On the third day of the baby's disappearance, Nuala and Master Druston insisted, against her protests, that Ophelia drink some milk of the poppy to help her sleep. She had eaten very little since the birth and her face was drawn and hollow. Constantine was not much better, but the despair that pervaded Ophelia's grim countenance turned into rage on his. He was furious and there was no place for his anger to go.

As Ophelia drank the pungent opiate brew, she felt a floating sensation come over her that was familiar to her, and yet not, much like a far away feeling she had experienced in a dream. *"I felt this before,"* she thought as she eased into a fitful sleep.

In her dream, she walked through hallways, opening door after door, looking for her child. She called to him, but in the dream, she called him "Phillip." They had not had a chance to decide on a name for the baby. Constantine refused to entertain names until he knew the baby was born safely and lived. Door after door, she opened, becoming more and more frantic with each empty room.

She heard her baby cry, faintly at first and then louder as she ran down the hall in the direction of his cries. "Phillip!" she shouted. "Mother's coming!"

She threw open the door at the end of the hall and found herself in the Queen's chambers where she had spun the straw into gold. There in the middle of the room sat Ducky in a rocking chair holding her son. "No Ophelia," she said. "Mother is already here. This one mine. You must stop looking for him and move on with your life."

"Give me my baby," Ophelia said. "Give him to me now."

"Oh no," Ducky said. "A deal is a deal. I have your blood oath that your firstborn is mine." She pulled a white linen cloth from the folds of her skirt and showed it to Ophelia, the dark taint of old blood smeared across the white. "I help you spin the gold and you give me your baby. That was the agreement."

A flood of memories washed over Ophelia in her dream, clearer to her now than the memory of another dream, long ago, had been in her waking mind. *"You can have my first-born son that does not exist."* Her own words rang in her ears again and again. She angrily beat her hands against her head to make them stop. "NO!" she shrieked. "You give him to me."

"I told you that magic always comes with a price," Ducky said. "Now the price is paid."

"How can you do such a thing? How can you take a woman's child from her?" Ophelia ranted.

"Women lose children all of the time," Ducky said, shrugging. "It's not so hard as all that. You can have other babies almost as handsome as this one. *Yes, you can!*" The last words she said to the baby in a chanting voice. The baby began to cry pitifully and Ophelia's heart ached.

"I'm sorry you lost your baby," she said. "But your baby died because you killed yourself. That was your own fault. You have no right to take mine."

Ducky was up in a flash, her face a mask of rage. "You mind what you say, young woman," she snapped. "You are speaking of things you know nothing about. *Nothing!*"

"You give him to me, you witch," Ophelia hissed. "I will hunt to the ends of the earth to find you if I must, but I will have my baby back."

"*A witch?* Oh, I am no witch, *dearie*. I am just an old woman who finally got her babe. Four queens I had to go through to get him, but here he is, a fine prince from Arthur's lineage, just as I wanted." As in her previously long-forgotten dream, Ophelia noted that the old woman's common accent was now replaced by a low and regal tone.

"What?" Ophelia said. "What do you mean you went through 'four queens?'"

"Oh, they were not as pliant as you. They were not ones to bargain, no matter how much they wanted what they wanted. You gave this little one away with almost no effort on my part at all. The other ones fought and fought for their children."

"But they died of natural causes!" Ophelia argued. "This is absurd."

"Did they now?" Ducky looked at her meaningfully. "The first one, Queen Eugenia was her name, refused me even as I was delivering the baby myself. All I needed was a simple yes from her and she could have lived, but no. So argumentative was that one, so she and the baby both had to go."

Ophelia listened in horror as the old woman continued. "It was easy, really. I just held the baby inside with my hand until they both stopped moving and to all who saw, it was naught but a misfortune of birthing. So common, you know. The second one, Queen Flora, she would not even speak to me and refused my special food and drink that would have made her more of a willing spirit for bargaining. As soon as she conceived, she tried to use herbs and magic to drive me away. I was having none of that. This is my home." Ducky said this as though Ophelia should understand the necessity of what came next. "It was just a matter of slipping some herbs into her tea to get her good and congested, then taking her breath away in the night as she slept."

"Queen Silvia was a sickly woman anyway and when she refused me, I was not much surprised. I offered her glowing health and still, she rejected me. Didn't matter. I knew her miscarriage was already starting. It was an easy thing to feed her the herbs so that she bled her life away when the child passed. Now Queen Agnes, she was even easier. She agreed to my offer straight away and she got the beauty she craved. God was not kind to that woman, let me say but I certainly was. With each day, she became more beautiful just as she wanted, but after she quickened, the stupid girl threw herself off the cliffs rather than let me take her baby. Oh, she begged and pleaded to be let out of the agreement, talking about how she'd rather not be fair of face, but have her baby to herself. I told her what I am telling you, *'A deal is a deal.'* You agreed just as she did.

"That's four queens gone because they crossed me. Will you be a fifth? It's easy, girl. Just walk away. Walk away and live your charmed life with your adoring husband and your healthy womb and all the other babies you can have."

"Never! And why do you not go find a baby who is orphaned? There are plenty of motherless children out there who need someone to care for them."

Ducky chuckled softly. "Idiot Girl, it is not any old baby I want. I could have had an ordinary baby a thousand times over. I want *Arthur's* child. This baby descended of the Pendragons, the last of them. That is why he must be mine. You gave him away to me. That is your burden to carry, not mine!"

"You tricked me," Ophelia seethed. "You made your deal like a coward while I was drugged and sleeping! You did not even have the honor to say who you really are or what you wanted. You pretended to be my friend."

"I am your friend," Ducky said. "This is just a business deal between friends. You wanted my services and I named my price. You accepted. That is it."

"I WAS ASLEEP! …AND DRUGGED!" Ophelia shouted. In the depth of her dream, she reached into her memories of the writings by Taliesin and grabbed onto the only recourse she could find. "I demand… I demand…a parley," she said with more confidence than she felt.

Ducky looked stricken. "A parley? How do you know about parley?"

"When a spirit has tricked a living person, the living person can demand parley if they offer more than the original terms, is that correct? I am a living person and you are a spirit. I demand a parley."

"Yes," Ducky said, "That is an unfortunate condition, but it is to me to accept or reject your offer. What can you possibly have now that I want?"

Ophelia's thoughts raced as she tried to imagine what this old woman could envy of hers and then remembered her earlier words.

"I will give you life," she said at last. "You tell me what I must do to get my baby back. If I cannot do it, I will give over my life and you can have my body and live as Queen. You will have your youth, your baby, and a wonderful husband. *You* can have the charmed life and I will have no life."

Ducky seemed to consider this for a moment. "I have your baby now," she said. "How do I know that you will honor the agreement? You're already backing out of this one…or trying to."

"You have my word as High Queen, but you have to make the task you choose something a human can actually accomplish. Nothing magical like spinning straw into gold."

"Fair enough," Ducky said thoughtfully. "It would be good to have a young body and handsome husband again, not to mention the running of the kingdom at my hand. Fine. You have a deal."

"But what *is* the deal?" Ophelia asked. "What do I have to do?"

Ducky smiled a broad, toothless grin. "Oh," she said, "nothing big. Just tell me my name."

"Your name?" Ophelia asked, puzzled. "Ducky?"

"Oh no, I mean *my real name*. Tell me what name I was given by my own mother when I was born and I will give you back the baby. You have until midnight tomorrow. Meanwhile, this little luv stays with me."

The baby cried louder and Ophelia begged, "Please, Ducky. Please. Just let me hold him and comfort him. He is frightened, can you not see? He is hungry. Let me feed him."

"I can take care of my child just fine," Ducky said resolutely. "Now, leave us. You meet me in this room by tomorrow midnight and one of us will walk away as High Queen with a baby. I believe I know which one it will be."

Chapter 37

Ophelia woke with a start with her baby's cries still ringing in her ears. Sunlight streamed through the windows and Nuala sat stitching an altar cloth in the chair by the bed. "Fee, what is it?" she asked when Ophelia sat bolt upright in bed.

"How late in the day is it?" Ophelia asked. "How late? Tell me?"

"It's mid-morning," Nuala said, "Ophelia, calm yourself, dear. Your body can't take this stress."

"I have no time for that," Ophelia said, pushing herself up out of bed. "Send Beth or Bess or whatever her name is in to help me dress. My hands are too shaky to do it myself. I need to speak to every servant in court who has been here longer than twenty years and I need the king's guard to go find anyone in the village who may have worked here more than twenty years ago."

"Fee," Nuala said gently. "You're delirious from the poppy. You must rest."

"NO!" Ophelia said with an edge to her voice she did not intend. "Just do it. As High Queen, I order it!"

Nuala pulled back, stunned. "Yes, *Your Highness*," she said, not caring to hide the hurt in her voice. "I will get to it straight away."

"Nuala," Ophelia said softly. "I am sorry, truly sorry. I just need this. Please. Now."

"Then it will be done." Nuala slipped silently away while Ophelia contemplated what to do next.

Less than an hour later, Master Solomon knocked her on her door and entered when she bade him to do so.

"Ophelia," he asked. "What are you doing? What is going on?"

"Where is the King?" Ophelia asked. "I have not seen him all morning."

"The King is in chambers with the council, organizing an extension of the search party through the village. Before, we had limited the search to the court itself, hoping to keep this unfortunate business under wraps. Everyone thought it best to let you sleep while you could, then word came of your orders. What is happening, Dear Child?"

She told him everything, from her first encounter with Ducky right up to the dream. He listened intently. "Have you spoken of this to the King?" he asked.

"No," she said, looking regretful. "I honestly had no memory of it until the milk of the poppy brought on my dream last night. Master Solomon, I have to take this chance."

"Of course, you do," he said. "But how to find the information? I cannot imagine. I was not in court while Bors was alive, although I have heard his name. I am trying to think of anyone who may have known him."

"Thank you for not dismissing this as the hysterical ranting of a grieving woman," she said.

"Ophelia," he said, "You are the most mentally sound woman I have ever met, even under such stress as this. If you say it is so, it is so. It is not yet midday. We have time yet. Let us take some time to think this through."

Together, they mulled the situation; each feeling there must be something they were missing. Master Solomon said, "As I recall, Bors and Ducky died almost twenty years past now. She was not of noble birth that I know, so there would be no record of her birth. She was midwife here for a while and there may be adults here in court who were babies delivered by her. She possibly midwifed in neighboring villages as well."

"How does this help us?" Ophelia asked.

"Sometimes the answer is right in front of us, dear Ophelia. We just have to talk it out. The more we know about her, the more we can trace back those who may have known her. Now think with me."

Sometime later, Nuala knocked on the door. "There are five here, My Queen, who have been in court for longer than twenty years. It is all we could find."

"Bring them to me," Ophelia said. "And thank you, Nuala."

Several minutes later, Ophelia and Master Solomon stood before four women and one man, all of whom were elderly. "Were any of you here when King Arthur was living?" she asked.

The four women and one man looked at one another and all shook their heads. "No one?" she asked.

"No," one of the women said. "Arthur is more than forty years gone now."

"What about Bors, the chamberlain who came after him?" Master Solomon asked. Did any of you know of him?"

"I did," one of the women spoke up. "I was a young woman just come to work in the tanning room and he was still chamberlain, yes."

"What about his wife?" Ophelia asked anxiously.

"Ducky? Oh, you don't want to be knowing about her, Your Majesty. She was crazy as a loon, that one was."

"You knew her?"

"A bit," she said. "So did Besina there." Another of the women nodded.

"Did any of the rest of you know her?" Ophelia asked.

The others shook their heads. "You may go," Master Solomon said, "The two of you stay."

The other three dutifully filed out. "Do not be afraid," Ophelia said. "I need for you to tell me all you know about Ducky."

The one called Besina looked at the other. Ophelia thought her name was Adula but was not certain. "Well," Besina began. "She was a right good cook. We loved her breads especially and she ran the kitchen well. She was also a midwife and did most of the birthing. She was a good bit older than we were, so we didn't much spend time together. She could be harsh and some said she dealt in the dark arts. You know…magic." She leaned in conspiratorially for the last word.

"Yes," Ophelia said, feeling her frustration build. "I know what the dark arts are. Do you know her real name?"

"Her real name? Adula, do you know?" Besina said and the older women looked at one another again.

Adula shrugged her shoulders. "Wasn't it just Ducky? That's all we ever heard. Don' reckon she had no other name than that."

"What did Bors call her?" Ophelia asked. "When he spoke to her, how did he address her?"

"Let me think," Besina said. The passing of time was maddening to Ophelia. "Just 'Wife' mostly, I think."

"A-yah," Adula agreed. "He called her 'Wife.' Never even called her 'Ducky,' I don' think."

"What else do you know about her?" Master Solomon asked.

Besina thought for a moment. "She was a good storyteller," she said.

"She told us about her births sometimes," Adula said. "Once she told us about a baby she birthed for a woman where the baby was covered all in hair, it was." Besina nodded in agreement.

"Then she told us about one time she cut twin babies out of a dead woman while the woman was not yet stiff," she said. "And the babies lived too."

Master Solomon was suddenly at attention and Ophelia wondered what he was thinking. "What became of the babies?" he asked.

"Why," Besina thought again and seemed to retrieve the answer from very deep inside her memory. "One, a boy, was put with a cook who worked in Lord Seaton's court. The other was a girl and was give to the miller a few villages over to raise up." Ophelia and Master Solomon exchanged a look.

"When was this?" Master Solomon asked.

"Oh," Adula said, "Maybe twenty years gone now. Not thirty yet." Besina nodded in agreement.

"Do you remember anything else?" Ophelia asked. "Anything?"

The two women looked at one another again. "No," Besina said. "I can't think of a thing."

"Thank you," Master Solomon said. "You may go. Should you remember anything else about Ducky, anything at all, please find me and tell me." He pressed a coin into the hand of each of the women, who smiled gratefully.

When the women left, Master Solomon and Ophelia looked at one another thoughtfully. "I need to think about this," Ophelia said.

"You're hearing the twenty-year old lost memories of two old women," Master Solomon cautioned. "Be careful what you take from it."

"I am willing to consider anything at this point," she said, weary from the day and her lack of sleep since the birth. "We have to get my father here." She pushed herself into a standing position and held on to the table beside her for support.

Gahren put his head in the door. "Your Majesty," he said, "A word?"

Ophelia bid him to enter. "It's the King," he said. "He has collapsed while in council. The guards took him to the royal chambers. Master Druston is with him now."

Ophelia and Master Solomon exchanged worried looks. "Go," he said. "I will manage the rest, but My Queen," Ophelia looked at him expectantly. "...it is already mid-afternoon. Whatever happens needs to happen quickly. Is your strength sufficient to carry on?"

"It will have to be," Ophelia said. "This is a battle I am not prepared to lose."

Chapter 38

Constantine lay ghost pale on the bed when Ophelia arrived and took his hand. The court physician was just completing his exam. "It's exhaustion," he told her softly. "But more. The man is broken hearted. He is losing the will to go on."

"Phillip," Ophelia said. "Phillip, wake up and speak to me."

"I have given him herbs to help him sleep," the Master Druston said. "He may not be able to wake. He needs rest and dreamless sleep. It may have been months since his injury, but he is still weakened. We will know more tomorrow."

"Tomorrow?" she said. "You expect him to be like this until tomorrow?"

"He must rest, My Queen. He needs time to…not think for a while. He is trapped inside his own mind with fear running courses in his head. That is not a safe place for a king to be. We will let it be known that the King is indisposed and if he is well enough for court tomorrow, he can begin to slowly return to power. For this moment, you and the council will have to rule as you do when he is away.

"You, however, do not look well. Are you still bleeding overmuch from the birth? How do you feel?"

"Exhausted. Weak. Angry. How do you think I feel?" Ophelia snapped. "Now I have no husband to lean on for support and I must also do his job as well."

The physician looked haunted. "My Queen, it is no secret that you are stronger than is the King in many ways. While it is regretful that you must take on such a burden at this delicate time, it is also good for all of us that you are here to do so. My regrets if I overstepped. If his condition changes, please do send for me." He bowed his head and left.

Constantine remained as still as death itself. Ophelia's hand shook as she pushed her hair back from her face.

"I have sent our fastest riders for your father." Master Solomon's voice at her side startled her.

"Thank you," she said. "That could be hours. What can we do in the meantime?"

"May we speak away from the King's rest?"

"Of course," she said. Leaving the room, she instructed guards to always attend the King and to bring Nuala to sit with him. Together, they walked to the bedroom where they had interviewed the women. "Ophelia, you are exhausted. You have to get some rest. If you will sleep, I swear to you, I will wake you the moment your father arrives."

Ophelia looked helplessly at her hands, trying to imagine one more thing she could do, ever mindful of the darkness that was falling with the setting sun and from her own fear. Her head pounded relentlessly with pain, her breasts were swollen, hard, and hot, begging for release, and her very life felt as though it was slipping away with every drop of blood she lost.

"The moment he arrives…" Ophelia said.

"I swear it," the old man vowed.

Ophelia slipped into the bed beside Constantine and pulled the covers around her. She knew she would be unable to sleep, but she needed time to think away from the influence of others. There was something sticking in her head and she could not figure out what it was. It was as a bee buzzing around that would not light on anything long enough for her to see it.

Sometime later, she jerked awake almost violently when Master Solomon squeezed her arm. "My Queen. Your father and his wife have arrived."

Quickly, she sat up in bed and tried to orient herself. It was late. Very late, from the lack of light in the room despite the glow of the torch Master Solomon had brought in with him. "Give me a moment and then meet me in the next room," she said. He nodded his understanding and left.

Ophelia washed her face and smoothed her hair back into place. When she pushed the door opened, she hardly recognized her father. Clear-eyed and smiling, she almost mistook him for a courtier.

"Fee!" he came to her and gave her a tight hug. "Are you safe? Is there any news?"

"Mills?" she asked. "Is it you?"

"Of course, it's me, dear daughter. Are you unwell?"

"No, it's just…Falia, it is good to see you."

She nodded to the woman who stood behind her father, who curtsied deeply and said, "My Queen."

"The baby," Mills said, his voice fraught with worry. "Have he been found?"

"No," Ophelia said cautiously. "I did not know that word had spread beyond the court about his disappearance."

"The knights who fetched us told us what happened, My Queen," Falia said. "I hope it was not inappropriate."

"Of course not," Ophelia said quietly. "I apologize. I am not myself and I have just awakened. Please, Falia. Call me Ophelia. You are my stepmother."

Falia nodded to her. "As you wish."

"Mills," Ophelia said. "You look so… different."

"I am a happy man," he said, giving his wife an affectionate hug around the shoulders. "You changed my life, Fee, when you sent this beautiful lady to my life. She whipped me into shape and made a new man of me." Falia lowered her eyes humbly.

"I cannot take credit for that," Ophelia said. "The King is the one who sent her and she is the one who was willing to care for you. I hope she is as satisfied with the arrangement as you are."

Falia smiled, "I am a happy woman," she said. "Your father and I have taken over managing the tavern for Forrest and his wife. We run a good business and have a fine life. But you… how are you holding up, my dear?" Her face conveyed genuine concern for the stepdaughter she barely knew. "You are barely out of the birthing bed and now this!"

Ophelia sat down in a nearby chair and Master Solomon joined her and indicated that Falia and Mills should also sit. "It has been a trying time for both the King and the Queen," he said. "We have learned, however, of a way that you may be able to help."

"Of course," Mills said. "Anything." Falia nodded her agreement.

"There are two women in our court," he began, "who claim that some twenty years ago, a woman named Ducky who was wife to the chamberlain here delivered twin babies of a dead woman, a boy and a girl. Do you know anything of this, sir?"

Mills looked uncomfortably at the floor.

"Sir?" Master Solomon repeated.

Mills looked up at Ophelia and then at Falia, then at Ophelia again. He started to speak several times but seemed unable to get the words out of his mouth.

"Mills?" Falia said, sternly. "If you know something that can bring your grandson back, it needs to be told and told right now."

He looked at his wife, nodded, and then spoke. "I do. Three and twenty years ago, it was, a woman who had been my foster sister came to our door and had a newborn babe in arms. She knew my wife, Eleanor, had longed for a babe and was barren. She told me, Ducky did, that this wee one's mother had died birthing her and a boy. The boy had gone to a kitchen woman in the court, but she'd secreted the girl away for us. I really don't see how this can help anything..."

"She was *your foster sister*?" Ophelia asked, feeling they were closer to hope than they had been for this entire nightmare. "What was Ducky's real name, Mills? You must know if you were raised with her. What was her name?"

Mills thought for a moment. "Fee, I never once heard her called anything but 'Ducky.' It is all I knew her name ever to be. They called her Ducky because of how she walked as a child. She followed my mum around like a little duck, toddling and waddling."

"Wait, she was your foster sister," Ophelia said, "so where did she come from? How did she come to live with you?"

"I don't rightly know," Mills said, looking puzzled. "She was a good bit older than I and already living with us when I was born. She left our home when I was but a lad of ten."

"All the times I asked you about my mother…why did you never tell me a word of this?" Ophelia asked.

"My Eleanor was so taken you that she didn't care one bit where you came from. You were her dearest child and she loved you to the ends of the earth, she did. She never wanted you to know you were not her own flesh and blood and made me vow never to tell you. When she took sick and died that winter, I did my best to care for you, Fee, but you know I did about the worst job of that I could. Eleanor…she was my whole world. I buried my whole heart right into the ground along with her. With her gone, it felt like I couldn't love anyone anymore. To think about her, even enough to tell you who she was, just hurt too much. I never thought to feel anything ever again…until there was Falia here. She opened my heart up again."

"The boy," Master Solomon leaned forward on his staff. "What happened to the boy?"

"What boy?" Mills asked, confused.

"The boy born with the baby Ophelia. Her brother. Do you know what became of him?"

"Oh, ho, ho," Mills laughed, "Now that's one hell of a story, it is. He went on to work in the abbey in our village and now is out there on Avalon parading himself out as the new Merlin of Britain Reborn. No ego there, I tell you."

The color drained from Ophelia's face and she started visibly. Her breath caught in her chest and she found she could not blink, could not breathe, and could not move. Only startled sounds like those of an injured animal came out of her throat.

The Merlin Reborn

Neve…Neve…

"It will mean nothing to you until the time when you need it."

"You will need it more than you have ever needed anything before."

"It is the name of the woman who cut me from my mother's dead body the day I was born."

"Oohhhhh," she said, her breath finally coming in jagged gasps. "Ohhhhhh. Ohhhhh. Ohhhh!!" Her eyes were wide and bulging and she clutched the bodice of her dress in a tight fist.

"FEE!" she could hear people around her screaming. "Fee, are you hurt? Fee?"

"The parchment!" She gasped. "The scrap of parchment." She touched her breast here the precious paper had lain beneath her bodice so long ago and started to laugh hysterically. "The paper!" Her breath came in fits and starts and she laughed to the point that it seemed she would take a fit.

"What paper, Fee? What paper??"

"It will mean nothing to you until the time when you need it."

"Oh God, the paper!"

"You will need it more than you have ever needed anything before."

"Think," she said and slapped herself on the head repeatedly. "Think, think!! Where is the paper?" She closed her eyes and clapped her hands over her ears to block out the shouting of the people around her.

"Ophelia!! Someone get the physician!" she heard Master Solomon say.

The paper.

It had fluttered. It had fallen. Fallen on the floor.

She had bent over. She had picked it up. She had put it...

WHERE? Where had she put it? In the dresser? In the trunk? ...no, no...

In the book!! She put it in the book she was reading!

Where was the book? So long ago!

"It is the name of the woman who cut me from my mother's dead body the day I was born."

Get The Merlin! We can get The Merlin! No, ridiculous, it would take far too long... no time left. No time left."

"I will not be able to be here to tell you this on the day when you need it most."

The book! Where was the book?? What book was it? The answer was in the book. The book. The Merlin...Taliesin!! Taliesin!

She had no idea how much of her thought processes she screamed aloud and how much she only screamed in her own head. She knew everyone in the room was looking at her as if she had gone mad.

She took a deep breath, let it out slowly, and opened her eyes.

"A Treatise on Interfaith Government," she said with as much dignity as she could muster. "*A Treatise on Interfaith Government* by Taliesin. Get it."

"Get it?" Master Solomon asked, confused.

"It is in the court library. Get the book! Get the book! We have to go NOW!" She pushed Falia aside, who had the misfortune of standing closest to the door, and raced across the courtyard, her skirts in her hand. How much time did she have? An hour? Maybe two? She had to get the book.

The priests had already left the library for the night. With shaking hands, she managed to light the torch after dropping the flint several times in a maddening fit of clumsiness. Like a woman possessed, she began pulling books off the shelves and tossing them aside. She knew where it should be. The priests kept he books meticulously arranged and there was never room for error. Where was the book? Where? She had returned it a few weeks later without a thought of what she had placed inside.

Master Solomon arrived some time later and gasped at the literary carnage in front of him. "Ophelia, these books. They are beyond value. What are you doing?"

"The book *A Treatise on Interfaith Government* by Taliesin," she said again, making direct, intentional eye contact with him. "I am not mad. It has the name in it. It has *her* name in it. The Merlin gave it to me when I released him."

"What?" he said in astonishment. "What?"

"HELP ME FIND THE DAMNED BOOK!" she shrieked.

"Ophelia," he said after they had searched every shelf. "It is not here. Someone must have it."

Without a word, she flew out of the library and banged on the door to the bungalow next door so hard that her hands started to bleed. "Master Leonard!!" she screamed. "Master Leonard, your Queen commands that you open the door at once!"

The old man who was the head scribe for the library opened the door, blinking at the frantic woman in front of him. "Your Majesty?"

"*A Treatise on Interfaith Government*... where is it? Who has it? I have to know!" She grasped the front of his robe and pulled the little man off the floor. "*A Treatise on Interfaith Government.* Tell me now!"

"Ahhh," he stammered. "A-a-a-rchbishop Augustine has it. He took it last week."

Without formality, she dropped the little man and turned to Master Solomon. "Do what you must, but you get me that book. Use whatever force is necessary."

Master Solomon and Ophelia hurried to the Archbishop's quarters, collecting several of the king's guardsmen along the way. Ophelia pushed Master Solomon away to beat on the door again, but he stopped her hand with surprising strength. "Allow *me,* this time," he said.

He knocked and within moments, the Archbishop, looking confused, opened the door to them. "Yes?" he asked. "What is it? Is something wrong with the King?"

"A book," Master Solomon said. "A book by Taliesin, the Merlin of Britain, is in your possession. The Queen requires it immediately."

The Archbishop looked shocked. "Master Solomon," he said. "You must know that I would never read material written by a dark sorcerer of Avalon." He nearly spat the words at the older man. "I have no such thing."

Ophelia moved forward, but Master Solomon stopped her. "Master Leonard is very certain that you collected the book from the library last week. By order of the Queen, I demand that you release it."

"I have no such.."

"GIVE ME THE BOOK!" Ophelia screamed, nearly knocking Augustine over as she lunged at him. The Archbishop's high-pitched shriek rang through the courtyard. Angrily, Ophelia pushed him aside and entered his quarters. They were immaculate, as she suspected they would be, and it took her little time to locate the book on a table near his bed. She pressed it to her leaking breasts, her breath jagged and labored. "Please," she prayed. "Please, please, please…"

She closed her eyes and opened the book upside down, allowing the pages to move freely. As she did so, the parchment fluttered to the ground. She picked it up, unfolded it, and calmly read the words written there. She put down the book on the table, nodded to Master Solomon, and looked gravely at the Archbishop. "It will not go unnoticed by myself nor the King," she said through clenched teeth, "that your willful deception may have cost us the life of the prince and heir to the throne."

He began to stammer out a response, but she held up one hand. "Do not speak to me," she said, "…ever again."

She pushed past the guardsmen and once she was out the door, picked up her skirts and began to run. She looked up at the sky and noticed the tracking of the moon. Less than an hour until midnight. She ran faster.

Chapter 39

By the time Ophelia got to the room in the castle where a year earlier she spun straw into gold, her adrenalin was waning and her energy was non-existent. Her legs felt like jelly and her entire body was shaking uncontrollably, much, she thought, as it had when she had given birth. The thought caused her to laugh and she realized that perhaps madness really was not all that far away for her.

As she neared the room, she heard the baby crying and pulled upon the last reserves of her strength to move even faster. She pushed open the door and rushed into the small anteroom. There, next to the spinning wheel, stood Ducky with the baby.

Blood streamed down Ophelia's legs, but she barely noticed. Her chest heaved in violent gasps and she spat out the words, "Give me my baby!"

"Oh Luv," Ducky cooed. "I didn't think you'd make it! So close to time now! Ohhh, you've brought me my new body all bedraggled and broken. No worry. A young, healthy body like that will rebound in no time. Then I will give pleasure to my King as he has never known and will rule this kingdom the way it ought to be done. He will be eating from my hand and from under my own skirts in no time."

"Give him to me," Ophelia said simply.

"Oh now, we had a deal, did we not? You took your time getting here and now here you are throwing demands around. Shall I assume you have failed?"

"Assume nothing about me, you heathen bitch."

"Oh my, you *are* in a mood, aren't you," she gloated. "Tell me, Ophelia. Tell me what you think you know before I begin walking your body around this castle."

Ophelia spoke loudly and clearly, "Demonia Belisama Margawse, I name you! Give me my baby and be gone from this place forever more."

Ducky got a startled expression on her face and her mouth began to work with no words coming out. Ophelia rushed forward and pulled the crying baby from her grasp. Ducky could not maintain her grip on the baby as her body began to tremble with the force of power running through her, much as Ophelia's had done minutes before. The trembling increased until the old woman's jaws were slamming against one another and she began to reel and pitch indiscriminately around the room, convulsions wracking her body.

Ophelia ran into the larger chamber of the room and with the baby firmly in her grasp, scurried onto the bed and huddled in the far corner, leaving a trail of blood behind her. "Demonia, Belisama Margawse," she chanted over and over. "Be gone. Be gone from this place and harm us no more."

As Ducky slammed her body into one wall and the next, into the dresser, into the bed frame, Ophelia continued to chant. She wanted to scream, but it came out a chant. "Demonia, Belisama Margawse…be gone. Be gone from this place and harm us no more. Be gone from this place and harm us no more."

"You BITCH!" Ducky seethed as she flew into the wall by the door, now leaving stains of greenish goo where she pitched and reeled and collided. "You devilish BITCH! Look at what you have done!" she shrieked.

"Demonia, Belisama Margawse…be gone. Be gone from this place and harm us no more."

As she careened through the rooms, Ducky's movements became even more forceful and erratic. She pitched wildly back into the anteroom and then…

…there was complete silence.

Breathing heavily, Ophelia got up off the bed and inched her way to the door of the anteroom. There was only a labored, barely perceptible creaking sound. She looked inside and saw Ducky's body impaled upon the spindle of the spinning wheel. The wheel was turning, creaking, turning, of its own accord. 'Round and 'round, it turned.

"On your fingers, through your fingers, around your fingers… gold flows through rock in veins, just like the blood in your body flows through you…the blood will make the gold stronger. Keep spinning, my sweet. Keep spinning."

Ducky's arms still twitched and waved madly in empty air. Her feet danced a little tattoo that would have sounded quaint had they been on the floor instead of suspended a hand's width above it. She watched as Ducky's body stopped moving and then began to contract into itself in an odd sort of condensation, emitting a foul, acrid smoke. She became smaller, her body mass pulling up onto the spindle until there was nothing but what looked to be a small strip of tanned hide. Nothing resembling a human at all remained on the spindle. The room smelt of sulfur and ozone as the wheel slowed to a stop.

Ophelia sank against the nearest wall and looked down at the stunned baby. He seemed healthy, but frightened. She held him close and felt tears sliding down her cheeks. She wiped them away with the heel of her hand, snuffled heavily, and thought, "Huh. So something *can* make me weep."

There was a commotion at the door and several people rushed into the room. She was unsure who all was there because her vision closed in on her with black invading from all sides. She pointed at the spinning wheel and said, "Burn it and what's on it." Then she knew no more.

Chapter 40

Ophelia awoke with a frightened gasp and immediately began shuffling through the blankets on the bed. "He's gone. Oh dear God in Heaven, he's gone," she cried.

"No!" Constantine said, holding her shoulders firmly. "No, Ophelia, look at me. He's here. He is safe."

"Safe?" she whispered, confused. "He's safe? He is here?"

"He is right as rain and right here!" Nuala smiled, bringing the small bundle to the bed. "Look at your fine son."

"Ohhh," Ophelia said weakly. She looked at Constantine who was beaming at her. "He's here." Her chin began to quiver and she was surprised when tears filled her eyes again.

"He's here," Constantine smiled. "And he is perfect. You did it, Queen Ophelia. While I slept through the madness like a coward, you went to battle and saved our baby. Everyone tells me that you were a fierce, warrior queen."

Ophelia chuckled. "Some fierce warrior queen, I can barely sit up."

"You have lost a tremendous amount of blood, Fee," Nuala said. You have not eaten for days and had not yet even recovered from birthing when you went through this trauma. Will you please stay in bed for a while now?"

She tucked her baby into the crook of her arm and offered him her nipple. He took it eagerly and she felt her milk release down into her breast at last with somewhere to go. Thankfully, her milk had not dried up while the baby was…missing. He gasped a little at the let down of milk and Constantine laughed. "Already he bites off more than he can chew. He will make a fine prince."

Their eyes met and she saw that his were also brimming with tears. She reached her hand up to cup his cheek and he kissed the palm. "Ophelia," he said, softly. "I am so, so very happy right now. Thank you."

All she could do was nod.

"Are my father and Falia still here?" she asked after a minute. "I have to thank Mills for giving us the information that would unlock the answer in my head."

"They had to return to the tavern," Constantine explained. "We will see them again soon if you wish. I understand there was some deception revealed while they were here. Are you…are you well with that?"

Ophelia's expression darkened. "I bear him no malice," she said, "but there is something I need to do and I suspect it will take you out of your own comfort."

"Name it," he said. "I will do anything you ask."

"Send to Avalon for The Merlin," she said. "I need to speak with him and if Archbishop Augustine says one harsh word against him, have him banished. I will tolerate no harm to him."

"Consider it done," he assured her.

"I am starving," she said.

"Good!" Nuala smiled. "Beth! Go get broth for the Queen!"

"And meat, cheese, and bread for the King," Constantine added.

"And meat, cheese, and bread for the King," she repeated.

"Oh, and wine for the Queen!" Ophelia said.

"And wine for three of us," she added and then sighed heavily. "After all these years of monotony, you two certainly know how to bring the world to life."

"I, for one, look forward to some quiet for a while," Constantine said. "But you know, we do have to give this young prince a name."

"Oh, it is Phillip," Ophelia said quickly. "Prince Phillip Henry Constantine Millhouse the First.

Constantine laughed and raised one eyebrow. "Millhouse?"

"Millhouse," Ophelia said.

"It is so ordered," he said. "We will have him christened in a few weeks and present him to the court then. For now…I want some time alone with my Queen and my son."

"It is so ordered," Nuala stood to leave.

"..and my aunt," he completed. She smiled and ruffled his hair as if the High King were a small child.

"Ophelia," she said, "You have certainly brought out the light in this one."

Beth brought in a tray loaded with food, even including some fruit and honeycakes in addition to what was requested.

"It looks like a feast," Ophelia said.

"Go slow and easy," Nuala cautioned. "Your body is not accustomed to eating."

Constantine caught Ophelia's eye and said seriously, "Someday, you will have to tell me everything that has happened. I am sure I do not know a tenth of what has befallen in my own castle, even when I was in court. In your time, when you are ready, my dear."

"I will," she said. "But truly, not today." She bit lustily into a honeycake and smiled up at him.

Chapter 41

"**Y**our Majesties," The Merlin said, bowing to Constantine and Ophelia in turn.

"I trust your reception was more gracious this visit than last," Ophelia said and was rewarded with a broad grin.

"It was and the accommodations are far more comfortable, My Queen."

"The last time we spoke, you said that there may come a time when you ask more from me than you did before."

"I did," The Merlin replied. "And I swore to you that it would never be more than you are willing to give. Am I to understand that the scrap of parchment I gave you came in handy?"

"Indeed," Ophelia said. "All you predicted came true. The paper meant more to me than life itself. In the course of using the paper, other information came to light."

"I see," The Merlin said. "Do you wish to share it?"

"May I ask how old you are?" she said.

"I am twenty and three," he answered, "Born on the Winter Solstice of that year."

The hairs went up on the back of Ophelia's neck as she remembered the times that Forrest had celebrated her birthing on each Winter Solstice, saying that Mills had told him it was so.

"Were you in fact raised as a fosterling in Lord Seaton's court near here, Lord Merlin?"

"I was," he said.

"And orphaned as a baby, before you were even born?"

"Yes," he said. "The prophecy that Taliesin wrote as The Merlin before me was that when he was reborn, it would be as a man born of no living woman and that I was."

Ophelia surveyed him critically. In the jail cell, she had not been able to see him well. Now, he was clean, well groomed, and finely attired. He was tall with broad shoulders and strong arms that were bare beneath his tunic and gold cloak. His hair was black as darkest night, falling loosely past his shoulders. His face was shaven and marked with blue woad in mysterious symbols that she did not understand. His skin was a reddish-brown color, much like mahogany, deeper even then her own olive complexion.

What drew her in were his eyes; almond-shape and dark, they matched her own and those of her son. "Are you my brother?" she asked without further pretense.

He laughed. "It is my belief that we are, in fact siblings. Closer than siblings even, as wombmates. May I be so bold as to hug the Queen?"

Constantine smiled and nodded. Ophelia stepped down from the throne and held her arms out to The Merlin, who walked into them and embraced her, even picking her up and twirling her around as he had done in the dungeon that night now almost a year gone by. She laughed and relished the familiarity of his closeness. Yes, yes indeed. She knew this man. She knew him as her own flesh and blood, the only flesh and blood that existed now for her other than her son and to him she owed the very life of her son and, as it turned out through her bartering of parley, her own life.

He kissed her fondly on the cheek. "Is it well with you, My Sister?"

She smiled at him and said, "It is well with me." She turned to Constantine. "My King, I ask to take leave to speak with my brother."

"Of course, My Dear," he smiled. "You know you have my blessings."

Her arm tucked into the crook of his elbow and each enjoying the closeness of the other, they walked to the court gardens. Constantine watched them leave and noticed how they both tilted their heads the same way and how perfectly matched were their paces. A part of him envied The Merlin for the closeness he had with Ophelia that no other could share. Most of him, however, was simply happy that she was happy. That was enough and more.

Chapter 41

“My name is Bran,” he said. “It is short for Brannon.”

“Such a continental name for one so exotic,” she observed. “May I call you by your name or are titles required between us?”

He laughed. “I will call you Ophelia and you will call me Bran,” he said. “We will leave the titles for the courtiers. My foster mother named me. She was Irish and quite a woman.”

“Was?” she asked.

“She died,” he said, “When I was very young. She was good to me, as was her son, Duncan. He taught me to be a farrier and a groom, but I followed my own path and went to study with the priests when I was twelve and left there two years past to go to Avalon.”

“It feels odd to me,” she said, “that we started the same, you and I, but you are someone as special as Taliesin reborn and I am so ordinary.”

“Oh, you are far from ordinary, Ophelia,” he said. “How else do you think a tavern wench could become High Queen? Why do you think you were not merely the only one who could defeat Ducky, but were, in fact, *the only one who could even see her*? Why,” his voice lowered and his tone became more intense, “do you think you could spin ordinary straw into gold and why do you think Augustine fears you as he does?”

His last words caused her to draw in a breath. “I could spin the straw into gold because of Ducky’s magic, not mine.”

“No,” he said. “Ducky knew you could do it. That is why she wanted your baby so much. She figured out who you were and knew that a child of your line and the Pendragon line would be powerful."

"But Ducky tried to take the babies of the other queens as well, not just my own" Ophelia pointed out.

"True, but that was before you arrived and she learned that you were the miller's daughter. Once she knew who you were and the lineage you carried, she was more determined than ever before."

"But I do not carry a lineage," she said. "You do, of many lives."

"And you carry my blood and your son does as well. Our mother was Marian, a priestess of Avalon, a healer, in fact. Her mother before her was Ninian, who was Lady of the Lake. Our mother was Beltane-gotten."

"Do you know who was our father? Were we too Beltane gotten?"

His face clouded a bit. "I can tell you, but it might complicate things for you a bit and you might wish you did not know."

"Well, now you have to tell me," she said.

"Very well," he looked at her solemnly. "Our father was Oswin, whose father was Mordred. Your husband killed our father in Londinium."

The breath went out of Ophelia. "I see." She thought for a moment. "Our grandfather killed Arthur, who was our own great-grandfather."

"Oh, Sister," Bran laughed, "It gets better than that, even. Ninian was Taliesin's daughter. I am my own great grandfather as well."

"That is wicked," Ophelia agreed. Her mind flashed back to the jest she had made in the tavern the night before her entire life flipped upside down. "*My mum was one of the faerie women from Avalon, priestess trained, she was. In fact, the Lady Morgan knew her personally and taught her the arts."*

"So" Bran continued, "because our grandfather was Mordred, that means our great grandmother was…"

"…The Lady Morgan…" she finished.

"…who was Lady of the Lake. She was born of the royal line of Avalon, and therefore, so are we. That means that your son is born of the same blood as Arthur in more ways than one. How do you know all of this Avalon history?" he asked.

She laughed. "Indirectly, you told me. I have read every book Taliesin ever wrote. In fact, it was *A Treatise on Interfaith Government* that held the parchment you gave me that saved my son." She was thoughtful for a moment, "What is it like," she asked, "being another person reborn?"

"It was hard," he said. "I always had voices talking in my head, memories that were not mine, and I could not sort them out. Father Francis, a mentor of mine, helped me with that."

"Father Francis?" she asked. "Of Seaton Abbey?"

"Yes," Bran said. "Do you know of him?"

"I know him well," Ophelia said. "He stayed in our home and taught me to read. Had he not done so, I would not have placed the parchment in the book and there is little guessing what would have happened to it." She paused thoughtfully, thinking of when he handed her the small scrap of parchment. "When I saw you in prison, you said nothing about any of this. Did you know then? You did! I remember now you called me 'Sister'."

"I did," he said, "but it was not yet time. All things happen in their time."

"That night, you told me that someday you might ask me for more, but that it would never be more than I was willing to give. What did you mean by that?"

"Your husband, I believe, is a good man," Bran said. She nodded in agreement. "Unfortunately, there are people around him, like Augustine, who are not good men."

"You must know," she interrupted, "That Augustine is no longer Archbishop. The King gave him the option of stepping down from his office or being publicly tried for…well, for a deception that nearly cost us the life of my son."

"I see," Bran said. "But Ophelia, you must know, he is relentless. Understand that no matter how long it takes, he will find his vengeance. He is a ruthless, dangerous man."

"I agree. I regret recusing myself from the decisions that were made regarding him on behalf of The Crown, but I did not trust myself to rule objectively. If I had my way, he would have been put to death."

"I understand," Bran said, "And what's done is done."

"And so, what is it that I can do for you?" Ophelia asked.

Bran looked pained as he said, "The priests of what they call the One True God have been torturing people of the Old Ways and have declared war on Avalon and on magic itself. Avalon is not only my home, but it is who I am. When you saw me in the dungeon, I was doing more than attempting to ally the kingdoms. I was trying to persuade kings and priests to assist me in eliminating the torture and to create an alliance with Avalon so that those of the Old Ways could be free to practice their faith just as the Christians are allowed to practice their own holy rites unhindered. We ask for no more than the same freedoms the Christians receive. We lived in harmony for many years in this land and could do so again, but not while people like Augustine are imprisoning and torturing people like me. You have the power to stop this, Ophelia."

Ophelia's mouth drew into a grim line. "Bran, already I feel love for you and a connectedness I have never felt before, but magic…I cannot support it."

"But it is what you are!" he said. "You are magic born and a priestess by right. Please, Ophelia. You cannot turn your back on your people. Both our mother and father were of the Goddess."

"I have no interest in denying my heritage," she said, "Although I will not willingly offer up that Mordred was my grandfather. I feel nothing for him or for some priestess who for whatever reason left Avalon with a full belly and found her way to Lord Seaton's barn to give birth to us. You are here in front of me now. You are real and I can feel our kinship. Bran, you must understand that magic very nearly took my son from me."

"And magic helped you to get him back," he countered.

"Without magic, I never would have had to deal with that hell in the first place," she insisted.

"Without magic," he pushed gently, "You never would have had your son to start with. Ophelia, you cannot unwind this from your life. It is there, encoded in your make up as deeply as your dark eyes and black hair. It is a part of you."

"No magic, not in Carmeliard. I cannot allow it."

"Good people are dying, Ophelia," he said. "Simple, good people are prevented from worshiping the Goddess in Her glory and are being tortured for refusing to bend the knee to the Christ. Their crops are put to torch so that they starve and their holy places are desecrated. Surely, you cannot accept that."

"No," she said. "I cannot and will not. What I will do is insist that the persecution ends. There will be no war against Avalon and Avalon can continue to live as they choose. In Carmeliard, however, there will be no magic allowed. Gwent is free to do as they so choose. Magic I do not want around me or my son."

"Well," he said, "I did promise that I would not ask you for more than you were willing to give, My Sister. If this is all you can give, then I will gladly accept it."

"For the past year," she said, "soldiers have been amassing on the shores near Avalon. Do I need to be concerned for the safety of my own borders?"

"No," he assured her. "That is for defensive measures only. The Glastonbury priests have become aggressive about broaching Avalon to wipe out the wise ones of the Old Ways who live there. The Priestesses and Druid Priests on that island are my family and of my closest friends. The attacks the righteous ones are committing in the name of the Christ are very personal to me. Ophelia, I have the full support of Rheged, Elmet, and Wales. Gwent, The Summer Country, and Cornwall refuse alliance. So long as there is no aggression against Avalon or the people who practice the Old Ways, there is no reason for any concern, nor shall there be. If the priests continue to persecute the people of the Goddess, there will be war in your land. It really is that simple."

"I give you my word that Carmeliard will not take action against those who practice the Old Ways. They honor their gods as they choose. The King himself is not over-fond of religion of any kind, so he will not tolerate the persecutions, nor will I. Whether you acknowledge it or not, Brother, magic is a threat and it can be wielded as a weapon just as easily as the swords and bows your soldiers carry. I have been at the business end of it and it was not pleasant. I will not have it put into the hands of irresponsible people in my kingdom."

"Anyone can take up a sword or a bow," he countered, "and they are deadly in the wrong hands. Will you outlaw those as well? Should we not strive more so to cultivate good and honorable people than to curtail practices and items that may or may not be used for evil as well as good? This stone," he picked up a rock from the garden, "can be used to kill a man. Should we outlaw it as well?"

"Magic is an act that must be learned and in being learned, it is subject to the intentions of both the teacher and the student. It is colored as it is created. A stone is a stone. It has no good or evil to it."

"I do apologize," he said. "I am dangerously close to breaking my promise of not asking for more than you are willing to give. I know that you have just experienced a trauma from the unethical use of magic by a disincarnate entity that apparently did wrong to your court long before you arrived there. I know this sways your thinking and I do understand why. Just know, precious Ophelia, that you cannot tear magic from your own blood. It is there and is your legacy and eventually, within you, there will come a time when it will no longer be denied. I will always honor what you choose, Sister, and I ask only that you honor my own choices."

"I know that you are a good man, Bran," she said. "I have no fear of you, with or without magic. It is magic in the hands of those with ill intent that frightens me. Perhaps that will change one day."

"Likewise," he said, "It is Christianity in the hands of those with ill intent that frightens me, and so shall we agree to be wary together?"

"Agreed,' she smiled. "Do you have a wife? Children? Is it for The Merlin of Britain to marry? I do not even know."

"I do!" he said excitedly and laughed a bit. "My wife is, in fact, Lillian, the Lady of the Lake. We have seven daughters."

Ophelia was visibly stunned. "Seven?"

"Born all at once, not long after I languished in your dungeon."

"That is…a lot to process!" she said, chuckling.

"For me as well," he said. "They are just over a year old now and walking. Their little hands are everywhere. They are…so busy…all the time."

Ophelia laughed. "Do you still travel? Surely the Merlin of Britain is an ambassador who is gone from Avalon a good bit."

"No," he said. "I rarely leave now and when I do, it is only for a few days like this. My wife…I have difficulty being away from her. She is my life. The girls…they are my life. They come first. It should be otherwise and my diplomatic duties should be more important, but that is not always the way it is. As the world moves forward, we all must adapt."

"Indeed," she said. "I cannot imagine that The Merlin of Britain was ever seen as a family man. I am glad you have someone who you love so much, Brother."

"And what about you, Ophelia? Are you happy?"

She smiled. "I am so happy," she said. "Especially now that I have found you." She reached and took his hand and together, they walked into the dining hall for the court's evening meal.

Later that night, she eased into bed with Constantine and nestled into his warm embrace. Phillip snored lightly, happily fed and tucked into his basket near their bedside. Ophelia was still uncomfortable with him being away from her and often would pull him into bed with her, slipping the child between them.

"Did you have a nice visit?" Constantine asked.

"I did. It was very informative."

"Do I want to know?" he asked, kissing her forehead.

"Not at all," she said, and slipped her hand around his warm, eager hardness.

Epilogue

Into the Darkness

A delicate balance between Avalon and the rest of Britain held true for many years. Ophelia was as good as her word and while she continued to reject magic both for herself and in Carmeliard, she worked aggressively with Constantine to stop the persecution of those in Britain who practiced the Old Ways.

There was tremendous resistance, primarily from the Christian priests, who vowed to extinguish all of the sorcerers, priestesses, Druids, and Pagans who refused to follow and conform to the new religion forced upon Britain. Carmeliard even supplied soldiers to protect Avalon's borders to assist in keeping the peace and provided supplies to the soldiers from other kingdoms who protected the shore lands.

Cornwall and The Summer Country also resisted, but King Marcus from Cornwall was Regent to Constantine, and as such acquiesced to the King's wishes and ended the persecutions in his kingdom as well. King Lucius in The Summer Country, bane to be the only lesser king in opposition to The Crown, also bent the knee and ended persecutions in his country.

For many years, although the atmosphere was tense in Britain, it was safe for people of all faiths to follow their own spiritual paths as they desired as, according to the tenets of Avalon, "it harmed none." The villages near Avalon prospered with the abundance of the harvests that Avalon supplemented and they shared their wealth with the soldiers and with other villages. Avalon itself was tranquil as well. Within a year, so confident was the Council of Elders on Avalon in the newly established security that the soldiers sent to defend the island were returned to their homelands.

For almost two decades, there was relative peace in the land.

Then, on a dark and cold Winter morning, some sixteen years after she first spun straw into gold, Ophelia woke up to find that Constantine had died peacefully in his sleep beside her. He did not die at the hand of an enemy as did his father and not at the will of his vices and excesses, as did his brother. He died of natural causes as a happy man of advanced age.

The Queen did what she always did: she took care of business. Nuala, Master Solomon, Master Druston, her father, and Falia were all long dead by this time. Many of those who served on the Council of Advisors were new, younger men who were bold with their intentions and ideas. Most were heavily invested in Christianity and the new Archbishop, while showing deference to Ophelia, quite obviously detested her.

"What was it about Archbishops?" Ophelia had wondered. *"Why must they be so hateful and angry?"*

Ophelia had fought tooth and nail to keep the promises she made to Bran years before. Constantine stood by her as her staunchest supporter in this and together, they stayed the hand of the church and the new wave of lesser kings who saw the intricate workings of the Christian church and the government of British lands as one and the same.

Constantine lay in state for three days and Ophelia knew he would have been moved by all who came to pay their respects to him, a king who never wanted to be king and who never felt worthy of the throne. In the end, many and more loved him. Although he was no King Arthur and had not aggressively fought back the Saxons from the land, he did stop the killings of the lesser kings and ended the persecutions of those of the Old Ways. There were those who spoke behind their hands about how Queen Ophelia was the real power behind the throne and that Constantine was no more than a figurehead. Anyone who mattered, however, cared not.

On the same day that Constantine was entombed with honor, Phillip was crowned King and Ophelia was made his Regent until his eighteenth birthday. Bran and Lillian attended both the funeral and the coronation, lending their support to Ophelia. Many felt it was improper for those of the so-called Devil Island to sit in such power with the Queen, but in this instance, it was Ophelia who cared not at all.

After Constantine died, slowly but surely, the lesser kings began to work more independently of Carmeliard once again, much as they had done when Constantine focused on his crusades against the Sons of Mordred. As the persecution of non-Christmas began to resurface, Bran left Avalon to negotiate alliances with the kingdoms. Although all acknowledged him as The Merlin of Britain and his wisdom well established in the land, they refused him audience. His life was not in danger this time, but neither was he humored. By the time his negotiations ended, only Carmeliard and Cornwall remained in support of Avalon and those bonds were tenuous at best.

Ophelia and Phillip traveled with Bran on several journeys to appeal to the lesser kings. Although agreeing to adhere to the rule and laws of King Phillip when in his presence, it came to be that as soon as he left their kingdoms, the lesser kings followed the will of the persistent and ever-present priests rather than a boy king and his mother who were out of sight and out of mind. Raids were once more conducted on those who lit the balefires for the old sabbats and villagers known to work magic were again imprisoned.

Ophelia and Phillip met with the Council of Advisors daily to attempt to draw together what was falling apart around them. The new advisors blamed the tolerant attitude Constantine and Ophelia had shown to the non-Christians for the increase in Saxon attacks, saying it was God's vengeance on Britain for straying from a singularly Christian nation. Ophelia's head hurt from repeatedly pointing out the obvious: that it only made sense that when a country was vulnerable from a king's death that those greedy for more land would become more aggressive.

The priests countered that during the reign of Arthur, the country had known peace only because Arthur was a Christian king and ruled Christian lands. She argued that Arthur had sworn to defend Avalon and then died in defeat and ruin after he foreswore his vows. Most often, she felt more of an orator than a queen. So much attention did they place on the campaign to wipe out those who practiced the Old Ways and force all under British rule to bend the knee to the Christian God that Ophelia felt that they blatantly overlooked the fact that their own civil war was killing as many people as the Saxons ever did.

Every day she felt more as if she fought a losing battle. Although Augustine had not served as Archbishop for many years, after Constantine's death, he managed to work his voice into the ear of the advisors and his presence seemed to become more prominent with each passing day. He was, in the parlance of his own faith, her cross to bear. How could it be so that so many good people had died while his ancient, angry old face still stared down at her from across the Council Hall?

It came to the point that for the first time in her entire life, she dreaded opening her eyes in the morning. She would first look to the empty side of the bed her husband had lain so many times beside her, where he had smiled at her so fondly, where they had oh-so-carefully made their baby Phillip.

No other babies had come to them; not even a suspicion that she might be breeding. Constantine never complained and instead reveled in their son, insisting that he never expected to have even one heir, much less one as splendid as this one.

In all their years together, Constantine had never so much as had a cross word for her, not one reprimand, not one stern look. He enveloped her with love almost from the first moment they met. Up until the day he died, he held her hand, almost delicately as though afraid he would hurt her. He kissed her fondly and often in front of others and more passionately and urgently in private, even though they had been together for such a long time. He told her how beautiful he found her and how much he admired and respected her. Such adoration and loyalty she never imagined she would have in her life.

To her memory, there had never been a single instance where he had opposed her in matters of state, always supporting and welcoming her opinion, regardless of how unpopular it may have been with the other advisors. Under their rulership, the lesser kingdoms and Britain overall had prospered in a way it had not done since the Romans had ruled, just as Constantine had predicted.

Now, the king was dead and the rats were scurrying. Their faith in young Phillip diminished quickly from the smear campaign the priests enacted against her for her defense of Avalon. Once again, magic was compromising her when she herself in no way practiced. She could not condone torture and persecution of anyone for matters of faith. Who cared what gods a person called on to fortify their spirit? Why was it the business of one to dictate the worship of another and why should leaders insist upon only one faith? Her brother always insisted that all gods were one anyway. No, the church held sway because the church was growing in financial abundance. The more of the masses that converted to Christianity, the greater their larders grew with tithing and when one had means, one had power.

Ophelia could clearly see the gradual influx of zealotry in those who were selected as advisors. As the older wise ones died out, those who had been more tolerant of harmonious living between those of different faiths were replaced by the narrow-minded and intolerant pinch-faced tyrants who single-mindedly focused on converting the country to one faith that they overlooked the more obvious and invasive threat of the Saxons.

Ophelia had little to no experience with battle and frankly, neither did anyone she knew. Other than the crusade against the Sons of Mordred, which had largely happened before Ophelia's time as a queen, there had been little warfare in the past two decades save for the conflict between Pagans and Priests. The Saxons had temporarily quelled their attacks on British lands during

Constantine's reign with Ophelia when the kingdoms were united, but once his death and the relative instability of the country became known, the sieges and rampages began again with earnest. Those who best knew how to fight from horseback and who were champion warriors were no more. There had been no need for aggressive battlefield warriors and as such, it was largely a lost art. The extent of battle for nearly twenty years, almost the entire lifespan of the average knight, had been limited to minor skirmishes that were quickly settled. No sitting knights had been involved in aggressive battle.

Ophelia refused the luxury of women attendants who would dress her as though she were an infant, so each day, she went about her own toiletries and dressing, then braced for a battle of words as she went to engage the council. Some days, she felt so weary that she wished she could be like other queens and hide herself away in the castle great rooms, weaving, spinning, and doing fine stitching, oblivious to the matters of state and government.

As she had done many times, she wished that Phillip had a proper teacher who could mold him into the king that the country so desperately needed him to be. Less than a century before, great leaders actively conspired to unite the bloodlines of Avalon and the Pendragons to create a leader that would save the nation. That very blood ran in her son, but without proper guidance, there was no hope he could do more than stave off the inevitable downfall of the country. What civil war did not destroy, the Saxons would. The futility of what they tried to do clung to her spirit like a wet cloak, dampening her every day.

On what would be her last day as Queen Regent, Ophelia's heart was heavy when she made her way across the courtyard to the daily meeting with the Council of Advisors for another session of arguments and postulating. She came from a fine breakfast with Phillip, who had been in good spirits. It was a bright point in a day that was otherwise set to be challenging at best and maddening at worst.

After they broke their fast together, Ophelia excused herself to check on Clara, one of her ladies who had not been feeling well the day before. She found her abed, weak and gaunt looking. For all of her flaxen beauty, Clara had never married. She still had her razor-sharp wit and love of gossip, so Opelia enjoyed spending time with her. Today, however, although she was glad to see Ophelia, Clara had little energy for chatting.

"I fear my time is upon me, My Dear Queen," she said.

"Oh Clara, you are always so given to the dramatic. You will be up and around in no time."

"We have come far, you and I, haven't we?" Clara smiled. "It seems just yesterday that I was scraping away at those mad eyebrows of yours."

Ophelia smiled. "Just yesterday and yet a lifetime ago and now here we are, two old crones trying to find what to do with ourselves."

"Speak for yourself," Clara said. "I am only nine and thirty. You are older even than I."

"Just barely, my friend. Shall I send 'round the court physician? He is quite kind on the eyes."

Clara smiled weakly. "He is, isn't he? You can send him if you like, but he is overly pious for my tastes. He forever wishes to pray for me in his course of healing. I have oft told him that I pray for him as well, just not quite in the same fashion."

"Your wit is still sharp, dearest," Ophelia smiled. I will send him to you and you can both pray in the form that suits you best. You could do worse than to have him lay hands on you."

Clara shrugged. "Perhaps I should feign a cough for a complete chest examination." She practiced a weak clearing of her throat and even that small exertion obviously wearied her.

Ophelia leaned over and hugged her friend gently, kissing her forehead. "You have a fever. I will send fresh water to you as well. Do you feel chilled? Do you want warm bricks at your feet?"

"No," Clara said miserably. "I just want to sleep. I have no strength at all. It is as though my spirit has left me."

"Then sleep you shall," Ophelia said. "I will put one of the young girls to tend to you and you are to want for nothing. I will send you the court physician and some clean water and good broth. Take in liquids until you feel stronger."

As she turned to go, Clara caught her hand. "Be careful, Queen Ophelia," she said softly. "I fear there are ill times at hand."

Ophelia smiled, "I will take care."

Clara's words rang in her mind as she arranged for the woman's care and then made her way to the council hall. Philip would already be there, wondering what had taken her so long. She thought about the new king in Gwent, Caradoc, who had only taken power shortly before the King had died. He was aggressive and confident, overly eager to her mind, and something about him made her entirely uncomfortable. After Constantine died, Caradoc insinuated himself into a kingship on Gwent where no king had previously held court. He had the backing of several members of the Counsel of Advisors. She knew Augustine made frequent trips to Gwent to meet with the king and always returned filled with renewed anger toward her. Augustine seemed to be the primary force that manipulated Caradoc onto the throne through his influence with the new advisors. She supposed that fact alone was a good part of what made her suspicious of the man.

Her mind was so lost in thought when she pushed open the door to the Council Hall that it took her several minutes to register what was going on and what she was seeing. People filled the room, which itself was unusual, and not just people, but soldiers. None of them she could see was of the King's Guard and oddly, in fact, none of the King's Guard was present.

"Where is the King's Guard?" Ophelia asked, her eyes falling to Phillip, who was standing at the head of the council table with his arms behind his back. "Phillip, what is going on?" She lost the formality of "My Son" or "My King" in her startlement and instead addressed him by name.

"The Guard has been relieved of duty for the time being, My Lady," Master Lionel said. She noted that he looked uncomfortable and pointedly avoided the use of the usual title of "'My Queen.'"

She saw that many of the council members were noticeably absent. Archbishop Gregoras stepped forward and Augustine slipped in beside him as though the two were conjoined at the hip. "Lady Ophelia," the Archbishop intoned, "You are hereby charged with the crime of high treason against the throne of King Constantine."

"High treason?" she said, confused. "That is absurd!"

"Madam, did you or did you not release from our confines a prisoner who was deemed an enemy of the state by the court?"

Ophelia felt herself flush. "Are you serious?"

"Archbishop Augustine, your testimony declared that while High Queen, Lady Ophelia conspired against the throne and against the One True God and released a known sorcerer and traitor after he had been rightfully apprehended. Is this true?"

It was obvious that Augustine could barely contain his glee. Clearly, he had waited long for this moment and wished to enjoy it to the fullest. "It is," he loudly intoned, "So help me God. I rightful confined the man claiming to be the Merlin of Britain to await the King's justice upon his return. She slipped in the dark of night into the confinements below and forced a king's guardsman to open the cell and release the prisoner."

"And is Lady Ophelia known to have familial connection to the evil isle of Avalon?"

"She is," Augustine continued. "In fact, the prisoner that she released who the Druids have named The Merlin Reborn is, in fact, her birth brother. She is known not only to frequent his company but has taken his advisement in matters of state and aggressively and flagrantly influenced this council to his favor. No doubt she bewitched the wise men on the council and even our king into doing her will and that of her brother and the very devil himself."

"This is ridiculous," she protested. "Of course, I see my brother and I never influenced this council using magic. The men who came before you saw the wisdom in ending torture and unifying our kingdoms."

"Madam," Archbishop Gregoras said, "Did you or did you not obtain the position of High Queen by way of magic?"

"I obtained the position of High Queen because the King asked me to marry him!" Frantically, she looked around for any sign of support from the council members present and found none.

"Madam," Augustine said, smoothly taking over the questioning from Gregoras, "Did or did not the King ask you to become High Queen because of an act of magic?"

"I will not answer to you. If anyone here is treasonous it is you. You were removed from office for lying to the Queen and jeopardizing the prince's life. You have no cause to address me."

Gregoras cleared his throat, "Then you will address me, My Lady. Did or did not the King ask you to become High Queen because of an act of magic?"

"Among other reasons…yes." She intentionally did not offer superfluous information, but she was not going to lie to them.

"And did you or did you not order the prisoner, the Merlin of Britain, released from his cell?"

"I held the King's proxy and yes, I did. The King had, in fact, given me authority to dismiss Archbishop Augustine if he came into conflict, but I refrained from doing so."

"I am certain the country benefitted from your considerable restraint if not your wisdom in prisoner management," Gregoras said grimly. "And is indeed, the man who fathered you not Oswin, son of Mordred, the slayer of King Arthur and enemy of The Crown?"

Ophelia was stunned. How could he possibly know this? She had told no one.

"Lady Ophelia," Augustine said almost gently, his eyes twinkling, "Answer the question."

"My father is the miller in the village of Seaton," she said quietly.

Gregoras sighed heavily. "Is the man who fathered you not Oswin, son of Mordred, the slayer of Arthur, High King of Britain?"

"I never knew any father other than Mills," she said honestly. She looked at her son. "Phillip, are you going to allow this to happen?"

His eyes showed both fear and helplessness. "Mother, are these allegations true?"

"They are, but the context has been distorted dramatically."

"Madam and the esteemed members of the Advisory Council," Gregoras continued, "It is known that a boy who is not yet a man cannot act as High King without a Regent and this woman stands accused of High Treason…"

"Where is the rest of the Council?" Ophelia interrupted. "You cannot make a summary ruling without the full consent of the council."

Augustine cleared his throat and spoke. "The remaining members of the Advisory Council are unable to be here and send their proxies with attending members."

"Mother…" Phillip stood tall and proud but looked as though he might weep at any moment. He had mentioned nothing of this at breakfast. Had he known?

Surely not! She noticed that he held his hands behind his back still and saw with a shock that *they were tied there.*

"Madam, it is the decision of this council that you will be removed from the status of Regent and sentenced to life in prison in grateful consideration of the years you have provided in service of The Crown." Gregoras pronounced sentence with the aplomb of a man who had just announced that the races were about to begin.

"Life in prison?" she gasped. "Life in *prison?*"

"All who agree?" A chorus of "Aye" rang through the hall.

"All opposed?"

"I am opposed!" she said angrily.

"As rightful King, I object," Phillip said.

"The sentence is passed," Gregoras clapped his voting stone into the table in final herald.

"But Phillip is King," she said. "His word is absolute!"

"Not until he is an adult," Augustine said, "and he has no Regent to speak for him."

"Is there no one here who will act as his Regent?" she asked.

Augustine laughed. "Dear woman, they were many here who would gladly act as his Regent, but none would speak in your favor. Am I correct?"

There was murmuring in the room, but no one stepped forward. Ophelia suddenly felt as though a heavy weight were crushing her chest. "Phillip is the rightfully born King, descended from the Pendragon blood!"

Master Menas, a quiet man who rarely spoke, said, "Madam, kings are overthrown regularly in Britain, especially in these strife-filled times."

"Overthrown?" Ophelia said, not believing her ears. "Is that what this is?"

Archbishop Gregoras said, "King Tiberius of Cornwall has graciously agreed to allow you to be housed in Tintagel out of respect for Cornwall being King Constantine's homeland. You may choose to go there for the rest of your days and remain within the walls of Tintagel or you may remain here and be imprisoned as a traitor and a sorceress. So be it."

Once again, Ophelia searched the room for any sign of support, for any kindness, for any softening expression. Phillip said nothing and she realized in a flash that it was because she had never taught him what to do in this situation. How could she have imagined he could be High King with no one qualified to teach him how to do it? How do you teach a king how to be overthrown when no High King has been overthrown in over a century, not since Uther Pendragon overthrew King Vortigern?

"And what of my son and your rightful High King?" she asked.

"Phillip," Augustine said, weighing his words heavily and avoiding the use of any titles. "You may remain here and act as King with me serving as your Regent or you may go to Tintagel with your mother and be banished from Carmeliard for all of time. The only other choice you have is the one offered to your witch mother, and that is to remain here and be imprisoned."

"Of what crime am I charged and how have I failed the Crown?" he asked solemnly.

"Phillip, you supported your mother in the ongoing rebuke of our Lord and Savior Jesus Christ and actively opposed the advancement of this country as a Christian nation. You knowingly cavorted with sorcerers, Druids, Heathens, and Witches and you interfered with this council's ability to effectively govern Britain as a Christian land *and all of this before you have even fully taken the crown.* No charges are being brought against you formally as they are your mother, but know this, you will not be king without me as your Regent."

Ophelia watched with horror as Phillip met and held Augustine's harsh gaze. Unflinching and fierce, she knew with both pride and fear that it was her own tenacity welling up inside of him and not his father's timidity. Or perhaps it was the anger Constantine had channeled into the defeat of the Sons of Mordred that Phillip tapped into in that moment. Regardless, Phillip's eyes turn to glistening hatred and she knew her son was, in that moment, being forever. *"No,"* she thought. *"Please do not harm him. Please do not harm my baby. He is such a good boy. Please."*

His eyes were like dark embers with fury glowing behind them. "Augustine," he said, sounding older than his years. "I will reign in lowest level of Hell with Lucifer himself as my Regent before I will spend a moment on your mummery of a throne with you breathing your words of pious filth into my ear. My mother has given her entire adult life to this court and has ruled as a good and just leader. If she used my father's proxy and released a man from prison, it was because it was in the greatest good of this country and no other reason. My only regret is that she did not use her proxy to rid the world of vermin like yourself. She has more good sense than the lot of you combined and while you are busy genuflecting to one another and torturing the good people of this land, of *my land,* it will serve you right when the Saxons take you unaware and rape your sisters and enslave you all.

"I feel my vomit rise that men who have been put into such position of esteem and good faith by my own father would stoop to such underhanded and low-brow behavior to gain control of a throne to serve your own angry God and to force others to do so against their will. A true God does not need to torture people into His worship. He will command their adoration by his goodness and mercy, not by the sword of ego. It will be that God, the *true* God, who will smite you and one day take you to your knees but in all His mercy, he will wait until I have had my moment to destroy each of you."

With his hands still bound behind him, he jerked his head violently and the golden circlet that he wore as a crown, one that had been his father's before him, flew off his head and bounced onto the floor. "Take it! Take it, you foul, cur dogs and fight over it as you will like the simple beasts you are." He spat in the direction of the crown. "If I do so come from the royal line of Avalon through Morgan, know now that I curse you all, every one, and call the vengeance of the Goddess scorned onto each of you and your houses. Be damned. Be damned every one of you."

There was complete silence in the Council Hall. Ophelia could not keep her jaw closed, stunned not only by the vitriol of his words and the terminology which she had no idea he knew, but because like his father before him, it was the largest number of words she had ever heard him put together at one time.

Phillip stood taller and where a young boy had been previously, now there was a man grown, a very angry man. For the first time in his life, Phillip – so like his father, seemed formidable and regal. His eyes blazed and his posture was defiant. *"They are going to kill him,"* Ophelia thought to herself. *"Right here, right now, I will watch my son die before me."*

"Phillip of the Pendragon, you are banished from this kingdom," Gregoras said. "You will depart with your mother and return here no more. May God have mercy upon your soul, son."

"I am no son of yours and by all that is sacred, I vow that you *will* see me again," Phillip promised. "You will see me again and my wrath will be upon you. Mine will, in fact, be the last face you see before you claim your well-earned Heavenly reward."

"Take them away," Gregoras said, and waved his hand dismissively.

Ophelia thought the soldiers would take them directly to the dungeon, but instead, they were marched through the courtyard and castle and each taken to their chambers. Soldiers brought trunks for each of them and they were allowed no contact with one another or anyone else until their departure the following morning. They were allowed no goodbyes and were given no food or water beyond what was already in their rooms.

It was in Ophelia's defiant nature to leave with only the simplest of dress, similar to what she had arrived in all those years ago and take nothing of her own possessions. *No, she told herself. I am the Queen Regent with or without their endorsement and I shall present as one."* Carefully, she packed every item she owned and asked for and received even more trunks so that when she left the next day, there was not so much as a thread or crumb left in the room.

She asked for two of her favorite servants to attend to her and that they be granted the option to travel with her to Tintagel if they so chose. These requests were denied to her. She asked to ride one of her own horses and was denied this as well. The convoy would transport her and Phillip in a guarded litter. Either of them on horseback would make escape too easy.

Phillip was already in the litter when the armed guards assisted her into it before sunrise the following morning. It would take days to ride to Cornwall, especially at a litter's pace, and she dreaded the idea of containment in such close quarters. She was grateful that it was a cool Spring, so at least she would not be sweltering. She could open the curtains of the litter, let in the fresh air, and perhaps even feel the sun on her skin.

He had been beaten...badly. She thought to herself that his father had not looked this wounded when he had returned home from being blooded in battle and had a warhorse thrash about on top of him.

"Are you spitting blood?" she whispered?

"Only from my loose teeth," he said thickly, his words slurred through swollen lips.

"None from your lungs?"

"No."

"None when you pass urine?"

"No."

"Can you breathe well?"

"My nose is broken, I believe, but air passes."

"Can you walk?"

He laughed a little and then winced at the pain it caused. "Barely. I do not believe any major bones are broken. My body has argued that I should have curbed my tongue yesterday, but my pride insists that I did not say enough."

"Where did you learn to speak that way, my son?" Ophelia asked. "Surely you knew they would kill you for it."

"Uncle Bran taught me," he said simply. "And no, I knew they would not kill me. I am the true King, Mother, and nothing will ever change that; certainly not this court of jesters. I was born for this and if what I heard from them is true, that I am not only Pendragon, but also great grandson to Mordred the Terrible, then that means I am of not one, but *two* royal lines. When I say that I will destroy them for what they have done to you, my good Mother, it is not ego that speaks, but birthright. You are royalty twice over, both chosen and by birth. I *will* be your champion and these jackals will rue the moment they ever crossed me."

The events of the previous day, in particular his words, ran through her mind like a litany. Initially, she had considered his defiance the day before had been purely posturing to the circumstances. Now, she realized with tremendous clarity that something at the same time awesome and furious had awakened in her son. "What are you going to do, Phillip?"

His answer was immediate. "I am going to spend a good amount of time in Tintagel figuring out exactly that," he said. She felt he would have clenched his teeth but for the pain it would cause. "I am going to find a way to confer with Uncle Bran and then I will teach those traitors to never let the true King survive when you stage a mighty coup." He laughed again and looked away from her. She could see a single tear sliding down his cheek. "What were they thinking, Mother, letting me live anyway?" His voice was so sorrowful that she feared her heart might break. "See?" he said, "It is obvious they have no idea how to run a kingdom."

The litter lurched forward as the horses drew out of the courtyard. Ophelia looked out onto her kingdom for what she presumed well would be the last time and watched the scenes of ordinary life pass by the open windows of the litter.

Deadlocked

"**N**o!" Lillian said firmly. "Absolutely not."

The Arch Druids and High Priestesses looked pitifully at Bran who looked back at them with equal helplessness.

"Do something!" their silent expressions said.

"You know how she gets when she's like this!" his own expression answered back.

"Will you stop talking about me as if I were not in the room?" Lillian demanded, although no one except her had spoken in some time.

"Without Ophelia and Phillip on the high throne, Avalon and the people of the Old Ways are in serious jeopardy," Bran said. "That is a fact that cannot be denied and even if we turn our backs on those who have walked the path for so very long, that does not change the assurance that the war will not only come to our door, but through it and into Avalon. We must act and act quickly."

"We are not warriors!" Lillian protested. "…and our daughters are especially not warriors. I cannot be a party to sending them out into a world that they do not know that is hostile toward magic. How can you even imagine such a thing?"

"My Lady," Danu said, "I have lived longer than anyone sitting at this table and I have seen the ravages of war as has none other here. The mistakes made by our forbearers that you have studied in sacred writ they made before my very eyes. Ego and faithlessness created their destinies. Do not make that same error. It is ours to learn

315 | P a g e

from the mistakes of the leaders gone before us; not to repeat them."

Lillian closed her eyes and tried to still the panic that pounded in her head. "Mother, do you not think I know this? In ways no one at this table understands? *I was the one who made many of those errors!* In past memories known to me, *I* manipulated lives by enforcing my own will over that of the Goddess. *I* played at Deity by attempting to infiltrate magic into a world unwelcoming of it. You dare to use my own missteps in argument against me when none knows better than I of the consequences?"

"Lillian!" Bran said sternly. "I realize you are upset, but *do not* reprimand our elders and advisors as if they are children! I will not allow it, wife or no. I like this situation no better than do you and how dare *you* to say that you know better than any other at this table for *I* sit at this table and *I too* have memories of mistakes past. Yes, we must be wiser and have greater faith in where the Goddess leads us than did our predecessors. We must grow and learn from the ego-based, grievous errors of the past, especially our own."

Lillian was stunned to silence by his rebuke.

"My Lady, my wife, my dearest love, do you not think this idea pains me as well? Still, we must look at the evidence before us. Did you not confide to me of your vision at the well when you were carrying our daughters? That they would be the salvation of the Goddess Herself? Can we deny the miracle that we created *seven* daughters when there are *seven* remaining kingdoms of Britain? We have raised these girls, all of us here have done so, to be wise and fearless and their wits, their reflexes, their magical abilities are without equal, even from ourselves.

They learned swordsmanship and battle skills from the highest and best masters of weaponry so that they are likely better trained than the very soldiers of the court! It is as though their lives prepared them for this task with it unbeknownst to us why until now. *Think* with your head and with your spirit, Lillian, and set your heart and your mother's womb aside for one moment. See the path that is before us, I beg of you."

Lord Baric, the new Arch Druid, a very solemn and reflective man, said, "Lord Merlin, Lady Lillian, one of the greatest wisdoms that has evolved from experiences of the past is that if an organism does not grow, does not learn, and does not evolve, it is dead. It is my belief, and I hope others here share this notion, that this concept applies to matters of spirit as well as matters of state. Our faith and our political standing have both changed considerably in the past many years. This is only "bad" or "good" when viewed through our own experiences and emotional filters. The idea that Taliesin promoted, for instance, that 'all Gods are one God'…that is a new concept to us, but we endorse it because its truth is felt in our own spirits.

"We are still here. We are still strong, though in ways different from before. The false Merlin who succeeded Taliesin knew this, although he applied it wrongly when he attempted to give the holy regalia to the priests for their own ceremonies. He underestimated the power of the regalia and it cost him his life and threw the title of Merlin into scandal until you reclaimed it. Still, the concept is viable and strong.

"I was a young man when your beautiful daughters were born and there has been no brighter blessing given to Avalon during my life time, I am quite certain. We all love these beautiful young priestesses as if they were our own daughters and sisters and not one of us would ever wish to put them into harm's way.

"Avalon has evolved, as is evidenced by the fact that The Merlin of Britain and The Lady of the Lake have joined in marriage and have a family. This has never happened in our known history. As such, our leaders of Avalon have rarely had family matters to consider regarding politics, yet here we are, working with all of the consequences of our own ability to adapt.

"In the two of you, we have the unique merger of centuries of genuine historical memories. This gives us an unprecedented and unparalleled gift of having the wisdom of the ages at our access and for our usage. As Lord Merlin has said, we must be careful to allow that wisdom to flow cleanly through us to reveal the direction the Goddess has chosen for us, whatever that may be, and not have it redirected by ego, fear, or doubt.

"One of the greatest strengths we have on Avalon at this time is not only the joining of our two leaders, but also what has grown of the relative peace we have enjoyed for decades now. This has allowed us all to focus on matters of magic rather than matters of state. While our political power has dwindled, our magical power has grown beyond calculation. My observation is that the strong focus we have invested for all these years has caused our magic to become a formidable force in and of itself. Our advantage is that the outside world does not know this. We have lived an isolated life for many years and I would hazard a guess that perhaps only one in ten or even one in twenty of those living on Avalon today have ever stepped foot off of its sacred shore.

"When we consider the events that have brought us to this table, it is breathtaking. A young man who was orphaned and raised as a fosterling is the Merlin Reborn. This happens around the same time that the Lady of the Lake is reborn to us here on Avalon and in their joining, these seven beautiful daughters are created. A simple miller's daughter becomes High Queen through an act of magic and is found to be the twin sister of our own Lord Merlin. None of the girls have been called to the Beltane fires despite being well of an age to do so. Does all this not seem pre-ordained?

"In the past, our leaders schemed and plotted and manipulated the lives of others to achieve the goal that was given unto us with no effort at all on our part: the merging of the two royals lines in Phillip and arguably the strongest leadership Avalon has ever known. Now I must ask this honored assembly, does this not seem to be leading us in a definitive direction? We cannot believe that these miracles happened for no reason and now that Queen Ophelia and King Phillip are no longer positioned to protect us, does it not make sense to use the power that we developed during our time of protection to bring the magic back to Britain and put Phillip back in power? They protected us for all these years and allowed us to grow in strength. Now it is our turn to do the heavy lifting."

A wave of murmuring came over the table and even Lillian found difficulty in arguing his points. She drew in a breath and rubbed her aching temples as he continued.

"I will belabor this point no further, but this I do ask. If you do not favor the advice of this council, Lady

Lillian and Lord Merlin, would you accept the word of the Goddess in this matter?"

Lillian looked confused. "Of course, I would," she said.

"Then," Lord Beric said, "Allow us to adjourn this meeting for the day while the two of you go to the Sacred Well and await Her word. There is little more that can be said here and we are teetering on the slippery edge of argument versus debate, which will do none of us good. We are a holy and sacred people. Let us call Her word into command rather than arguing our own."

"Agreed," Bran said. "Lillian?"

"I agree," she said reluctantly. "My Druids and Priestesses?"

"Agreed," the voices carried throughout the hall and then were silent as though all were afraid to move beyond the table and know what came next. Lillian broke the spell and pushed back her own chair. Arm in arm, she and Bran left the great hall and went back to the bungalow to prepare for their stay at the well.

At the Well of the Goddess

Ｎone knew how Lillian had winced inside when Lord Beric mentioned going to the well to hear the words of the Goddess. She had fought off this urge since the idea of sending the girls into the world as secret ambassadors of the Goddess had first come up a week ago. She knew well that she was the only impetus to this idea and she also knew that none would move forward with the idea without her endorsement. There was much and more that she knew, such as the fact that they were right; she was allowing her emotions to rule instead of her head. She knew that Bran was just as reluctant to let the girls embark upon this odious and dangerous task as was she, but that he was being the greater leader in putting his fears aside.

She knew they were both sick with worry over Ophelia and Phillip, who claimed they were being treated well at Tintagel, but were allowed no visitors. They could exchange handwritten messages, but others censored all correspondence between each passing and letters sometimes arrived with words or sentences inked out so that they were unreadable. Both Lillian and Bran were able to read beyond the words they did see to the true meaning and know that it was true that while their loved ones were in no immediate danger, they were prisoners in the great fortress, much as Ygraine had been all those years ago while Gorlois rebelled against Uther.

She knew that the news from Carmeliard was not good. The priests were wielding tremendous power and taxation on the lesser kings had increased more than twenty-fold to support the rise of the Christian church in Britain.

She knew that Saxons were broadening their borders with renewed aggression and brutality, killing or enslaving all of the Britons in the villages they invaded. The forceful movement of the Saxons, the Angles, and the Jutes had reduced Britain by more than half. Lothian had fallen, as had nearly all the East and the North.

Britain was changing and changing quickly. It was as though the Britons had nothing to fight for or believe in after Arthur's death and so they meekly rolled over and showed the invaders their delicate white underbellies. Far from the victorious Battle of Mount Baden where Arthur and his men drove back the entirety of the Saxon army, this was nothing other than slaughter.

Yes, she agreed, they must do something, but why must her daughters be involved?

Mostly, she knew that they were right. It was far from accidental or incidental that circumstances had conspired as they had done. Part of her incredible reluctance to go to the well was that she felt she already knew what she would see there and did not want to know.

Carrying only a bit of cheese, a loaf of bread, and some wine, Bran and Lillian made their way to the Sacred Well without speaking; Lillian sat on the edge of the well but did not yet look at the water which was only a very few inches from the top. It pulled its flow from the groundwater of the Sacred Spring that flowed down the hills and into the lake below. It was forbidden for any manmade item to touch the waters, either above or below, from its bubbling beginning near the top of the Tor until it reached the lake and became one with the vast body of water that separated them from the outside world. When pilgrims came to take the holy water back with them, they had to use their cupped hands to funnel it into their vessel, never allowing the vessel contact with the water.

The water had healing properties and was a strong life force to imbibe. The priestesses, Druids, and other people who lived on Avalon of course drank exclusively of the water, as well as the juices of the fruits borne by the trees and the wine made from the grapes of Avalon, all of which received their hydration from the same water source as ground water. This meant that rarely did any form of illness ever reached the island. The water sustained them and the water protected them from those on the shore who wished the harm. The mists that concealed Avalon also rose from that same sacred water.

Lillian shuddered as the bells of the Glastonbury cathedral rang faintly in the distance. It was rare now that the sound of the bells, calling the faithful and pious to prayer, were heard now that Avalon had moved so deeply into the mists, but now and again, the sound drifted across the water to them. Lillian again wondered that the Christians had to be called to prayer in a building rather than praying to their God within the Nature that had been created for them where God and Goddess most fully present. Certainly, she could well work magic within walls so long as the elements of earth, air, fire, and water were present in some capacity, but it was so much stronger when her bare feet touched earth and she could feel the sky above her and smell the water of the lake. How could it not be so for them when their god was the same?

She thought about Vivienne, the shrouded bones that had acted as the vessel for her spirit on this earth before, now rotting in the tomb Arthur had created at Glastonbury. She had never been there and felt no need to attend the manmade shrine built on orders of a king who had betrayed Avalon and broken his vow to honor all paths rather than only the Christian faith. That time, the greatest machinations of The Merlin and the Lady of the Lake had failed miserably, resulting in misfortune and death for all concerned. She shuddered that the same might happen again, only sevenfold over. Why would the Goddess intentionally lead them on a path to such catastrophe for everyone?

As if reading her thoughts and likely doing just that, Bran said gently, "It was the frailty of man and woman before that brought the outcomes of death and destruction, not the frailty of God and Goddess. Arthur fell victim to the madness of Guinevere and the ranting of the zealots around him. The false Merlin was a broken spirit who wanted to be accepted and revered. He attempted to use the holy regalia to buy his way into favor with the priests, not because the Divine Power led him to do so. Lady Morgan allowed revenge, greed, and pettiness to cloud her wisdom."

"And we are also human, Bran, and must think well before manipulating the lives of others; not only our good daughters and priestesses, but also the kings and families to which we send them. We cannot escape the fact that what we propose is treason and look at where your sister sits now for the simple treason of releasing you from a dungeon cell. This is so much more than that crime."

"This is true, My Love. It is not without danger and certainly, it is a tremendous act of faith if we do this; faith in the Goddess to protect our girls and faith in the girls to use their own cunning and wisdom to do what they must. Yes, we are human, but the people we were before acted in secret, of their own counsel. We have the wisdom of the whole of Avalon to guide us in that great hall and we have our own centuries of experience from which to learn.

"Dearest, we have been protected for so long. Since I returned to you on Avalon that Beltane night, we have but rarely had to be apart. We were blessed to raise our beautiful daughters in peace and magic. As Lord Beric said, we have had more than a decade and half again to refine our magic and build its power without fear or threat to our safety. Now, we must repay that gift by sending magic out into the world. I like it no more than do you, but I can feel the authenticity of it and I know that you do as well. We have agreed to follow the will of the Goddess, so let us do so."

He reached beyond her into the water of the well and scooped his cupped hands in to gather some of the water. He brought it to his lips and drank deeply. She turned and did the same, then spoke the sacred words that would show them what they needed to see.

At first the images where muddled and ran together in an indiscernible array. As they waited and watched, the images began to break apart into separate views: a tall stone tower, a woman in a red cloak running away from their view, a tall staircase, a vast library of books, a small cottage in a dark forest… Lillian passed her hands over the surface of the water and the ripples carried away the images. It was like turning a page in a book.

They could see their own reflections and the foliage behind them and then a new picture began to appear. At the furthest edge of the water, an arch formed that was made of seven crowns, each different from one another in detail. At the nearest edge of the water, the image of seven flowers became clear: a violet, a rose, a lily, an iris, a jasmine, an aster, and a dahlia. The flowers and crowns almost made a perfect circle in the well but for the blank spaces on the left and the right, separating the crowns from the flowers. As they watched, the flowers floated toward the crowns until the crowns slipped neatly over the flowers.

And so it was done.

Where Angels Fear to Tread, Yet Priestesses Do Not

The entirety of Avalon gathered on the Tor and every soul from the tiniest baby to the oldest elder stood together in a circle within the ring stones, around the girls, Bran, and Lillian. Each of the girls was given to the Ceremony of the Blade, wherein a dagger was held at their breast and they vowed that they entered this covenant with Avalon and the Goddess by their own free will and without coercion. Lillian herself felt a stab of dismay at the lack of coercion it took when the plan was revealed to her daughters. Each one had been eager, excited even, to take on the dangerous task laid out before her.

All seven girls vowed in the name of the Goddess that they were committed to their tasks and all seven vowed to honor their obligation with their last life's breath. Lillian looked at the beautiful garden of daughters that stood before her. Some wore veils, some had flowers woven into their hair, and some were adored with beautiful leaves and vines. Some were blond, some were brunette, and some were crimson-haired. Some were tall, some were short. Some were slender and some were full-bodied. Some were shy and reserved and some were boisterous and gregarious. All were beautiful, strong, wise, and highly empowered.

Their trunks were already packed and waiting at the launch near the Avalon barge. Divinatory processes assigned a kingdom to each of the girls, as well as a magical tool to aid them in their quest, specific to their own personality and interests. Each girl chose a companion to travel with them and lend support when needed.

It was rare in their lives that Lillian had spent even a day away from them. Twice, she and Bran had traveled to Carmeliard in support of Ophelia and Phillip, but never had they been away for more than a few days at a time. Only the sight and the little news that traveled to Avalon would tell her if they were safe and she had no idea of when they would return. She drew on every moment of priestess training she possessed to maintain her focus and composure during the ritual, constantly reminding herself that she must be present as The Lady of the Lake rather than as a worried mother.

Lillian had spoken at length with each of her daughters in turn, looking for any sign of fear, reluctance, or hesitancy in them. Had she found any, she felt she would have, Goddess or no, refused to continue the mission Each of the seven made it clear that this was their manifest destiny and that they embraced it with open arms. Somewhere in a deep and secret place, the pride she felt for her daughters was overwhelming.

Earlier in the day and just prior to the ritual, Bran took her alone to the Tor. She wondered at his purpose until his mood became very serious and he turned his own dagger to her breast. She felt the power of the Horned God come over him as had done so many times before. Even as the Goddess welled up inside of her at his invitation, she could not help but feel slightly humbled as the aura around his face began to radiate. She knew that the name "Taliesin" meant "Radiant Brow" and never failed to think how aptly named he was in his previous life. Brannon seemed like such a small, ordinary name for such a grand man as this.

She felt his blade press against her breastbone and he said to her, "Lady of the Lake, I feel the fear and grief in your heart. Hear me now and know that these emotions will taint the power of the magic we are sending forth into the world. If ever before you have had faith in the Goddess and where She leads, you must have it now. These young priestesses need the investment of your assurance and the energy and power we send into this undertaking must be pure and strong with no doubt or hesitancy in your heart.

Lillian knew what words he would say next and they were sacred. *"Know now that it is better to rush upon my blade and perish than to proceed with fear in your heart."*

For a moment, she was compelled to rush upon his blade, not only because she felt she could not possibly purge her heart of all worry, fear, and grief, but also because a part of her felt he deserved to have her die at his hand, through the God or not, for insisting that she do this. She felt bullied into this action by him, by the Council of Elders and yes, by the very Goddess. She was angry, hurt, and terrified and felt betrayed by them all and yes, it was true. Vivienne whispered to her that those feelings would deeply contaminate the magical process. She pulled away from the blade, sat down on the very altar stone where they had given their daughters life and wept as though her heart would break.

Bran sat beside her and wept as well, his sobs wracking his body and his tears dampening her tunic. It was as though all the personal fortitude he had invested in pursuit of this idea dropped away and he was as she: a parent devastated by what must be, embroiled in a process outside of their own power and understanding.

They held one another until the weeping ceased, then made love on the altar, comforting and gently at first, but becoming more passionate and urgent as their need built. Afterward, she felt the last of her energy spent. She was no longer angry or afraid, but instead, resigned and ready. She could not ever say that she was in love with this plan, but she was at peace.

By the time they again crossed into the circle of standing stones on the Tor with the entirety of Avalon around them, she did so as a High Priestess committed to the will of the Goddess. As Christ had himself prayed, *"Not my will, but thine be done."* She reflected on the thought that not long after surrendering himself in such a fashion, he had, in fact, been crucified.

The day seemed to careen forward like a horse out of control, carrying her in its wake and moving much too fast. It felt as though no time at all had passed before the ritual was ended and they were standing at the launch, watching the trunks being loaded onto the barge by the men whose task it was to attend the vessel. Their skin was dyed deep blue and they lived in the outlying areas around the shore. They were silent as priestesses in their tasks, their wiry muscles flexing as they easily transferred the heavy cargo from shore to deck.

When the young priestesses arrived on the shore of the mainland, each would receive two horses and a cart to transport their belongings. Some were going to nearby lands, but some would travel for weeks or even months to reach their destination. As magical beings, they would travel through many areas hostile to them; in danger not only from the Saxon raiders, but also from their own people should any discover who they were.

The girls had never left Avalon before and few outside of Avalon would recognize them, which served to work in their favor. Certainly, none would imagine that young priestesses of Avalon would be traveling throughout the mainland without proper escort. Their anonymity would be one of their many strengths and their real identity could remain hidden if none saw them work magic.

Not only was Lillian saying goodbye to her daughters, but to her dearest friend as well. Maia would accompany Violet on her journey as her chosen companion. Lillian suspected that Maia was praying one of the girls would choose her to go and it came as no surprise that Violet, who had been closest to her since birth, did so. Although she would miss her best friend desperately, she felt relieved that such a wise and powerful priestess would accompany one of her daughters.

The other girls chose their closest friends as traveling companions and admittedly, Lillian wondered what it would be like to be eighteen again and to embark on such an exciting and important adventure with Maia by her side. She looked up at Bran who affectionately wrapped his strong, brown arms around her, and thought of how her own amazing life adventure started at the same age.

"May your adventure be as delicious and rewarding as mine," she said so softly that no one could hear.

Together, they watched as the barge disappeared into the mists, taking the seven priestess princesses of Avalon to their own unique and life-altering destinies.

But those are stories for other books to come and for now, I will leave you with a preview of what happens next:

All hell broke loose.

The End

About the Author

Katrina Rasbold has provided insightful and guidance to countless individuals over the past three decades through both her life path consultations and her informative classes and workshops. She has worked with teachers all over the world, including three years of training in England and two years of practice in the Marianas Islands. She is a professional life coach who holds a PhD in Religion. She is married and she and her husband, Eric, co-authored the Bio-Universal Energy book series.

Katrina lives in the forested Eden of the High Sierras of Northern California near Tahoe. Katrina is a hermit who lives inside her beautiful mountain home, pecking away at her computer keyboard. She frequently teaches workshops on different aspects of Bio-Universal energy usage in the El Dorado, Sacramento, and Placer counties of California. She has six children, who are grown up and out there loose in the world.

Other Books by the Author

Energy Magic

Energy Magic Compleat

Beyond Energy Magic

The CUSP Way

Properties of Magical Energy

Reuniting the Two Selves

Magical Ethics and Protection

The Art of Ritual Crafting

The Magic and Making of Candles and Soaps

Days and Times of Power

Crossing the Third Threshold

How to Create a Magical Working Group

An Insider's Guide to the General Hospital Fan
Club Weekend

Made in United States
North Haven, CT
14 November 2022

26745605R00186